He wanted her

He needed her.

He couldn't have her.

Not now.

Not ever.

A faint whimper escaped her in her sleep. Cathlynn's eyelids fluttered with the mad movements of a dreamer dreaming. Dark shadows of distress slipped across her innocent face. Fear spread her breaths raggedly through her parted lips.

Fear. Yes, she had a right to fear him, Jonas thought, watching her sleep. He'd do her no good. Having Cathlynn pretend to be his wife so he could acquire the trust fund was the most important thing in his life now. He needed the money to continue his work, to save his life and his brother's. He would sacrifice anything to find the cure.

His dreams were grounded in reality, in his vision for a brighter future for all, not in fantasy. He had to remember that. In two weeks, Cathlynn would be gone, and everything could go back as it was.

Anger rose. A disturbing anger that shook him to the core. Damn Cathlynn and her irresistible appeal!

Dear Harlequin Intrigue Reader,

Sunscreen, a poolside lounge—and Harlequin Intrigue: the perfect recipe for great summer escapes!

This month's sizzling selection begins with *The Stranger Next Door* (#573) by Joanna Wayne, the second in her RANDOLPH FAMILY TIES miniseries. Langley Randolph is the kind of Texan who can't resist a woman in trouble. Can he help unlock a beautiful stranger's memories...before a killer catches up with her first?

Little Penny Drake is an *Innocent Witness* (#574) to a murder in this suspenseful yet tender story by Leona Karr. The child's desperate mother, Deanna, seeks the help of Dr. Steve Sherman. Can Steve unlock her daughter's secrets...and Deanna's heart?

Dr. Jonas Shades needs a woman to play his wife. Cathlynn O'Connell is the perfect candidate, but with time running out, he has no choice but to blackmail his bride. Each minute in Jonas's presence brings Cathlynn closer to understanding her enigmatic "husband" *and* closer to danger! Don't miss *Blackmailed Bride* (#575) by Sylvie Kurtz.

Bestselling Harlequin American Romance author Tina Leonard joins Harlequin Intrigue with a story of spine-tingling suspense and dramatic romance. She's created the small town of Crookseye Canyon, Texas, as the backdrop for *A Man of Honor* (#576). Cord Greer must marry his brother's woman to keep her and her unborn baby safe. But is it fear that drives Tessa Draper into Cord's arms, or is it something more than Cord had hoped for?

Indulge yourself and find out this summer—and all year long!

Sincerely,

Denise O'Sullivan
Associate Senior Editor
Harlequin Intrigue

Blackmailed Bride
Sylvie Kurtz

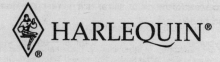

HARLEQUIN®

TORONTO • NEW YORK • LONDON
AMSTERDAM • PARIS • SYDNEY • HAMBURG
STOCKHOLM • ATHENS • TOKYO • MILAN • MADRID
PRAGUE • WARSAW • BUDAPEST • AUCKLAND

ISBN 0-373-22575-X

BLACKMAILED BRIDE

ABOUT THE AUTHOR

Flying an eight-hour solo cross-country in a Piper Arrow with only the airplane's crackling radio and a large bag of M&M's for company, Sylvie Kurtz realized a pilot's life wasn't for her. The stories zooming in and out of her mind proved more entertaining than the flight itself. Not a quitter, she finished her pilot's course and earned her commercial license and instrument rating.

Since then, she has traded in her wings for a computer keyboard, where she lets her imagination soar to create fictional adventures that explore the power of love and the thrill of suspense. When not writing, she enjoys the outdoors with her husband and two children, in addition to quilt making, photography and reading whatever catches her interest.

You can write to Sylvie at P.O. Box 702, Milford, NH 03055.

Books by Sylvie Kurtz

HARLEQUIN INTRIGUE
527—ONE TEXAS NIGHT
575—BLACKMAILED BRIDE

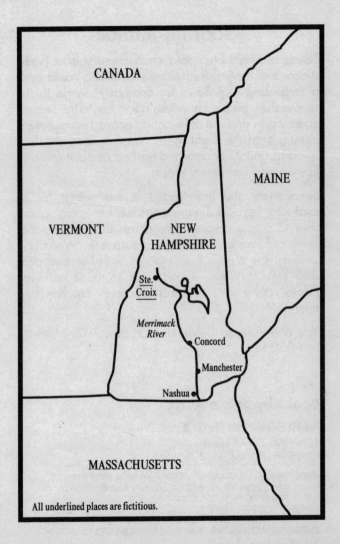

All underlined places are fictitious.

CAST OF CHARACTERS

Dr. Jonas Shades—With time running out, he had to convince a beautiful stranger to play his wife for two weeks. Yet how far would his "marriage" go once she was by his side...?

Cathlynn O'Connell—She was playing the role of a lifetime. What price was she willing to pay to get what she wanted?

Alana Chandler Shades—The faithless socialite was missing. Was it by choice? Or was it murder?

Sterling Ryder—Did the family lawyer and trust fund's trustee have a motive of his own to see Alana dead?

Geoffrey Chandler—Alana's cousin. Greed was always a good motive for murder.

David Forester—Jonas's trusted assistant knew everything that went on between the thick monastery walls.

Meara O'Connell—Would Cathlynn's grandmother appreciate the sacrifice her granddaughter made for her sake?

Lorraine Forester—The local seamstress was happy to oblige Jonas's every request.

Bertha Lane—There was no love lost between David's grandmother and the mistress of the monastery.

Scott MacPhearson—The private eye was a bulldog when it came to tracking down a clue. Jonas had paid his salary, but no man could buy the truth from him.

To my grandmothers—for the fond memories.

Prologue

A paper-thin moon hung in the ink-blue sky, mutating grotesque shadows behind the three crosses in the courtyard of the Ste-Croix monastery in rural New Hampshire. But Alana Chandler Shades didn't care. The creepy place with its eerie shadows and haunting chant-like winds had ceased to frighten her a long time ago.

Now, it merely bored her.

At thirty, she'd wasted almost half her life in this godforsaken place. As she hurried over the courtyard's cobblestones, she smiled, ignoring the ominous whispers of fall leaves from the nearby woods. Soon she'd be free. She threw her head back and laughed, defying the morbid sounds of night. She'd waited a long time for this freedom—a freedom she'd earned with her filial duty; a freedom which would now be greatly enhanced by her coming inheritance. She'd have plenty of time to make up for all the deprivation she'd endured over the last thirteen years.

As she opened the garage door, it creaked. For now, she'd settle for the simple pleasures of the flesh. Her latest conquest was strong and virile, and Alana licked her lips in anticipation of the feral passion they'd share.

She hopped into her red Miata and roared into the bleak night.

Too bad that husband of hers had found the papers and ruined his Christmas surprise. He'd been amiable enough about the whole situation, with her conditions. But with him, who knew?

Their love had died a long time ago, hadn't it? Had they ever truly been in love? She'd been too young. Her dreams hadn't had a chance to gel yet. She'd realized too late the price she'd paid for her father's approval. And he'd made sure with his manipulations of her trust fund that she couldn't undo the damage until too late. All this sacrifice and for what? A miracle cure that would never happen; a marriage that was doomed to fail before it began.

And the differences in their backgrounds, the five-year difference in their ages so exciting at first, had soon grown into rifts, then chasms. The fool, he'd turned such a brilliant future into nothing with his misguided vision and his righteous anger. An anger that had grown over the years, and sometimes managed to frighten even her.

But not tonight. Tonight was her weekly escape from tyranny, and she was determined to make the most of it. The car rattled over the loose boards of the old covered bridge, echoing like thunder into the oppressive night. Alana hid the Miata in the thicket of pines and slipped into the small one-room cottage.

She sensed movement from the bed. "You're here already. Why didn't you light the lamp?"

She lit the hurricane lamp, blew out the match and turned to her new friend. A black-robed monk stepped forward from the shadows, his face hidden by his cowled hood, his hands buried in opposite sleeves. She smiled when she saw the way the robe strained over broad shoulders, the way the thick cord at his waist defined his trim hips.

"Ah, so you like to play little games, do you?" Alana laughed. She unbuttoned her coat and flung it on the bed. She started toward him, shedding her scarf, then her sweater. "Shall I play your sacrificial virgin?"

The monk's hood fell back. Malevolence burned in his eyes. Laughter froze in her throat. Her fingers went rigid against the zipper of her tailored pants. His hands came into the light. A rope snapped between them. Fear paralyzed her limbs, her voice, her breath.

The rush of adrenaline came too late.

Chapter One

Cathlynn O'Connell glanced around the living room of the monastery turned mansion, looking for her treasure with, she hoped, what passed for cool composure. Her heart fluttered with excitement, but she forced herself to present her usual calm professional appearance. People expected that from her; she'd built her reputation as a top-notch antiques dealer with her fairness and levelheadedness.

Where was the sculpture? What if— But no, she wouldn't even entertain such a thought. The auction brochure had clearly printed the description, and the picture had left no doubt.

The Aidan Heart was here—somewhere.

Cathlynn removed her wool hat and gloves and dropped them on one of the folding chairs. A storm brewed outside. Strong winds pummeled the ancient stone structure—one of three buildings on the grounds. The promised inclement weather hadn't kept people away from the auction. Cathlynn didn't blame them. *Nothing* could have kept her away today.

She'd raced the dark, billowy clouds all the way from Nashua to the small village of Ste-Croix on the western edge of the White Mountains, and the old Ste-Croix

Monastery. Slate skies had met white snow with nothing in between to give the illusion of depth except somber evergreens and the gray branches of winter-bared maples and beeches. Taking a wrong turn along the twisty country road, she'd almost ended up in the treacherous depths of the Ste-Croix River which fed eventually into Lake Winnipesaukee. But she'd made it.

And ten years of searching for the Aidan Heart would end today.

Inside the gray stone main house, people milled about, creating a soft buzz with their chatter. Curiosity seekers or competition? The cordial fire glowing in the hearth mellowed the wind's strong bite, but couldn't quite keep the chill out of the air. Cathlynn scanned the room once more. The fact the walls' only adornment was a series of paintings portraying the austere monks of the Order of the Holy Cross in black-hooded habits didn't help. It almost seemed as if the monks followed her every move, especially the one over the fireplace whose eyes glowed red in the firelight's trail.

What kind of person would choose to live in such a bleak environment? An involuntary shiver slid down her spine.

As she crossed the room, she recognized several rival dealers and nodded a greeting. Noticing a side room from which people emerged, and guessing the auction goods' location, she headed in its direction.

On a series of tables a collection of high-quality antiques crowded the small adjoining room. Cathlynn looked at the rich offerings, feigning interest while her heart beat strong with anticipation of finding the Aidan Heart. She spotted a lamp and several glass bowls she could easily place with her clients, but knew she wouldn't bid on them.

She'd come to Ste-Croix for one thing and one thing only—the glass sculpture her great-great-grandfather had fashioned for his bride almost a hundred years ago. A gift of love tragically lost when Aidan and Deirdre O'Connell had left Ireland for the United States.

Now she held the precious gift in her sight.

As she approached the twelve-inch sculpture, Cathlynn held her breath. Though shaped like the pylon paperweights popular in the late 1800s, the similarity ended there. Rather than tool the glass into shape, the artist had handblown it so the glass folded over itself, forming hanging layers of translucence from light pink to dark purple to pure transparent, with a three-dimensional heart suspended, as if by magic, in its center. The whole rested on a flat square base.

It was perfect. More beautiful than she'd imagined. The glass spoke to her, flooding her with sensations of the past, of love, acceptance, happiness. She breathed deeply to tamp down the tears of joy threatening to fragment her careful composure.

With discreet awe and a trembling finger, Cathlynn reached out to touch the object of her intense search. The glass felt warm beneath her finger. She picked it up, feeling its solid weight in her hands for the first time. Turning it over carefully, she inspected every facet. Not a chip, not a scratch in sight. The room grew unbearably warm around her, making the glass pulsate with heat, coating her hands with sweat. Even the walls seemed to shimmer in a feverlike hallucination.

Her lips trembled. She clamped them down. She had to get hold of herself. She couldn't let herself be drawn in by emotions. Staying cool, calm and collected—that would get her the prize, not foolish emotions.

With a deep reluctance, she set the sculpture down on the table once more and turned back to the main room. Maybe the imminent storm would keep most of her competition away. Few people realized the value of the piece, but perhaps some would be drawn into the bidding by its simple yet elegant charm.

No use worrying. She'd get the Aidan Heart even if she had to sell her soul for it.

By bringing the sculpture back to its rightful owner, she hoped to give a final glimpse of magic to her dying grandmother. Gram had done so much for her. Her summers at Gram's house had brought a measure of peace to her chaotic childhood, the stories of Aidan and Deirdre's love, the magic of belonging. And with the sculpture she'd brighten her grandmother's last days, see the light of recognition shine one more time in her eyes. She owed her at least that much.

Two elderly ladies shuffling through the door blocked her exit from the room. Cathlynn stepped aside to let them pass.

"Do you suppose he'll show up?" asked the one leaning on a cane.

"Who?" asked the one whose purple feather on her hat bobbed to a palsied rhythm.

"Jonas Shades. Who else?"

Jonas Shades. Why did the name seem so familiar? Where had she heard it before?

Purple Feather cocked a hand on her hip. "Bertha, you've no intentions of buying anything, do you? You dragged me out in this weather just to add fodder to your gossip fuel. I've a good mind to drag you right back home."

"You'll do no such thing!" Bertha pretended indignation, then leaned closer to her companion's ear. "My David says he's been impossible to work for since his wife disappeared, that he's lost his edge. Hasn't been able to do anything. The research; it's stopped. David says the man spends most of his days pacing. And you know how it is.... Well, I had to see for myself."

Purple Feather's eyes rolled toward the ceiling. "Your grandson is as bad a gossip as you are."

Bertha picked up a trinket from the nearby table and replaced it with barely a look. "David says that's why he's having the auction. David says he desperately needs cash for his research. Think of how it would affect the village if he left."

"Someone else would come. Someone always does." Purple Feather tried to pull Bertha along.

"Yes, but at what price to us? Remember what happened when the family lost the monastery after Jeremy Shades died? The village almost disappeared."

"Come on." The hat's purple feather dipped wildly as the woman forcibly pulled her companion along. "The auction's about to begin. Let's go take our seats."

Cathlynn followed the old ladies out the door. Bertha stopped abruptly, and Cathlynn nearly crashed into her.

"There he is," Bertha whispered to her companion. "Oh my, he doesn't look good at all, does he? I wonder if he'll cancel the Christmas fete this year. What a disappointment that would be for everyone. But who could blame him with all this tragedy hanging over his head?"

Despite herself, Cathlynn couldn't help following the old lady's gaze to the tall man standing in the corner. He leaned his long, athletic frame against the wall, studying the room with undisguised contempt. His dark brown hair looked as if it had recently been raked by fingers. Deep-set eyes the color of squally clouds hid beneath low eyebrows, giving him an appearance as frosty as the winter storm announcing itself outside. Prominent cheekbones and a square jaw negated the promise of sensuality offered by his full mouth.

Not a man to tangle with, yet Cathlynn found herself drawn to the sheer power of his presence. Even when he tried to melt into the shadows, he filled the room.

Their gazes met and held for longer than was comfortable. The intensity of his gray eyes traveled all the way to her soul, and buffeted her with feelings she didn't dare name. She put down the exciting sensation thrilling through her to the prospect of owning the Aidan Heart, not to the brooding man who stood in the corner.

Unexpectedly, the protection of her coat felt like candy glass, thin and transparent. She tightened it around her despite the insufferable warmth tingling her body. An echo of something she couldn't quite put her finger on pinged deep inside.

The illusion of warmth faded from his eyes. When she realized his stare had hardened into hate, she shivered and turned away.

Why? She made her way back to her chair. *What did I do?* She removed her coat and self-consciously smoothed the skirt of her burgundy wool-blend shirtdress, then picked up her brochure.

Jonas Shades. Where had she heard the name? She read the brochure's cover and found the auction sponsored by the Monastery Company. She searched through the catalog of her mind, but came up empty. She'd never met the man—would have remembered if she had. Power that potent wasn't easily forgotten.

She shrugged. It didn't matter. She hadn't driven all this way to solve the mystery behind the pained look in Mr. Jonas Shades's eyes.

Suddenly, the front door blew open. Wind whipped through the opening. It whistled and snarled down the makeshift aisle, snapping the folding chairs in the back row to the ground with its unexpected ferocity. The audience turned in one movement.

"Do you suppose it's her?" Bertha whispered to her companion.

"Who? The monks' virgin sacrifice?" Purple Feather scoffed.

"*Her.* You know, his wife. The one who disappeared last month. I've heard people say they've seen her ghost about the place. Some even say he killed her himself in a fit of rage."

Purple Feather jabbed Bertha in the ribs with her elbow. "There you go again, gossiping. No one's sure she's even dead. You should know by now people love to exaggerate everything because nothing ever happens here. The monks' legend is just that—a legend."

"Well, there's always a grain of truth in every story. The monks do have a bloody history."

"It's just a myth!"

A heavy thump boomed and resounded down the corridor as a young man dressed in a suit too formal for the occasion closed the door, straightened the downed chairs, then took a seat in the back row.

The auctioneer banged his hammer and got the sale under way. He proceeded at a fast pace, for which Cathlynn was thankful. Turning her gaze to the corner of the room, she found Jonas Shades's icy stare on her once more. The faster she got her prize, the sooner she could escape and leave behind the uncomfortable feeling settling in her gut.

"Now we have item number one hundred and thirteen. A piece of experimental Irish glass circa 1900 from the Summers Glasshouse. The artist is unknown, but the piece is often referred to as the Aidan Heart. Who will give me..."

She knew the market value, but she also knew she wanted the piece no matter what it cost. And that put her at a disadvantage. Would puffers, seeking to inflate prices, prey on her vulnerability? Would the auctioneer call phantom bids when he sensed the intensity of her desire? She'd bid tentatively at first to feel out the opposition. If she simulated a lack of interest, she might get the piece for below its market value.

Cathlynn waited patiently, breath held, while someone signaled to cut the opening bid in half.

"Ladies and gentlemen," the auctioneer continued, "this is the finest example of Irish glass I've seen in a long time..."

The bidding went fast and furious. As the price of the piece rose to its market value, Cathlynn tightened her hold on her bidding card and tried to remain calm.

"This is no money for such a fine example of Irish glass..."

Beads of moisture formed along her hairline. Cathlynn put up her card.

"Remember, this is an original, ladies and gentlemen. You would pay more than this for a reproduction. Who will give me..."

The bidding was too high. Cathlynn's armpits prickled with sweat. She crossed and uncrossed her ankles. As she calculated her options, her mind whirled.

I want it.

I need it.

No amount of cool reasoning could counter the irrational demand of her yearning.

She *had* to have it.

She put up her card.

"This should be a part of any serious glass collection..."

One card went up. Then another. She'd never dreamed the price would go so high. Oh God, she was going to lose the Aidan Heart after searching for it for ten years. She couldn't let it go.

Licking her dry lips, she flung up her card, not sure how she'd manage to pay.

Jonas interrupted the auctioneer. A frantic whispered discussion passed between them, and Jonas, nodding once to someone in the back, left through the back door.

What was going on? Why had they stopped? Dreadful premonition swamped through her. No, they couldn't stop. It wasn't legal. She was so close. Her rapid pulse hammered her brain. Her hands unconsciously tightened around the bidding card, scrunching the flimsy cardboard.

The auctioneer cleared his throat and resumed his pitch. "Ladies and gentlemen..."

From the back of the room came a bid. A bid so ridiculous it took an instant to register into her brain.

"What!" Cathlynn jumped to her feet amid agitated whispers. She whirled, knocking her chair to the ground. "You can't do that!"

The polished young man who'd closed the front door smiled at her, tilting his head sideways and lifting his eyebrows and shoulders in mock regret. Not a single black hair fell out of place. Not a single crease marred his expensive suit. Not a wrinkle worried his handsome features.

"David?" Bertha scrunched her eyes and peered at the young man. "Is that you?"

"Any further advances?" the auctioneer asked. He looked around the room. "Going once! Twice! Last time!" He brought his hammer down. The sound of finality exploded in Cathlynn's mind. "Sold to number one for…"

She'd lost.

Cathlynn couldn't believe it. After all this time, it couldn't be true. Her heart banged painfully against her ribs. As her vision narrowed, the whole room swirled into a vortex, twisting everything into rushing black specters speeding toward her. The roar in her ear thundered over her thoughts, dousing them in a quagmire of thick, dark slime. Her limbs shook, ice-cold, numb. She couldn't find air. She pulled in a harsh gulp. The air vanished before it found her lungs.

"Are you all right?" A strange voice pierced the dark abyss spinning all around her, releasing her.

"I'm fine." She devoured the air in great mouthfuls. "I'm fine."

Someone righted her chair and helped her into it. When she realized who stood above her, she trapped the young man's hands in hers. "I want to buy the Aidan Heart from you."

"Sorry." He smiled apologetically and a contrite expression glimmered from his warm brown eyes. "I'm just the buyer's agent."

"Who's the buyer?"

He nodded toward the back door behind the auctioneer. "Him."

The dark and mysterious Jonas Shades.

Dizzy, she reached for her hat and gloves, knocking them to the floor. Bending down to retrieve them, her head cleared, returning the room to its original shape. She sat on the edge of the hard chair and closed her eyes, willing herself to wake up and find this had all been a terrible nightmare.

"Now we have item one hundred and fourteen...." The auction resumed.

Pain ripped through her heart until it seemed as if blood dripped from her chest. It wasn't fair. It wasn't right. Light-headed, she wavered once as she rose.

She had to think. She couldn't give up. She'd find the buyer and make him understand he couldn't have the Aidan Heart. Searching the back of the room, she couldn't find him. The man seemed to have disappeared. Shakily, she made her way to the entry hall and gripped the auction room's doorjamb, drawing strength from its solid form.

"Is J.T. in?" A British-accented voice carried like a wave from farther down the corridor. Cathlynn caught a glimpse of the receding figure of a man bundled in a heavy black overcoat, gray scarf and felt bowler.

"Dr. Shades was not expecting you today."

Dr. J. T. Shades!

Now she remembered where she'd heard the name Jonas Shades. He was the brilliant researcher who'd made waves last year when he'd denounced his sponsoring company's intentions as fraudulent and ended their association.

What did *he* need the Aidan Heart for? What could he possibly want with her piece of glass? Her breaths quickened. Her free fist clenched by her side. She stowed the helplessness away in a deep corner, and let anger swell and crest, needing desperately to latch on to something other than the pain mauling her heart.

If Jonas Shades thought she was going home empty-handed today, he had no idea who he was dealing with.

JONAS HAD EXPECTED Sterling Ryder to show up, just not this soon. He turned swiftly into the small room adjoining the living room, plucked the registration card for bidder 168 from the Secretary's desk and strode through to the door at the opposite end.

The rumors, of course. Alana had threatened to leak the less than idyllic state of their marriage to knowing ears, but she'd been drunk when he'd found her sprawled with the papers—drunk and vindictive. She'd vowed he'd suffer for the isolation she'd been forced to endure. The deal she'd outlined had shades of Satan all over it. He'd wanted to strangle her. In the end, he'd accepted. A little humiliation was nothing compared to the good his research could yield. Had she whispered her secrets out of spite to her cousin Geoffrey, realizing he'd have a keen interest in the outcome?

Jonas ripped open the door in his path.

"Jonas!" He nearly bumped into David Forester, his assistant, who carefully cradled the Aidan Heart in both his hands. "What do you want me to do with this?"

He handed David a key. "Put it in the cellar with the rest of the paperweights. In the safe."

Without waiting for a response, Jonas forged ahead in the corridor, and let the door slam behind him. His butler and the old man weren't far behind, but he'd reach the library before they did.

Ah, dear Alana! She'd kept at him and kept at him with her barbs and her threats—until he'd exploded.

Now she was missing. Had been for four and a half

weeks. And it wasn't like her to leave without a scene. Something wasn't right, but the investigator he'd hired had uncovered nothing. It was as if she'd vanished.

Purposefully or not, she'd conveniently left him with a suspicious lawyer to appease and no devoted wife to prove his wedded bliss. He didn't like being backed into a corner. And he surely didn't like the thoughts poisoning his mind—thoughts he wouldn't normally entertain. But images of the woman sitting at the auction floated back to him.

She could help him.

He turned a corner, feeling as if the walls of the home he loved so much were closing in on him, and pushed open the library door.

She'd had a glow about her that had caught his attention. He'd admired her catlike grace and the self-assurance with which she moved. His attraction to her had been immediate and powerful. A fact Jonas found both intriguing and disconcerting. History repeating itself? How long had it been since he'd allowed a pretty face to turn his head? And what price had he paid?

He wouldn't make the same mistake again.

Jonas blazed on a light and marched to the fireplace. He threw a log in and watched the sparks fly up like angry bees disturbed from their nest. He'd found her glowing face refreshing after the blasé cynicism he'd grown used to. Her light brown hair with its luxuriant profusion had him thinking of sex, hot and wild. The way the glossy strands caught the fire's light and reflected gold, he'd wanted to reach out and bury his hand in her hair to harvest the sheer life it exuded. He shook his head to dispel her image. He had to stay in control.

He banged a fist against the mantel, punctuating his determination. But she came back, her image haunting him in the erratic dance of flames in a way he didn't like.

Massaging the back of his neck with both hands, he saw her eyes again. They were the most beautiful he'd ever seen—brown that shifted to topaz, reminding him of his mother's tiger's-eye pendant. Yes, she vibrated with life, and he'd almost forgotten that feeling, dead as he'd been inside for so many years.

Jonas raked a hand through his hair to clear the sensual cobwebs weaving themselves into his brain, and headed for the silent butler by the sitting area. He plucked ice cubes from a bucket and dropped them into a glass.

When she'd turned and looked at him as she took her place at the auction, his whole body had tensed. At first he thought his impression had been a trick of the light, a quirk of his troubled mind, a ghost from his guilty conscience. But the similarities of her face to Alana's grew over the differences, bringing with them a host of emotions he didn't want to feel. Anger, betrayal—even hatred.

He poured whiskey over the ice and listened to the cubes crackle and pop.

Sterling's arrival for the signing over of the trust had only compounded the feeling of powerlessness that had slowly enveloped him since Alana's untimely disappearance. A feeling he'd felt only once before in his life and had sworn he'd never allow again.

He brought the glass to his lips, then slammed it down on the cart once more. Damn his blasted temper for getting him into this situation in the first place! He refused to lose a life's worth of work over one ill-timed flash of anger.

As he slugged back a swallow, the pale amber liquid

burned his throat. It rested in a fiery ball in his empty stomach, mixing with acid, bringing a caustic squall to life.

He'd watched the way the woman had sat up straight, then leaned forward with anticipation when the Aidan Heart had been raised to the block. The way she'd held her breath, waiting for the opening bid. The way she'd scanned the room, spotting each bidder and assessing them. They way the fear and hope had mixed, bringing her desire to the foreground. And when she'd turned desperate, an uncanny feeling of déjà vu had swept through him. That's when the mad idea had formed in his mind and wouldn't let go.

Sterling's early arrival had served to imprint the idea further. The woman's cry of outrage as David had placed the winning bid repeated in the chambers of his mind like a ghost's tormented lament. He didn't like resorting to a ruse, but he'd make it worth her while.

His future, his life, and those of his siblings, depended on it.

He picked up the bidder's registration card and studied it. Cathlynn O'Connell. An antiques dealer from Nashua. For now, he'd let her cool her heels. Then they'd talk. If he'd read her right, the bait he'd dangle would be irresistible to this tiger hiding in a sleek cat's skin.

They'd both get what they wanted.

The idea was so crazy, it might actually work.

CATHLYNN TOOK a few minutes to compose herself, but the raw fury refused to be tamed. She tromped down the hall where she'd heard the voices floating. The farther down she went, the darker and colder the atmosphere got. Soundless shapes reached out for her, then retracted into their dark crevices along the walls and ceilings. Tall candles protected by brass-trimmed sconces hung unlit, question marks along her path. Didn't Jonas Shades believe in electricity? Maybe his cash-flow problems were as bad as the old lady had insinuated. That would serve him right, after he'd stolen her treasure from under her. Cathlynn snorted silently. He'd snuck away before she could face him with a counteroffer. Now she'd get her chance to face him, and he'd bear the full brunt of her disappointment.

Trailing her hand along the cold stone wall, she moved cautiously on the faded red runner. The stones seemed to come alive beneath her fingers, undulating mute portents into the marrow of her bones.

Beware. The warning pulsed directly into her brain. Her head snapped back to see who stood behind her. Nothing but the entry's heatless light met her gaze.

Shaking her head to dismiss the creeps crawling over her skin, she followed the sound of muffled voices. She turned back every now and then to make sure she wasn't being followed, unable to quite shake the feeling that someone was watching her. She passed several more arched wooden doors with black iron hardware and tested the latches. Why were all the doors locked? What dark secrets lay behind the cloistered portals? What skeletons?

The voices got closer. Through the half-opened library door, she spotted Jonas Shades. The arrogant snob chatted pleasantly with his guest as if nothing had happened—as if he hadn't pulled the rug out from anybody. Cathlynn regained her sense of purpose. Her anger billowed to new heights, and she reacted before thinking.

"How could you?" She cried. "How could you make such an outrageous bid?"

Two men turned toward her with startled expressions on their faces. Jonas recovered from his surprise quickly and stepped toward her.

"Alana, darling, no need for such a fuss." The rich, deep timbre of his voice floated pleasantly to her, but his smile was near-glacial when he drew her close and kissed her forehead with a featherlike brush of lips.

"Play along," he whispered.

"What?" Cathlynn tried to pull away, but his hand captured one of hers, and his narrow glare warned her not to defy him. What had her mad impulse propelled her into?

"We can talk about whatever's troubling you later, darling. Why do you think I bought back the Aidan Heart? For you, my sweet."

"What are you talking about? How could you? You, you—" As waves of conflicting feelings battered her, the insult stuck in her throat.

"Because you mean the world to me, darling." His smile held not a trace of warmth and his expression gave her the feeling the words left a rancid taste in his mouth.

Before she had a chance to respond, he turned her toward the distinguished-looking gentleman with the gray hair and neatly trimmed mustache, his palm wide and hot against the small of her back. "Do you remember Sterling Ryder, your father's lawyer?" Her mouth opened to speak, but he plowed ahead. "No? Well, thirteen years can change a man, can't they? He's come from London in time to celebrate your birthday in two weeks."

"Are you crazy?" What sort of game was Jonas

Shades playing? Calling her by a name not hers, and pretending it was normal, the man had to have a screw loose somewhere. Holding the Aidan Heart as ransom for her cooperation, how low would the man go to get what he wanted?

"Darling—"

"What do you—"

"Not now, darling." His gaze steeled and clouded dangerously. "Say hello to Sterling."

As he waited for her reply, his fingers tightened with admonition around her waist, making Cathlynn wonder what might happen if she *didn't* elect to play along with whatever perverted little game he was playing. Trying to loosen his controlling hold on her, and drown the speck of fear floating to her mind, Cathlynn pasted on a smile and offered Sterling her hand.

She'd play for now. For the Aidan Heart. Then Dr. Jonas Shades would see he wasn't the only one who could bluster like a blizzard.

"Nice to meet you again," Cathlynn managed to say, covering her stunned dismay. Who was Alana anyway? And why would Jonas pretend she was her? "How nice of you to come all the way to Ste-Croix for my birthday."

"Well, this is an important one and I wouldn't have missed it for the world." Sterling released her hand and eyed her curiously. "Besides, it will be my last official duty before I retire. I'm rather looking forward to it."

The last official duty or the retirement? Cathlynn couldn't help the sarcastic streak turning her thoughts sour. *Well, enough of this.* Satisfied at having played her part in Jonas's charade, she smiled at him.

"You could have told me you'd let me have the Heart. It would have saved both of us a lot of trouble, sweetheart.'' She gushed the endearment, secretly pleased at his camouflaged discomfort. ''Can I go pick it up now?''

''Why don't you wait a minute? Sterling was just about to go and freshen up. There's something I need to discuss with you. About the Christmas fete.''

I'll bet! Ooooh, would he have some answering to do! ''All right, sweetheart, but I don't have much time and a lot of details to see to.''

Cathlynn perched herself on a Louis XIV chair next to Sterling and waited while Jonas rang the intercom by the door. A worn Oriental carpet delineated a cozy sitting area, brightened by a fire glowing in the stone hearth. Three of the four walls held ceiling-to-floor bookshelves, with some of the tomes looking quite ancient. Idly, Cathlynn wondered which of the books she'd have to pull to disclose the hidden access to the dank and musty passageways which surely crisscrossed the bowels of this ugly monstrosity. The fourth wall showcased the fireplace, as well as two tall windows topped with heavy crimson velvet curtains that gleamed like wet blood in the flickering firelight. A garish medieval tapestry decorated the chimney above the stone mantel.

Sterling's gaze brought her attention back to Jonas's guest. Curiosity glinted openly in his pale blue eyes. An uneasy feeling quivered in her stomach under his scrutiny, but Cathlynn put it down to having to choke her anger so fast.

''I must say, Alana, you look marvelous,'' Sterling said. ''The years have treated you well. Why, I remember telling Jonas at your wedding reception, you were a rose that would bloom more beautifully with each passing year. And I was right, wasn't I?''

Wedding reception? Sterling thought she was Jonas's missing wife! What had she gotten herself into?

"How kind of you," was all she could think to say. She'd make Jonas pay for this.

"You have put on a few pounds, but it suits you. I always thought you were much too thin."

Cathlynn bristled at Sterling's misplaced mirth, and bit her tongue in order to keep her retort civil. The ten extra pounds she carried around were a source of aggravation. They clung to her no matter what she ate or how much she exercised. A failure in her docket of successes. She didn't appreciate the reminder.

"You seem to have held up quite well, too," she said. "Men your age tend to go to pot."

Sterling beamed at the compliment, not realizing she hadn't meant it that way. Jonas twitched uncomfortably in the background, and Cathlynn nearly gave away her pleasure at his discomfort by smiling. Let him suffer. He'd started this vile charade, not her. She didn't even know the ground rules.

"Well, one does what one can. I take pride in exercising every day. Sherry, my dear?" Sterling stood up to freshen his glass.

"No, I don't drink."

As he poured from the crystal decanter on the mahogany silent butler, Sterling raised a questioning eyebrow.

Jonas stood with mechanical discomfort.

"The calories," Jonas mumbled.

"Oh," Sterling said, but his expression gave away his doubt.

"Tell me, Sterling, what'll you do after you retire?" Cathlynn asked to twist the light away from an obvious faux pas.

Sterling sat down and leaned sideways, closing the gap between them. "I'm planning a grand history tour. I've always been fascinated by the stories behind the ghosts who haunt the castles of England. But with as many fingers as your father had in so many pies, there wasn't time for much else except work."

"You can get an early start on your retirement, then." Cathlynn placed a conspiratory hand on Sterling's arm, noting out of the corner of her eye Jonas's sharp glare. The ice cubes he dropped into his glass clinked a strident warning. The expensive material of his shirt shifted and stirred fluidly with each movement, but couldn't hide the caged tension beneath. She forged ahead anyway. "I've heard some people from the village say they've seen a woman haunting this place."

"Really, how interesting!"

"A local legend about monks and a sacrificial virgin," she said, repeating the rumor she'd heard earlier.

As he filled his glass with amber liquid, Jonas shot Cathlynn a look of silent condemnation. Had she gone too far? *Some even say he killed her himself in one of his fits of rage.*

"It's only gossip," Jonas said.

Just then the door yawned open and a uniformed butler with a beaked nose and thinning white hair came in.

"Valentin," Jonas said with obvious relief. "Please show Mr. Ryder to his room."

"*Oui, monsieur.*" The old butler bowed. "If you'll follow me."

Sterling picked up the briefcase by his feet and rose. "When can we go over the trust paperwork, Alana? I want to be sure you understand everything for the reversion and signing on your birthday."

"Tomorrow will be soon enough," Jonas interrupted. "Supper is served at seven. We'll see you then."

Sterling looked at Cathlynn and honored her with a smile that reminded her of a jackal's glee. He reached for her hand and brought it to his lips. "I wouldn't miss it for the world."

She shivered despite herself and snatched her hand away as soon as she could. There was something about the man that inspired no confidence. How ridiculous, when this old man's jovial good looks could be mistaken for a trim Santa Claus!

"And Valentin," Jonas said as the butler reached to close the door, "please return when you're done."

"Oui, monsieur."

The dark glower in Jonas's eyes, the grim set of his jaw, the coiled sensuality of his movement when he turned toward her had Cathlynn wishing Valentin had left the door open for an easy escape. Not one to lie in wait, she decided to turn the tide in her favor.

"Well, Dr. Shades, care to explain what all that was about?"

"Funny, I was about to ask the same question. What kind of game did you think you were playing?"

"You started it, you go first." Cathlynn sat back and crossed a leg over one knee, pretending a calmness she didn't feel.

Jonas turned and walked to the massive English walnut desk nestled in the corner by two banks of bookshelves, giving him height, width and breadth. Did he feel it, too, the strange thickening of air in the room? Did he need the exterior props to shield himself from it? Or did the viscous atmosphere originate with him? He pivoted to face her and skewered her with a dark glare.

"I need a wife."

"Pardon me?" As her foot slapped the floor, Cathlynn was sure her mouth hung open with disbelief. She leaned forward. Did he expect her to marry him, or just play the part?

"I need a wife," he said as if it were a perfectly normal thing to say. Chilling apprehension snaked coldly through her. The man was insane!

With his chin cradled over a fist, he cocked his head and looked her up and down. His slow appraising look made Cathlynn feel like one of the antiques he'd put up for auction this afternoon. "Your coloring and height are about right, and you seem to have fooled Sterling."

"Fooled Sterling about what?" Then it hit her. "You think I look like your wife?"

"Sterling thinks so, and that's what's important."

Cathlynn rose from her chair, sliding her gloves on. "I didn't come here to discuss my looks, to fool anyone, or to get engaged. I want the Aidan Heart, then I'll be on my way."

"Thirteen years is a long time and the changes are plausible," Jonas continued as if he hadn't heard her. His gaze lingered disquietingly on the curves of her body. "Alana was raised in Boston, so even your accent works."

"Thank you for your unadulterated show of approval. Now, about the Aidan Heart—"

"How much is two weeks of your life worth to you?" he snapped sharply, like a man who'd made a decision and didn't intend to have it contradicted.

"Excuse me?" Again, Jonas's unmitigated gall caught her off guard. My God, he meant it. She saw it on his face, the uncompromising look of a man used to getting his way.

''Two weeks, how much is that worth to you?''

Cathlynn sank to the chair and sat primly on the unyielding surface, elbows on the armrests. She held her chin high and looked him straight in the eye. ''More than you can afford.''

The fluid unfurling of tensed muscles as he rounded the desk and came toward her had her blood tripping through her veins at high speed. What fuse had she lit now?

Cathlynn had the compelling urge to jump up and run, but held her ground. She'd show him she was just as strong as he was.

He leaned down, placing his hands on her chair's armrest, his fingers brushing her arms accidentally, striking her like hot lightning. He trapped her there with his aura of power and physical might. The heat of his breath caressed her cheek, turning a wave of trepidation in her stomach. His woodsy scent caused a ripple of turbulence along her skin. The cyclone in his storm-darkened eyes pierced her soul and whirled a myriad of sensations, chief among them an acute feeling of danger.

''Play my wife until the Christmas fete, until Alana's birthday,'' he said in a deep low voice that vibrated through her like an approaching storm's warning thunder. ''And I'll give you the Aidan Heart.''

Chapter Two

"I won't do it." Cathlynn ducked under Jonas's caging arms, and moved toward the door—away from his magnetic aura, from his enchanting scent, from his piercing gaze, which both frightened and exhilarated her at the same time.

"Not even for the Aidan Heart?"

She hesitated, her hand hovering above the doorknob. "You can't buy me."

"Yours free and clear in exchange for two weeks of your time. It seems a fair deal for something you want so desperately."

Damn, he'd pinned her into a neat little corner, hadn't he? She'd spent most of her adult life looking for the darned thing, and most of her childhood dreaming about it. Now, to get the Aidan Heart, and see her grandmother's eyes shine once more, she'd have to compromise her standards. She'd have to live a lie when she was known for her honesty. She turned to face him. How far would he go?

"No. I'm sorry, I don't have two weeks to spare. I have a business to attend to, a grandmother who needs me."

"I'll make it worth your while," Jonas said after a

short silence. Not even a hint of remorse crisped his stern features. He moved to his desk and riffled through the mess of papers on it.

"I already told you. I'm not for sale. From what I hear, you're not in a position to make such a generous offer."

"Idle village gossip. I hadn't thought you the gullible sort." He opened a drawer, the solid flex of his muscles beneath the shirt uninterrupted by her barb. He searched the drawer's contents, slammed it shut, then started on the next. "Everyone has a price."

"You don't even know who I am." Arms crossed over her chest, Cathlynn waited for his next move, icy expectation standing between them.

He stopped suddenly. His shadow loomed long and spectral on the wall behind him. "Your name is Cathlynn O'Connell and you're an antiques dealer from Nashua."

His smile caught her off guard. It lit up his face in a most attractive way, and she almost forgot her anger.

"How did you know?" She turned away from the desk, eclipsing his smile from her sight.

He picked up an index card and let it float back to his desk. "Your registration card for the auction."

He resumed his search and came up with an antique silver frame, then handed it to her, his fingers hesitating for a moment against hers. She took the frame more to break the unnerving contact than anything else, but a warm shiver still managed to snake through her. Even as she focused on the picture, she couldn't stop the heated hum where skin had touched skin.

The photograph showed the face of a happy bride. The hair color, framed in white lace, was different than hers, she noted—darker, richer. The eyes also appeared darker, but the picture's colors had mutated with time. The facial features were similar enough that Sterling might put down to maturity the differences in their looks. Yes, the young girl in the picture might have grown into something like her. A shiver crawled along her scalp and slid down her spine.

"Uncanny, isn't it?" Jonas's voice startled her from her reverie.

"Yes." Cathlynn placed the picture on the desk and retreated to the fireplace. She needed warmth to thaw the cold ice clogging her veins.

"Think of this as a vacation."

"I haven't said I'll take your offer." She rubbed her hands and offered her palms to the heat emanating from the weaving flames.

"I saw the way you looked at that piece of glass." Jonas came to stand behind her. His presence pulsated along her skin, raising the hairs along her arms in static protest. "I saw how fervently you tried to hide your desire while you bid." His breath caressed her hair like a Chinook wind. "You want the Aidan Heart more than you want anything else in the world." His voice wooed her like a gentle spring breeze. "What's a few weeks of your life for something you want so much?"

His fingers reached for her shoulders and the possessive weight of his palms felt as if it burned a hole through her coat. "Cathlynn..."

Her name sang into her soul and echoed in her mind. He'd said it so gently, she could almost believe this dark man had a heart. And God help her, she couldn't leave without the Aidan Heart.

What were a few weeks when she'd searched for her ancestor's sculpture for most of her life?

A log in the fireplace broke in half and crashed on the hot bed of coals, sending up a shower of sparks.

"Why do you need me to pretend I'm Alana?" Cathlynn asked, trying to figure out exactly what she'd get herself into if she accepted. Her throat felt dry, her palms sweaty. "How do you expect to fool Sterling? What if he sees a more recent picture of her?"

"That won't be a problem."

Jonas slipped his hands from her shoulders, and Cathlynn found herself inexplicably bereft. "Won't he find it suspicious that there are no pictures lying about?"

Jonas returned to his desk. "Alana hated to have her picture taken. She didn't realize this picture existed. It's the only one I have of her. You'll do it then? You'll play Alana?"

"I haven't said so. I still don't know exactly what you expect from me. What if Sterling wants to talk about Alana's family, her past?"

"I'll coach you on the basics. You'll do your best to avoid him most of the time." Jonas sat down in the big leather chair behind his desk. "Basically, you need to be seen but not heard until Sterling leaves after Alana's birthday."

"Why?"

"Because there's a lot at stake." Guarded tension stretched his features taut. Secrets, dark and dangerous, oozed from his every pore, igniting her curiosity and firing urgent warnings along her strained nerves like the dots and dashes of Morse code.

"Like what?" Cathlynn dragged a chair by his desk and sat down. Even if the village gossip proved true, he needed her alive, she had nothing to fear from him.

"Like a trust fund worth millions that reverts to her in a few weeks' time on her 30th birthday."

Greed, always a good motive for murder. Why hadn't anyone else thought of it? But then, only the gossip of old ladies had Alana dead. To the rest of the logical world she was merely missing. And wouldn't he wait until after the signing over of the trust to kill her?

"As her husband, won't you inherit?"

Jonas picked up a pencil from his desk and tapped it on his other hand in an annoying nervous rhythm. His eyes hardened, putting more distance between them. "With Alana missing, there will be delays and I need my promised share now to continue my work. I'm close to a breakthrough. She couldn't have picked a worse time to…leave."

"That sounds awfully cold."

The pencil stilled; the eyes didn't. They seemed to bore deeper and deeper, past the cracks in her mask, to her soft inner core, and anchor. What was he looking for? What did he want from her? Jonas's unwavering scrutiny narrowed the room, making her edgy and stifling her breath low in her lungs. She smoothed the skirt of her dress to remind herself she was indeed fully clothed.

"There are mitigating circumstances," Jonas said.

"Such as?"

The corded tendons along his jaw drew tight, relaxed, then tightened again, but he didn't say anything.

"What if she comes back?"

Jonas dropped the pencil and stood up abruptly. He walked to the window, but Cathlynn could have sworn he didn't see the mad dance of snowflakes falling past the windowpane. The iron-stiff set of his face frightened her with its severity. Something ate at him. Guilt? What had happened between him and Alana to cause such unbending grimness? His skin had paled, making him appear even more formidable.

"What if she comes back?" Cathlynn found the courage to ask again, not sure she really wanted an answer. Her mind had already worked overtime on sinister conclusions.

"I doubt she will." His voice grated with something close to hatred. His jaw tensed, raising tiny knots along the muscle. He didn't amplify. Or was the harshness due to his loss? Could she be mistaken? Had he loved Alana, and were the ominous feelings snaking through her just a product of her fertile imagination fueled by the house's ghoulish grimness?

Cathlynn digested the information he'd given her while a dozen questions popped into her mind. If he loved Alana, why had she left? Why wouldn't she be back? Was it because of Jonas, or something else? Something permanent…like death.

Some even say he killed her himself…

"What about the people in the village, won't they know the difference?" Cathlynn asked, trying to sway her thoughts away from their direful direction.

"Alana rarely ventured there, and there's no need for you to leave the monastery. All your needs will be taken care of. Only Valentin, my butler, and David Forester, my assistant, will need to know the truth, and they've both proven their trust."

Trying to slow down her mind and make sense of the bits of information he fed her, she focused on the tapestry over the fireplace. A medieval battle took place. Knights in shining armor on trusty steeds fought for the Holy Grail, killing for their perception of Truth and Right.

Well, that didn't help at all. The bloody carnage darkened her already dismal thoughts. There were always two sides to everything, weren't there? Perceptions changed truth. Didn't all the wars in the name of God prove that? Would she really be compromising her honesty by accepting the role in exchange for her heart's desire? And there was Gram's to think of. A week, a month. The doctors weren't sure how long she had left; they could only say that her time was near. Would two weeks be too long?

Cathlynn studied the room, looking for an answer to her dilemma among the sullen whispers of the past swirling about the room. The stones seemed to pulse again with unseen life.

Beware.

The whisper into her brain chilled her to the bone. She looked around the room, but saw nothing out of place. She shook her head, and put the perceived thought to a figment of her overtired mind.

Oh, Gram, what am I getting myself into?

Could she live for two weeks in the coldness of this grim stone house, among the austere monks' ghosts and the cloak of sadness permeating the walls?

"Can't you get your funding elsewhere?" Cathlynn asked, trying to fill the heavy silence while she thought her alternatives through.

"My options are…limited. The income from the monastery's various holdings isn't enough to support the monastery, let alone my research."

"The Monastery Company. That's you?"

"Yes."

"Why stay here then?" Cathlynn asked. "Why not sell this place?"

He sat down, leaned his elbows on the chair's armrests and tented his fingers. "You want the Aidan Heart, don't you?"

She nodded.

"And there's no logical reason for it, right?"

"No."

He lifted his hands. "I love this place, and there's no logical reason for it."

For an instant, his eyes showed the truth of his words and his face softened. Just as fast, the fleeting impression vanished, leaving Cathlynn to wonder if she'd simply imagined it.

"As for my research," he continued, "I do it for a very personal reason, and the trust would enable me to keep it—and the monastery—going without worry. I won't be the only beneficiary of your kindness. A lot of people depend on me for their livelihoods, and maybe even their lives."

The reasoning seemed noble enough, yet Cathlynn sensed there remained much untold. Did she really want to know the truth? Shadowed fear fought with her soul's deep yearning.

"I can't afford to take two weeks off work," Cathlynn said, mirroring his seated stance. Years of dealing had taught her the fine art of negotiation. "I have to keep buying and selling merchandise." But they had been lonely years. "I have to keep visible." They hadn't taught her to manage these strange gut feelings, or the way this man's mere presence could short-circuit her usually ordered thinking. She fought now for her edge, for the safety of her professional mask, for the knowledge that his need matched her own in ferocity. How far would he go? "As much as I want the Aidan Heart, I do have to make a living. Then there's the complication of my grandmother. She may not have two weeks to live.''

His cold, gray gaze fixed on her. She didn't flinch. The silence grew between them until Cathlynn thought she would suffocate from it. His pointed stare made her want to squirm, but instinct told her she couldn't let her discomfort show. She kept very still outwardly, but inwardly everything buzzed.

Staring back at him didn't help, because she saw so much and yet so little in the vivid gray pools. Everything about him seemed so contradictory—sensuous lips and a hard demeanor; eyes that thawed and iced over with no rhyme or reason; a seemingly logical approach to everything and an illogical love for a place. Which was the real Jonas? The murderer of village gossip who'd killed his wife in a fit of rage, or the driven researcher looking for some mysterious cure?

''Over the years, I've collected a fair amount of antique glass,'' Jonas said finally, breaking his mesmerizing eye contact. Cathlynn swallowed her sigh of relief. ''I've put off my collection's appraisal for far too long. I'd like to hire you to do the job.''

''I—''

''I'll pay you your going rate, and I'll also give you free title to the Aidan Heart when you leave after the Christmas Fete.''

Jonas Shades was no fool. He knew exactly which string to pull. Cathlynn was sorely tempted. She wanted the sculpture.

She couldn't leave without it.

''I've worked hard for what I've earned,'' Jonas added, leaning back in his chair. ''I'd hate to see it go to my wife's cousin, who hasn't worked a day in his life and would squander it, when it could be put to good use. How much care does your grandmother need?''

''She's cared for physically. What she needs is my presence to tie her to reality.''

''Would a visit every few days work?''

If she accepted his offer, she'd have her treasure and money besides to increase her inventory of merchandise. Her work here would be legitimate, and the telephone would keep her in touch with Gram's condition on a daily basis, and with the outside world should the need arise. Professionally speaking, she'd be a fool not to accept. What about personally? Could she trust this man?

''Be assured, Miss O'Connell,'' Jonas said. He had the air of a man who'd had enough of negotiations and now played his trump card. ''As long as I'm alive, the Aidan Heart will never make its way onto the market. If you want it, make your decision. *Now.*''

The deceptive silky smoothness of his voice rang with implicit power. She didn't want to, but she yielded. She had no choice. Not if she wanted the Aidan Heart— for herself, for Gram.

But she wouldn't capitulate completely. She'd been her own woman far too long to submit meekly to anyone—especially someone who could buffet her like a rudderless ship in a storm.

''All right, I accept, but I refuse to do anything illegal. I won't call myself by your wife's name. I won't sign any documents. And if I find you're using me to defraud Alana, I'll report you to the authorities.''

HE WATCHED the woman leave the library. She was a complication. But he was used to those. Jonas had never made anything easy for him, had taken so much from him already. The woman's resemblance to the departed Alana *was* uncanny.

His memory drifted to the real Alana and their last night together. How sweet the taste of her final breath in his mouth! He tugged the cuff of his shirt over the faint scar of scratches on his wrists. The bitch. She deserved what she got. They all did.

Perhaps he could use this resemblance to his advantage. Use her to put the final screw in his revenge when he exposed her treachery. Then he'd set his trap and watch Jonas's world fall apart. Watch Jonas lose all claims to the trust fund, to his research, to his future. Watch Jonas as he realized he was doomed to die the same horrid death his father had died—painful, destructive.

Yes, he could make this work to his advantage. He would watch and manipulate. He would stir the pot of suspicion. The lies would be exposed. Then he'd have his revenge…and more.

CATHLYNN FOLLOWED Valentin up and down the meandering, dimly lit corridors to a set of stairs carved straight out of the gray stone. The cool, damp air chilled her to the bone. She tried to shake the uneasiness licking at her heels, then shifted her concentration to memorizing the path they followed, but one colorless stone wall pretty much looked like the next, and she lost count of the multitude of shadowed arched doors with black iron locks they passed.

"The place doesn't look this big from the outside," Cathlynn said, trying to dispel the gloomy silence between them.

"Non, madame."

"Do you ever get lost?" Cathlynn asked with a

forced chuckle. The eerie clipping of her footsteps behind the butler's silent ones on the stone stairs reminded her irrationally of a prisoner being led to his execution.

"Non, madame."

Valentin, it seemed, was not a man of many words. Between Jonas's glowering silences and Valentin's sparse conversation, this could prove to be a very long two weeks.

"It must be hard to keep up with the housework."

"Most of the house is closed, and in the summer we hire staff to keep up appearances for the weekend guided tours. Curiosity about the monks' legend brings them in."

"I'm not familiar with the legend."

"The curse of the Holy Cross Brotherhood."

"Ah." Cathlynn couldn't think of anything else to say as she followed Valentin's ramrod-stiff penguin gait.

When they turned into an upstairs hallway, the walls' wraithlike shadows reached out for her again. Their cold, clammy fingers snatched at her hair, prickling the base of her neck with a feeling of coming doom. She quickly reached back to brush the uncomfortable feeling away, half expecting her fingers to twine into the sticky ectoplasm of a ghost. Instead, they met only empty space.

Beware.

The whisper echoed eerily inside her head, erupting a series of shivers down her spine.

"Does anyone besides you and Jonas live here?" she asked, sure a logical conclusion could be found for her auditory hallucination.

"No one, *madame*." He paused for an instant. "Except perhaps the ghosts."

"Ghosts?" Cathlynn had a feeling Valentin wanted to scare her deliberately. Why? Whatever the reason, his tactic was definitely working. Cathlynn couldn't remember the last time she'd been this spooked about anything, and wondered again at the wisdom of her decision to stay. *I'm safe,* she repeated to herself like a mantra. The joy she'd bring her grandmother with the Aidan Heart was worth a few nights in a scary house. It couldn't be worse than the sleepless nights she'd spent after listening to some of her brother's ghost stories.

"The monks, *madame*. They lived and died here for a century before disappearing."

"What happened to them?"

"Their secret was discovered."

"Their secret?" She almost wished Valentin had stuck to one-word answers. The old geezer was giving her a bad case of the creeps.

He shook his head. "Too unspeakable to mention." He stopped by a door and clinked keys from a large brass ring until he found the right one. Probably enjoying the macabre echo they created as the noise bounced off the stone walls, Cathlynn thought. "Their legacy lives on."

His answer left her imagination to run rampant with dastardly possibilities. Fourteen more days of this. She'd scare herself to death before she could take the Aidan Heart home.

Valentin unlocked the door and handed her the key before he stepped inside the room and flicked on the lights. "This was Madame Alana's room."

The house's stony coldness extended to this room. Cathlynn felt out of place in the large room's opulence. Not that she didn't appreciate the fineries of life, but this room, despite its picture-perfect decor, lacked something. Her own house in Nashua might be small, but each room radiated a feeling of warmth, a feeling of life. She found this room's rigid formality depressing.

Yards of sheer material draped the large bed's canopy. A rich coverlet of emerald and gold, decorated with a dozen pillows in all shapes and sizes, lay over the mattress. Valentin snapped open the heavy emerald brocade curtains trimmed with gold, covering the single window. The darkening gray sky didn't allow in much light. If anything, it heightened the caged feeling, increasing Cathlynn's uneasiness.

A huge English walnut wardrobe crowded the back wall. Valentin opened the double doors. "I doubt many of these clothes fit you, but..."

Cathlynn stuck her tongue out at the butler's back. Not that she'd want to fit in them, anyway. From what she could see, Alana's taste in clothes might be expensive, but it lacked subtlety. "I'll get some of my own stuff tomorrow."

"As you wish, *madame*."

Cathlynn walked to the small vanity and trailed a finger along the dust on the old wood. This house with all its empty rooms and cavernlike corridors would dampen her natural optimism if she let it. Was that why Alana had left? Had the incredible sadness of the house finally overcome her?

"What was she like—Alana?" Cathlynn asked as she picked up a silver brush scrolled with a fancy S from the tray on the vanity.

"It is not my place to answer your questions." Valentin bustled about at amazing speed for someone so frail-looking. He heaped the decorative pillows onto the carved trunk at the end of the bed, turned down the coverlet, then opened the heavy wood door next to the vanity. "The bathroom is through here. There are fresh towels behind the door."

"You don't approve, do you?" Cathlynn asked as she replaced the brush in its exact position, then turned to face the stern butler.

"It is not my place to pass judgment."

"I'm not trying to replace her."

"As I said, *madame,* it is not my place to say. But…"

"But what?"

Valentin's balding pate, beaked nose and loose jowl skin reminded her of an aging eagle. He searched her face with a narrowed gaze, then as if changing his mind, he shrugged. "Madame Alana's disappearance has saddened us all."

"I'm sure it has…" Cathlynn felt sure he'd wanted to say something else.

He bowed and backed out the door. "If you need anything, *madame,* the intercom is by the door. Ring the service button and someone will answer."

He made it sound as if the house teemed with servants. "Thank you, Valentin."

"Soyez prudente," Valentin mumbled as he left.

What had he said? Before Cathlynn could ask for an explanation, Valentin shut the door with a resounding boom that echoed down the empty corridor like a small explosion. She looked at the ancient key in her hand. At least he hadn't locked her in. She could leave at any time. With a sigh she went to the window. Maybe she should leave.

The snow fell in fat weighted flakes that stuck to the glass with the wind's force. Shapeless white blanketed the cobbled courtyard. The last of the auction goers were leaving, their headlights cutting bright arcs across the darkening sky. Only her own Volvo remained—a white mound in the flat yard.

She sat on the window's stone ledge, leaned her head against the frigid glass and blew against the pane, clouding it with her warm breath. With a finger she squiggled a random doodle.

As Cathlynn's mind drifted to her childhood, a circle of pines replaced the monastery's shadowy landscape. The roses of her grandmother's garden bloomed all around her. Gram's finest china and linen graced the flaking wooden picnic table. Cathlynn saw herself carrying a plate heaped with cakes and tarts as Gram poured the tea into cups. She remembered well the taste of the tangy lemon curd sauce she heaped onto scones. But most of all she remembered the way her grandmother's face lit up when she spoke of Aidan and Deirdre's love. Cathlynn had felt so secure, so safe in that circle of pines, surrounded by the scent of roses and her grandmother's friendship. Was it so wrong to want the feeling back? Was it so wrong to want to see that bright light in Gram's eyes once more?

She studied Alana's room again. Secure was the last thing she felt right now. She was cold and alone, and if truth be told, a little scared. What did she know about Jonas Shades? What if he *had* killed his wife? If the house wasn't creepy enough, her unseemly reaction to its master would be enough to shake her confidence. But he needed her alive, didn't he? Until this mysterious Christmas fete she would be safe—then she'd be gone with the Aidan Heart.

Cathlynn sighed wearily. She didn't have long to wash up before Jonas expected her to put in her first performance. She couldn't let herself fall prey to the house's dreary mood.

She crossed the room and went into the bathroom. Again the opulence caught her by surprise. Who would have thought the plumbing could be so modern? A sunken tub, big enough for two, took up most of the room. Had Jonas and Alana shared loving baths here? She giggled at her image of Jonas surrounded by frothy scented bubbles—not too likely!

Alana's toiletries still stood on a mirrored tray. How odd. Cathlynn picked up a half-used blood-red lipstick and replaced it before trailing a finger through the assortment of bottles and jars on the tray. Wouldn't a woman bent on running away have taken at least some of her toiletries with her? Wouldn't she have taken some of her clothes, too? How fast had she fled, and why?

Some even say he killed her himself...

A shudder shook her. Her gaze shifted to the wooden tray at the opposite end of the counter. She picked up the cologne bottle made by a local perfumery. Inhaling the scent, she realized it held the same woodsy tone that Jonas wore, which had so muddled her senses earlier. Had Alana picked it out for him, or was it his choice? For an insane half moment, she hoped it was the latter.

Curiosity led her to the wooden door opposite the one leading to her room. Jonas's room? Her hand hesitated for a second on the knob, but when she found it turned, she pushed it and went in.

She smiled. Now *this* room looked lived in. Unlike Alana's pristine room, this place was a delightful mess. Magazines, papers, maps lay in disarray over every piece of man-size furniture. Clothes had been dropped in a heap on an easy chair and forgotten. Even the bed was mussed. Either Valentin's housekeeping skills weren't up to par, or Jonas didn't like his privacy intruded upon.

Cathlynn expected the red, green and blue plaid comforter had been chosen more for comfort than eye appeal. She sat down on the edge of the bed in the darkened room, feeling its coziness while she ran a hand over the blue flannel sheets. She'd much rather sleep in this room than share the other with Alana's ghost.

How long had it been since Alana and Jonas had shared a room? A bed? What would it be like to sleep with Jonas here? Would she feel secure or defenseless? Would he show her his blustery side, or would the sensuality promised by his full lips come through?

She blushed at the thought. She didn't want to know. Not really. Because to know, she'd have to expose too much of herself, and she couldn't afford to do that.

So lost was she in her daydream that she didn't hear the footsteps behind her. When a hand buried itself erotically in her hair, she screamed and jumped off the bed. With her heart beating a hundred miles an hour, she whirled to face her attacker, hands forward in a defensive position. She found herself looking straight into Jonas's remote face and desire-darkened eyes.

"Didn't anyone ever tell you it's dangerous to come into a man's room uninvited?"

Chapter Three

"Didn't anyone ever tell you it's not nice to scare people out of their skins?" Cathlynn said, raising a hand to her tripping heart while the panicked rush of her pulse tried to regain its balance. Gray, like smoke, his silhouette had no sharp edges in the bedroom's dusky light, Jonas looked more intimidating than ever. She shook her head to bury the primal betrayal of her body to his erotic touch of her hair.

As she moved to put distance between them, seeking to remove the disturbing threat of his nearness, his gaze fixed her unblinkingly. But she wasn't fast enough. His hand caught her wrist, circling it like a warm manacle, holding fast like tempered steel. Her pulse bumped beneath his thumb, unmasking her cool exterior.

"A man's room is where he dreams, where he conquers." His free hand buried itself in her hair once more, bringing her face close to his as he whipped her cuffed hand behind her and pressed her body against his. Her lips parted involuntarily in anticipation of his kiss. A stab of fear pierced her gut at the violent storm in his eyes. Her skin snapped and crackled with static where their bodies met.

"Unless you're prepared for the consequences," he

said, his breath vibrating against her lips, "I suggest you keep out of my room."

She swallowed hard, wishing he'd let her go, hoping insanely he'd kiss her. "I'm sorry," she said lamely. "I didn't mean to intrude."

He let her go abruptly. She fell back. Rubbing the wrist he'd held, she recalled his steely warmth, the echo of his pulse beating in opposition, then in rhythm, to hers, the rush of heat it had stirred in her blood. She wondered how his lips would have felt against hers. Would they have been soft as their fullness promised, or hard like the rest of his face?

Why did she care?

She shot him a quick glance. He grabbed a blue-heathered sweater from his dresser and pulled it over his head, nonchalantly, as if nothing had happened between them. And nothing had, she reminded herself, except for the temporary short-circuiting of her brain. The wool molded over his shoulders, accentuating their breadth, their might. He centered the knot of his tie between the starched collar of his white shirt. She looked away, not wanting to be sucked into the vortex of his strength once again.

It had been a long time since she'd dared let a man touch her, let a man make her feel vulnerable. And as out of place as it seemed, she had wanted him to touch her, to kiss her. With his hard eyes and soft lips, Jonas Shades would be the wrong place to start looking for easy companionship. There was nothing easy or companionable about him, especially in the lengthening shadows of the room.

Yes, the stony set of his face almost guaranteed she'd get emotionally bruised and battered in this relationship.

And when he was through, there would be nothing left of her in the splintered remnants spit out of his twister.

But he would escape unscathed—as she suspected he always did.

"What did you want?" he asked, his voice filled with impatience. The clandestine light of dusk shifted around him, shielding the mirror of his eyes from her view.

"Nothing. I—I..." She didn't know what to say. That was a first. Cathlynn O'Connell at a loss for words! She recoiled farther away, closer to the bathroom, closer to escape.

"It doesn't matter." He dismissed her stammer with a wave of his hand. "I needed to see you anyway. There are a few things we need to go over."

He snapped on the overhead light, throwing garish light over the room, playing sharp black shadows against the gray stone walls. After clearing the clothes from the easy chair, he gestured for her to sit. "Come, we don't have much time."

She shook her head at his invitation and crossed her arms protectively over her chest. "What kind of things?" The chair would cage her, and she needed to feel free.

"Alana's history."

"Oh, yes. I suppose that would help." A soft sigh of relief escaped her. Away from his formidable proximity, she regained her poise.

"I wish you'd sit," he said.

"So you can tower over me? Forget it. I'll stand."

His eyebrows rose and he gave her an odd look. "Suit yourself."

Jonas paced the room with studious purpose, pulling facts from the files of his mind. His hasty movements took him in and out of the shadows as if he belonged equally in the worlds of light and dark. Lover or murderer? She shook her head to dispel the grisly thought.

"Your name is Alana Chandler Shades," Jonas said. "Your mother's na—"

"My name is Cathlynn." She couldn't help it. Submitting meekly wasn't her style. "I told you I can't use hers."

He stopped pacing and stood hands on hips. "Must you be so difficult? We don't have time to waste."

"Why, yes, I must." She mimicked his voice, his movements, and felt a smile tug the corner of her mouth. Yes, this was better. Having Jonas unstrung and struggling for control was much better than the other way around. This she could handle.

"My wife's name is Alana, how do you expect me to explain the discrepancy?"

"Use your imagination."

He grumbled something about cursed luck under his breath and resumed his pacing, giving her a terse history of his life with Alana.

They'd met while he'd interned over summer vacation at the U.S. branch of Chandler Pharmaceuticals. Encouraged by Alana's father, their attraction had grown swiftly; the summer had passed quickly. Promises had been made and honored a year later.

"Alana is British?"

"By birth. She was raised in Boston."

Jonas's voice faded and Cathlynn waited for him to continue. He'd recounted his story with factual dryness. Flat and cold like the air in the room. Were the memories too painful, or had deeper feelings never existed?

"What happened?" she prodded when he didn't speak.

"We married. I finished my degree. I was offered a

permanent research position with Chandler Pharmaceuticals.'' He flicked on the bedside light as a distraction to the obvious pain flitting through his expressive eyes, making him human, vulnerable for a moment. The chiseled sternness returned swiftly, making her wonder if she'd been mistaken.

He stood silent by the window, offering her a view of his profile. The crisp creases in his winter-weight wool pants matched the furrowed lines on his face. Sadness or guilt? Unexpectedly, Cathlynn wanted to hold him and unburden him from his grief. But she didn't move. Being a wife wasn't part of the deal, only acting.

He stuck his hands in his pockets, tightening the fabric of his pants over his buttocks, and stared deep into the dark thickness of night. ''Both were a mistake.''

A mistake? Curiosity had her longing to pursue that thread, but she sensed it would be a blunder.

''Is there anything else I should know?'' she asked. Watching him stare blankly out the window made her uneasy because she didn't know what to expect—from him; from her. ''What about preferences—food, drink, activities, et cetera?''

For a moment she thought he wouldn't answer, then he turned from the window and leaned his trim backside on the sill. ''She liked everything expensive. Quality didn't matter, only price. She drank a lot. To forget, she said. As for activities, I'd prefer you not emulate her in that department. I suggest you simply act naturally. Sterling's bound to sense a forced performance.''

He glanced at his watch. ''It's time. Why don't you run a brush through that mane of yours, and we'll go down to dinner.'' Flexing his thighs, he pushed himself off the sill.

"You'll be all right?" he asked, giving her a queer little look that shivered all the way to her toes.

"I'll be myself," Cathlynn said. Her smile cracked her face despite an attempt to suppress it. As long as she fought him, she wouldn't fall.

Being herself was no problem, but it might not quite meet Dr. Jonas Shades's expectations.

THE DINING ROOM proved as formal and gloomy as the rest of the house. Wraithlike shadows played across the tall ceiling. Three multitiered crystal chandeliers hung evenly spaced over the table's length. The long table could have seated twenty-four easily, but the crisp white linen cloth was set with only three places. The tall red and gold–upholstered chairs dwarfed their occupants. The heavy sideboard stood empty. Here again a series of solemn black-hooded monks stared at them from their gilt frames on the striped wallpaper, passing judgment, it seemed, at the affluence denied them in life.

All that's missing is the cobwebs and the rattling of ghostly chains, Cathlynn thought as she sat in the chair Jonas held for her.

Valentin pushed a squeaky cart laden with silver-domed trays while Sterling regaled them with the woes of his transatlantic flight. His voice boomed with disquieting loudness in the cavernous room. "Can you imagine being stuck beside such a chap for all those hours?"

Cathlynn downed her chuckle with a sip of water. Her pity sided with Sterling's unfortunate seatmate.

"Are you still afraid of flying, Alana?" Sterling asked, then tested the wine in his goblet.

"Please call me Cat—"

Jonas tapped her ankle under the table with his foot and glowered an icy warning at her. She stomped slyly on his toe with the heel of her shoe while she smiled graciously at Sterling. Jonas's pinched lips told her she'd found her mark.

"That's Jonas's pet name for me, and I've grown rather fond of it over the years."

She snatched a roll from the bread basket, tore off a piece and slipped easily into her role. She had to play it well; her dream was at stake, not only Jonas's. But playing it Jonas's way wouldn't work, and as much as he scared her with his frosty charm and tempestuous eyes, she had nothing to fear until he held the trust— then she'd be gone before she could suffer his wrath.

"If I'd gotten over my fear of flying," Cathlynn continued, "I'd surely have flown to England to visit you. I'd forgotten what an interesting person you are. But there's just something about trusting your life to a shell of metal thirty thousand feet above the ground." She scrunched her shoulders and feigned a shiver.

"It's really quite safe, you know." Sterling picked at the plate Valentin placed in front of him, removing the orange sauce from the chicken breast with the side of his fork. "Tell me, dear boy, is that butler of yours the only servant you've got left? I rang the service bell for half an hour before I got an answer."

Jonas sawed his meat. His jaw twitched once before he answered. "Times have been hard lately. We do the best we can."

Sterling pushed the peas around his plate, tasted one, then rejected the rest. "I dare say, you'll be happy when the trust money starts flowing, won't you?"

"It will ease my mind."

"And you, my dear, how have you stood the isolation all these years?"

"Boston isn't that far. Neither is New York. I've got plenty of distractions to keep me occupied. Then, of course, I have Jonas." She smiled widely, playing her role of adoring wife to the hilt, enjoying challenging Jonas's silent warnings.

"Yes," Sterling said, putting aside his knife and fork, and studying her. "I can see how you feel. How nice to know the bloom of love could have survived for thirteen years without fading. You're a lucky man, J.T. But then, you always were."

"How's cousin Geoffrey doing?" Jonas asked, pushing his plate aside and reaching for his wineglass.

"Splendidly as ever. Anne's health, on the other hand, has suffered. But the doctors think she'll carry to term this time." He sent Jonas a pointed stare. Jonas didn't flinch, but downed another sip of wine. "I'm looking forward to playing adopted granddad to the baby. When will you two add an heir to the Shades clan?"

Cathlynn looked down at her plate, her cheeks flaming with embarrassment. This was a subject she'd rather not touch. Babies weren't a likely part of her future.

"We still have plenty of time," Jonas said without missing a beat.

Sterling moved on to business matters, family and mutual friends. Cathlynn ate without tasting, and listened to the slight undercurrent of tension building beneath the idle chatter. She fell back easily on the conversation skills she'd cultivated over the years, and kept the ball rolling when it threatened to grind to a halt and squash the brittle lie of their deceitful game.

As Valentin served dessert and coffee, Cathlynn noticed the tired lines along Jonas's eyes. Were the constant reminders of Alana creating the stress, or was it simply playing the charade? She hadn't thought of that angle before, and watched him with renewed interest.

Citing a long day ahead of him, Jonas excused himself. Cathlynn and Sterling rose to join him. They all walked up the long, dark and lonely corridors together, stopping by Jonas's room to say good-night.

"Separate bedrooms?" Sterling said as Cathlynn and Jonas reached for different knobs. "Do you expect to produce an heir this way?"

"Of course not." Cathlynn placed a hand on Sterling's elbow. She pointed her chin toward Jonas and spoke in a loud whisper. "He snores like a car without a muffler, and as much as I love that dear husband of mine, a girl does need her beauty sleep. The connecting door is always open for, you know…" She let the rest of the sentence hang.

Sterling roared with laughter.

"I'll see you tomorrow, Sterling," Jonas muttered.

"Sleep well, dear boy." The twinkling in Sterling's eye suggested the slightest tinge of envy.

Cathlynn stepped into her room, clicking on the light before she moved to close the door. Jonas followed her in and shut the door decisively. He covered the space between them in two long strides. When she looked at him in surprise, his hand reached for her chin.

"You had your fun tonight." His voice caressed her with false gentleness, his hand, warm and hard, held her like a steel snare, imprinting her mind with the tiniest shadow of fear. Anger flashed like lightning in his eyes. "If you're not careful, Sterling will read through your act."

"What do you mean? I followed your orders. I was

being myself." Despite her outward indifference, Cathlynn found it hard to swallow.

"There's a lot at stake here." His grip on her arm tightened. "Remember, there's a price to be paid if you fail."

Cathlynn swatted his hand off and spun away from his grip. "Hey, wait a minute! I get the Aidan Heart no matter what."

Jonas ran a hand through his hair, then kneaded the back of his neck. "Not if you're going to deliberately blow your cover."

"How do you expect me to play the role of someone I've never met after you've told me next to nothing about her?" She snagged his arm as he moved toward the bathroom door. "I'm doing my best."

He stopped and stabbed her with a piercing gaze. "I *must* be able to trust you."

"Trust has to go both ways." She wasn't sure he'd heard her words over the explosive slam of their connecting door.

TRYING TO DISPEL her frustration, Cathlynn plopped onto the bed and called the hospital to check up on Gram and give the nurses the number where she could be reached. Nothing had changed in Gram's condition—which was both a relief and a worry. Then she called her friend and partner, Claire Martel. For her own peace of mind, Cathlynn needed someone on her side. Predictable Claire was right where Cathlynn expected her to be—at home, at her desk, even at ten on a Saturday evening.

"Why aren't you out being romanced by a handsome young man?" Cathlynn teased.

"Someone's got to do the books."

"Isn't that why we hire an accountant?"

"Did you get caught in the storm?" Claire asked, deftly avoiding Cathlynn's prying.

"You could say that." Cathlynn told her about her adventure with the Aidan Heart and its dark owner, and her decision to stay in Ste-Croix.

"Are you sure you know what you're doing?" Claire asked.

Cathlynn could hear Claire drum the eraser end of her pencil on the desk. Even her frown managed to telegraph itself across the wire.

"Of course I do." Cathlynn tucked her bare feet beneath her and switched the receiver from one ear to the other. "It's time someone took Dr. Shades down a notch or two."

"I don't know…"

"Stop worrying. I'm perfectly safe."

"Your shimmering walls aren't going to make sure nothing bad happens to you."

"Not him, but the monk's sacrificial virgin will." She forced a light chuckle while Claire groaned. She could just see Claire with her eyes rolled toward the ceiling in exasperation. How the two of them, with such different personalities, had become friends was one of life's mysteries. "No, look, I'm safe. I've got a lot in my favor. Number one, he needs me alive until he gets the trust. Number two, those self-defense classes you're always dragging me to will make me able to hold my own—"

"And number three, you take too many risks," Claire cut in. "What about the pickle you got yourself into last year when you thought Mr. Chin was trying to use you for some illegal smuggling operation?"

Cathlynn reached for her purse on the night table

beside the bed and searched for her brush. "Not one of my swiftest moves, but you've got to admit, he was acting awfully suspicious, and I was trying to protect our business and our reputation."

"That's not the point. The point is you were wrong."

"Not completely. He did have two wives who didn't know about each other."

Claire groaned once more, and Cathlynn heard the crack of her pencil breaking in two.

"I'm not wrong this time," Cathlynn continued, stroking her hair into order while scanning the colorless walls with all their shadowy cracks and crevices. Once again they seemed to come alive before her eyes, pulsating, shimmering like hot asphalt on a summer day. She swallowed hard. "If you saw this place, if you felt it, you'd understand. Besides, I always land on my feet."

"Yeah, but you've also used up at least eight of your nine lives looking for that stupid piece of glass."

"Then that leaves me with one more before the final goodbye." Cathlynn returned her brush to her purse. "And I've got you looking out for me. Pack me a suitcase. I'll come pick it up tomorrow when I visit Gram. And stop worrying. I know what I'm doing."

"I sure hope so." Claire sighed, obviously unconvinced. "Promise you'll keep in touch. If I don't hear from you every day, I'll call the police."

"You worry too much. But I promise I'll keep you up to date." Cathlynn twirled the rubbery telephone cord around her index finger. "Thanks, Claire, for caring."

"Yeah, well, I need you to keep business flowing through our shop door. Just make sure you don't bury yourself in too deep over there."

After saying goodbye to Claire, Cathlynn steeled herself for a night in this inhospitable room. Her gaze strayed to the closed door separating her from Jonas. She might have taken a dozen self-defense classes with Claire, but they'd been ineffective enough this afternoon when Jonas had trapped her with a mere look, paralyzing her with his stormy eyes and magnetic aura of power. She remembered, too, how she'd wanted his kiss, trembled with desire for it—a willing victim. Her uncharacteristic response to him could prove a liability in the future if she didn't immunize herself against him.

She sighed heavily as she rose to find a change of clothes. She'd tripped into an intricate web, but was she the spider or the fly? Shaking her head, Cathlynn searched the contents of Alana's dresser, looking for a nightgown. The room around her pulsed, raising her anxiety to new heights. She hated it when the walls seemed to take life like that. She hunched her shoulders and steeled herself for the ghostly echo in her mind, but this time the clammy shadow fingers didn't penetrate her skull.

The fact she wasn't seeing any of the clothes she touched didn't register. Jonas Shades could be creepy when he wanted, and he could make her angrier than anybody she remembered, even her mother.

Now he had her caged and shackled. If she left, she'd never own the Aidan Heart. If she failed to convince Sterling she was Alana, she'd lose, too. With an impotent groan, she closed the drawer and went on to the next.

Did Jonas know Alana was dead and not merely missing? Was that why her performance was so important to him? If he did know, how had he acquired the knowledge? Firsthand? And why was there no police investigation into the matter? Was his influence that strong?

But he needed Alana alive to earn the trust money. He wouldn't have killed her until *after* it reverted to her.

Cathlynn stopped short. "Listen to you!"

She shook her head and dipped her hands once more into the luxurious folds of silk filling Alana's drawers. Her hands hit something hard. She lifted them and found a leather folder. Curiosity got the best of her. She pulled the snap and drew out the legal document folder trapped inside.

Divorce papers.

When she noticed the date, the sheets quivered. Four and a half weeks ago. Wasn't that when Alana had disappeared? Cathlynn quickly refolded the document and stuffed it into the folder, willing her mind to stop buzzing with unanswered questions, willing the fear and doubts zipping through her veins to stop their frantic race. It didn't matter. It wasn't any of her business. She was just playing a role—for the Aidan Heart, and nothing else.

She didn't have to get involved. She didn't want to. She couldn't.

But she was.

She snatched a silk kimono-style bathrobe from the wardrobe and headed for the bathroom. A warm shower dulled her fears and doubts, and brought the drowsiness of dinner back. For good measure she secured both the bathroom lock and her bedroom door.

Wearing Alana's perfumed robe, wandering the perimeter of Alana's room, pretending to love Alana's husband gave her a queer feeling of inadequacy. She tried to shrug it off, but it stuck like cobwebs in an old attic as Alana's imposing ghost traipsed invisibly behind her.

"It's an act," she reminded herself. She didn't have to feel beautiful, she didn't have to feel like the mistress of the house, she didn't have to feel in love; she only had to pretend.

She punched the satin-covered pillow and covered herself with the cold satin sheets. But when she closed her eyes, gray squally seas drowned her mind with the uneasy feeling it would take a long, long while before she forgot the magnetic appeal of Jonas Shades.

JONAS COULDN'T SLEEP. As he twisted and turned in his bed, all he could think of was Cathlynn and the way her small hand had lovingly stroked the dark blue of his sheets this afternoon. He needed her here now, to sweep away the haunting loneliness of the winter night. A loneliness that hadn't bothered him until he'd seen her on his bed, looking for all the world as if she belonged there.

He could still see her eyes, vague and distant, her thoughts lost somewhere in the depths of her daydream. Had she been thinking, as he was, of their bodies entwined beneath the soft heap of bedclothes?

He jumped from his bed and grabbed his navy bathrobe from the post. Tightening the belt around his waist, he paced the length of his room, feeling every one of his muscles contract and extend with each motion of his limbs. He rolled his shoulders to relieve the tension. He rolled his head. He blew out a long breath and dragged in a slow one.

Nothing worked.

He needed her. He wanted her with every fiber of his

body. Wanted her like he'd never wanted anyone. Wanted her with a fierceness that scared him.

A woman could take away a man's power faster than anything else.

He shouldn't want her.

He shouldn't need her.

He couldn't afford to.

An irresistible impulse propelled him across the bathroom. He found her bedroom door locked, and reached beneath the mirrored tray for a key. Then he was in her room.

He hesitated, listening. The wind threw flecks of wet snow against the window, landing in soft plops, then sliding to the bottom of the pane in a curved heap. The wind moaned balefully around the house. Funny, he'd never thought of this place as sad before. Yet now, the wind seemed to cry an echo of his empty soul.

The sleepy rhythm of her breath caught his attention. His reluctant attraction drew him closer and closer to her bed.

Her brown hair fanned out on the cream silk pillow like a lion's mane. One hand curled in a soft C next to her cheek, the other lay peacefully atop the emerald coverlet. The deep V of the pink robe exposed the creamy sides of her firm breasts, making him hungry for a taste. Her parted mouth telegraphed an invitation to kiss.

Of its own volition, his thumb reached out to gently stroke the soft skin of her lips. He ignored the tremors running rampant through his body as he remembered the tempest that had flared fast and furious through him when he'd held her, the lightning that still sparked between them.

When she sighed, he snatched his hand away and

watched as the cream-colored sheet and emerald coverlet rose and fell with each of her breaths. Her head turned. A strand of hair fell across her face. He pushed it aside, feeling the smooth skin beneath his index finger.

A slow anger intertwined with the basic instincts of a man long denied.

He wanted her.

He needed her.

He couldn't have her.

Not now.

Not ever.

A faint whimper escaped her. Her eyelids fluttered with the mad movements of a dreamer dreaming. Dark shadows of distress slipped across her innocent face. Her head turned again. Her eyebrows bunched. Fear sped her breaths raggedly through her parted lips.

Fear. Yes, she had a right to fear him. He'd do her no good. Acquiring the trust was the most important thing in his life now. He needed it to continue his work, to save his life and his brother's, to assure that his sister didn't pass on the inherited mutant gene to any of her future sons, to help all the others inflicted with this dreaded degenerative disease. He would sacrifice *anything* to find the cure. Hadn't he paid a hefty price already for his choices? They'd caged him into a loveless marriage. They'd cost him his funding. And if he didn't find a solution soon, they could cost him his future. Yes, it was much better that she fear him because love, his love, would poison her life just as it had poisoned Alana's, and he couldn't bear to see those golden-brown tiger's eyes look at him with hatred.

His dreams were grounded in reality, in his vision for a brighter future for all, not in fantasy. He had to remember that. In two weeks, she'd be gone, and everything could go back as it was.

Anger rose. A deep, disturbing anger that shook him to the core. Damn Alana and her tricks. Damn Cathlynn and her irresistible appeal.

With numb, trancelike movements, he turned toward his room, feeling as if he'd just condemned himself to hell on earth.

CATHLYNN'S HEART pounded savagely against her ribs. Mad images flickered against the screen of her lids. She was dreaming, she knew, but couldn't seem to escape the disjointed vision playing itself before her.

Chanting, black-robed monks queued in an endless row, slowly circled the crosses in the courtyard. The dying sun bled the crosses red, and the forest's shadowy backdrop disappeared in a thick, roiling fog. A woman appeared from nowhere in the middle of the circle, her pasty, blank face zombielike in the fading light, her dark hair a sharp contrast to the flowing white of the dress she wore. Then she lay suspended in midair, levitated by some unseen strings above the ground.

The chanting increased, growing louder and louder, stronger and stronger, with each beat of her pulse. A long, silver blade gleamed in the last speck of sun. And as the last ray of light buried itself beneath the horizon, the blade fell.

The woman's body jerked once.

Her death-dulled eyes opened, turning toward Cathlynn. Her blood-red lips moved.

"Beware the monk," she said, her voice flat and hollow.

Then her eyes rolled back into her skull. The knife rose again. But this time the sharp, blood-tainted tip headed toward the dreamer. Just before it sliced her throat, the picture against Cathlynn's lids splintered.

Cathlynn's eyes snapped open. She jerked up, gasping as her hand reached for her heart. Fear-streaked sweat ran between her breasts. She glimpsed a shadow moving stealthily across the room. It disappeared into the wall. She rubbed her eyes with disbelief. It had been a dream, hadn't it? Yet she could have sworn the shadow wore a long, black-hooded habit.

A scream rose from deep inside and lodged in her dry throat, refusing to take shape. A manic thought infiltrated her brain, rooted and grew like Jack's magical beanstalk. It twisted and turned, encroaching on logic with its insidious branches until its tenacious fingers gripped her mind in its evil prison, forcing her to face what she'd wanted to deny.

Alana had disappeared.

Jonas knew she wouldn't be back.

The papers she'd found this evening beneath the silk of Alana's drawer, formed the perfect motive. With the divorce, he'd lose the trust fund. Was a missing wife still a wife in the eyes of the law? But he'd taken care of that with a stand-in, hadn't he?

Too clever, too sharp.

The ghost of her dream had warned her.

Alana was dead.

Chapter Four

Hiding behind his morning paper, Jonas tried to ignore Cathlynn's entrance, tried to ignore the speeding of his blood through his veins, the yearnings tugging at his heart.

Except for the way she wore her hair, this morning Cathlynn looked every bit as elegant as Alana. A barrette clipped her golden-brown mane in a ponytail. Jonas itched to set it free, to see the strands ripple with light in the morning sun. The cinnamon-colored dress she wore stretched to cling to Cathlynn's enticing curves in a way they never had to Alana's angles. She'd draped a gold and emerald scarf artfully around her waist to disguise the tight fit of the dress, and wore a pair of heavy gold earrings he'd given Alana for their third anniversary. They drew attention to the golden life of Cathlynn's skin. He thought of sun and heat and cleared his throat, slanting his attention back to the paper in his hand before he got burned. Even her scent matched Alana's, causing a caustic ripple in his stomach. His spine stiffened as suspicion crawled along his skin. She's not Alana, he reminded himself.

''Good morning,'' she said, taking the chair next to his.

Her voice spread through him like warmed molasses, thick and sweet. He grumbled an answer.

Valentin squeaked his cart to the sideboard and unloaded several silver-domed platters onto it.

"I need to go to town today," Cathlynn said.

He frowned at her over the edge of his paper. "Why?"

"I need a few amenities. I may be playing Alana and be stuck trying to fit into her too tight clothes for now, but I draw the line at using her toothbrush. Besides, we had an agreement. I can visit Gram every few days."

For the first time in months, he felt a genuine smile wanting to erupt over his lips, but didn't allow it. "Valentin, make sure David readies Alana's car." He returned his attention to the business pages of the *Boston Sunday Globe* to keep his seesawing emotions under control.

"Non, monsieur." Valentin poured a cup of coffee from the silver carafe on the sideboard and placed it in front of him.

Jonas dropped his hands, folding the newspaper like an imploding building. Had the whole world turned against him? "Valentin?"

"The roads, *monsieur,* they are impassable. The village plow was never fixed after the last snow. It will be a day or so before a private truck can come this far out."

"Who's leaving?" Sterling asked as he walked into the room.

"No one apparently." Jonas bristled inwardly at Sterling's appearance. His sense of timing was impeccable as always. Like a hound on a scent, Sterling was looking for traces of deceit, for any excuse to revert the trust to Geoffrey. Jonas had long suspected the reason, but there was no hard evidence, and until he could find some, he was at Sterling's mercy.

He glanced at Cathlynn as she sipped a glass of orange juice. He'd provided a decoy, but he was quickly learning he couldn't control her behavior. He'd have to hope Sterling and Cathlynn's meetings were few and far between, and that he was always present to avert disaster.

"Where were you planning on going, my dear?" Sterling asked. Curiosity bordered with an inquisition-like command tinged his voice. He lifted each silver dome on the sideboard and inspected the fare below.

"Shopping," Cathlynn improvised. She glanced at him, a mischievous twinkle in her eye. Jonas silently warned her to watch her step. But defiance lifted her shoulders and tilted her chin up. A ripple of apprehension raced through him. Jonas held his breath as he lifted his paper once more, steeling himself for the unfolding scene, feeling his control over the situation slip like water through a fist.

"I need a new dress for the fete," Cathlynn added. "And I'm in a shopping mood today."

"I've never known a woman who wasn't." Sterling poured himself a glass of orange juice, dropped dry toast on a plate and added a slice of melon before seating himself at the table.

"Coffee, *madame?*" Valentin asked.

"Please."

She whispered her answer as if she needed the caffeine to jump-start her day. What kind of nightmare had caused her face to contort in sheer horror last night? Had she slept any after waking up from her dark dream? The dark circles beneath her eyes said no. He'd heard her switch on her light, heard her pace. The light had still been on at dawn when he'd woken after a restless sleep. He'd half expected her to put an end to their bargain and leave. Her decision to stay pleased him more than he cared to admit. For his research's sake, he rationalized.

Carafe in hand, Valentin turned to Sterling. *"Monsieur?"*

"Tea. Darjeeling." Sterling never looked up as he picked seeds from his cantaloupe with disdain. Some things never change. Jonas had always wondered why Sterling thought of himself more as one of the family than an employee.

With a haughty lift of his eyebrows and shake of his head behind Sterling's back, Valentin duck-walked to fill the lawyer's request. Cathlynn suppressed her laugh with a sip of coffee, and Jonas with a bite of his tongue. He agreed wholeheartedly with Valentin's attitude.

"How did you sleep in our humble home?" Cathlynn asked Sterling a little too brightly to sound natural as she slipped into her role as hostess.

"Like the dead." Sterling stared at her for a full minute before his mustache twitched into a smile. Jonas saw her shudder in recognition that Sterling suspected something. He had to get them apart before Cathlynn tripped. Valentin shuffled in again, teapot in hand.

"Is Harry here?" Jonas asked curtly, folding his paper then placing it on the corner of the table. Harry was reliable, but would the boy trudge through the snow from his house in the village to take care of the horses after such a heavy storm?

"I do not know, *monsieur,*" Valentin answered. "He has not come to the kitchen yet."

Jonas pushed his chair away and rose. "I'll go see to the horses, then."

He stopped by Cathlynn's chair, touched her arm firmly, bracing himself against the lightning that sparked between them. "Care to come?"

He'd said it like a command, not an invitation, and she didn't miss the authority behind the question. The gold of her eyes swirled into the brown, drawing him in like a light at the end of a dark tunnel. She swallowed hard and gingerly placed her cup on the saucer. "I'd love to."

Oh, what a tangled web we weave, when first we practice to deceive. The quote floated through his mind. He wished he'd never had to start this farce. But he had no choice. His vision for the future was more important than his temporary discomfort. And now that Alana had forced him into fraud, he had to follow through.

Sterling watched them go, and Jonas felt the first knot snag in his web of lies. He'd caught himself. He'd made a mistake.

The real Alana hated horses.

Sterling knew it.

"I THINK STERLING SUSPECTS something," Cathlynn said to Jonas as she followed him out into the thick snow. Her nightmare had almost caused her to change her mind about staying, but eventually logic had won over emotion. He needed her until the fete. She was safe until then. But Sterling's suspicions could change everything.

"He wouldn't if you didn't make it so obvious you're uncomfortable here." Jonas's voice sounded brittle, like the thin ice over a puddle in early fall.

"You told me to act naturally. I did." She slipped on a patch of ice beneath the snow. Jonas caught her elbow before she fell all the way to her rear, and let her go as soon as she'd regained her balance.

"Perhaps if you toned down the overly happy hostess act."

"Well, perhaps if you'd tell me more about Alana, I could act in a way that pleases Your Majesty," she said, mimicking his pinched tone. He could make her spitting mad without trying. "What do you expect from me?"

He gave her one of his queer looks that seemed to see through all the locked doors in her mind. "The impossible."

He surged on ahead, and Cathlynn followed, frustration swirling an acid eddy in her stomach.

Despite the bitterly cold wind blowing outside, the inside of the stable was warm and cozy. The sweet smell of hay and the clean scent of leather filled Cathlynn's nostrils as she stepped into the fieldstone building. Soft nickers from three horses greeted them, and Jonas's face underwent a transformation. The lines erased themselves from his eyes, his mouth and forehead, taking years off his strained expression. And his smile as he greeted each horse in turn took her breath away.

Upon hearing the commotion of their entrance, a boy of about thirteen poked his strawberry-blond head over one of the stall doors.

"Hey, Jonas!"

"You're here, Harry. How did you make it past all the snow?"

The tall and skinny youth smiled and pointed at the cross-country skis leaning against the wall. "Glidepower."

"Good for you!"

"It would take more than a little snow to keep me

from Cloud.'' The boy eyed the large white horse with love, and the gentleness of his touch on the horse's neck echoed the tenderness in his voice. He looked like a rangy colt himself, all legs and arms and unbounded energy.

"How's school going?'' Jonas scratched the mare behind the ear, but she bumped his arm away and nuzzled his hand. From his pocket, he produced a section of carrot, and the horse crunched it greedily.

"Excellent. You'll see. I'll have the best report card you ever saw.'' The boy patted Cloud's obviously pregnant side. "You'll lose your bet.''

"I certainly hope so. I don't have time to take care of a foal this year.'' Jonas chuckled, and once more Cathlynn found her breath halted by the joyful sound. He glanced at her. "When was the last time you went on a sleigh ride?''

"I don't think I've ever been.''

"Care to try?''

Alone? With you? A strange yearning lodged itself low in her stomach. Food poisoning? Certainly not Jonas's smile. She wasn't that easily swayed.

"It would give us a chance to talk,'' he said as if sensing her hesitation.

"I'd love to.'' The words were out of her mouth before she could stop them.

He turned back to Harry. "Can you help me get Cirrus and Nimbus ready for a sleigh ride?''

"Sure thing.''

Harry stared at her for a minute before turning his gaze away with a fiery blush burning his face. Jonas had said Alana never ventured into the village. Had she not made it as far as the stables? What kind of life had

Jonas and Alana shared? The mystery grew thicker and thicker.

The boy mumbled a greeting, then hurried out of the stall and hung his pitchfork on the wall. He snagged a bucketful of brushes to groom the horse in the far stall.

Jonas took the second bucket and headed for the first stall. The dappled-gray horse pawed and nickered with anticipation, and on cue a treat appeared from Jonas's pocket.

"Easy, Nimbus." Jonas's deep chuckle swelled Cathlynn's heart with its genuine warmth, confusing her further.

The horses were groomed and harnessed, then taken outside where a sleigh waited. Cathlynn watched the whole process in utter amazement. How could one man be so different from one moment to the next? In the house, he'd seemed weighed by some unknown burden—guilt, more than likely. But out here, the load had lifted completely. Could guilt be disposed of so easily? For the first time since her nightmare, she wondered if she hadn't judged him too hastily. Could someone else have murdered Alana? Was Jonas's brooding darkness due to the loss of his wife? Yet, when he spoke of her, there seemed to be no love lost between husband and wife. But then, who else had a motive to murder Alana? What would she find as she peeled away the layers of this rotten onion?

Jonas helped her onto the sleigh's leather seat and tucked a quilt around her legs to keep her warm. Nimbus snorted and pawed one of his forefeet while the other horse stood patiently.

"Easy, Nimbus. We'll get going soon enough." Jonas picked up the reins and nodded to Harry, who released his hold on the bridle. Nimbus reared, but didn't get far. Cirrus nipped him into order. The horse puffed clouds of warm breath into the cold air with his impatient snort. Cathlynn gasped, grabbing the side of the sleigh and one of Jonas's forearms to keep her balance.

"Nimbus is just a baby," Jonas said, turning to Cathlynn and chuckling. "He's still learning the ropes and tends to get a little excited. But don't worry, Cirrus will keep him in line. He's an old hand at this." He jiggled the reins. "Giddyap!"

The ride possessed a strange air of unreality. It was like being transported to a fairyland. The sun shone on a wide expanse of virgin snow bordered on all sides by snow-laden evergreens. Dry flakes lifted by the soft wind sparkled around them like jeweled dust. The sleigh bells on the horses' harness, the swish of runners below them and the *clomp clomp* of horses' hooves sounded happy. At the edge of the woods, a deer warily watched them go by, but didn't run, as if it knew that today no harm could possibly come to it. Birds dipped and flew above for the sheer pleasure of being alive.

"Tell me about yourself," Jonas said, breaking the easy silence between them.

"There's not much to say. I have a brother. He runs a flight school in Nashua. My mother is dead. And my father is hibernating in Florida."

"How did your mother die?"

"Liver failure." Her bitter childhood soured her thoughts for an instant, then she pushed it aside. Because of her grandmother, she'd survived, and she'd rather dwell on the happiness she'd found at Gram's house than the nightmare she'd lived at home.

"Sorry to hear that," Jonas said, sincere in his apology.

"It's just one of those things," she said, shrugging. "I had Gram. She was a no-nonsense type person with the energy of three." She smiled. "And the gift of gab. She could weave stories…"

"Don't stop."

She never talked about her family, yet Jonas's relaxed charm and gentle questions had her spilling her guts, telling him about Gram and the magical summers she'd spent at her house. Was it because of the sunshine and the hypnotic rhythm of the sleigh bells?

"She sounds like a special lady," Jonas said.

"She is."

The shadows on Jonas's face had stayed behind as if they'd belonged to the house, and here out in the boundaryless outdoors, he could slip his guard and relax.

"How about you, do you have a family?" she asked him, fearing if either stopped talking for too long the magic would end. She wanted this precious morning of sun-dappled snow, sleigh bells and Jonas's dimpled smile to last forever.

"A brother and a sister. My parents are dead."

"How did they die?"

The muscle by his jaw tightened.

"My father died of a degenerative disease. My mother of a broken heart."

She worried the blanket's edge with her gloved fingers. "That's so sad. Are you close to your brother and sister?"

"Not particularly."

"Why not?"

He frowned, and she thought he wouldn't answer. "There's too much pain between us."

She wanted to say something that would heal the wound the torn relationships seemed to cause. Usually she would know exactly what to say, but today words came in floods or droughts, and she seemed stranded in a particularly arid patch.

He pointed to a spot near the forest's edge. "If you come out early enough in the spring, you can see does and their fawns graze here." A little farther out, he drove to the top of a rise. "There's a watercolor artist who's well known for the landscapes she paints from this vantage point." He dipped down to a spot near the river where two stout oaks stood guard. "I like to walk here in the summer. It's a great spot to think when I'm stuck for an answer in my research. I keep thinking that one of these days I'll install a hammock between those trees."

Cathlynn hadn't expected this softer side to him, hadn't known it could exist in this hard man.

As they skirted the village, heading toward the monastery once more, she looked at Jonas's face as he spoke of Ste-Croix, entranced by the warmth his voice held. "The village has managed to hold its own in the last few years. The Planning Committee has been able to revive a few of the dying arts, brought tourists and a few businesses in. Some kids are even staying now, instead of running to the city the first chance they get. It's been—"

He stopped midsentence and gave her a quizzical look. "What's wrong?"

"Nothing," Cathlynn said, shaking her head. She shifted her gaze to the countryside, afraid the nascent feelings she didn't quite understand would show through. Maybe she was getting sick after all. How else could she explain the weak feeling in her knees, the uncharacteristic trembling of her fingers, the heat and need flushing her skin all over? "It's all so beautiful. Thank you for taking me along."

He stopped the horses and looked at her with his stormy eyes abrew. His hand reached for a loose strand of hair with a leather-covered finger, and tucked it back into her woolen cap. Her breath stuck in her throat, making her uncomfortably aware of her speeding pulse.

"Thank you for coming."

His voice was almost a whisper and replete with tenderness. Her mouth opened, her captive breath escaped. His hand slipped to her nape. He pulled her forward. She melted toward him like snow under the spring sun. And when his lips touched hers, her skin sizzled, awakening a soul-deep hunger she'd hidden all her life.

He pulled her closer. She wrapped her arms around his neck and kissed him back willingly. His woodsy scent intoxicated her. His heady taste besotted her. His touch warmed her like nothing had since she'd arrived at the monastery.

Jonas broke off their connection abruptly and took up the slack reins. Clucking to the horses, he set them into motion.

"Don't ever change," he said, his voice filled with melancholy.

She didn't know if she'd heard him right over the sleigh bells' noise. Her lips tingled as ice crystals formed a protective layer over his brand. Every nerve in her body hummed with frustrated need. And a sinking feeling weighed her heart to the bottom of her boots.

Something was definitely wrong with her. She, Cathlynn O'Connell, had never before succumbed to mad impulses when it came to men, and here amid the magic of snow, sunshine and sleigh bells, she feared she could lose her heart to a man who would never love her.

A married man at that.

You're not his wife. You're playing a part.

The thought lingered in her mind, creating a sadness so heavy she thought it would crush her.

She swallowed hard and concentrated on the eerie beauty of the winter landscape. Wrong, wrong, wrong, she tried to convince herself. This strange feeling was all wrong. It wasn't real. She was under the spell of the day. A beautiful, magical day of fairy-tale quality. Like Gram's stories. Might as well enjoy it, because days like this never lasted very long. The summers never had.

With a resigned sigh, she settled on admiring the countryside and stuffed Jonas's nerve-tingling kiss and the ache in her heart into the tight little box in the corner of her mind where she kept all the things she didn't want to think about.

Safer that way, much safer.

Children's laughter and playful shrieks came from nearby. Half-dozen children skating on a cleared section of ice. In the distance stood the quaintest covered bridge. Red in the sunshine with sparkling snow on its roof, it looked exactly like a postcard should.

"Oh look! Where does the bridge lead? Can we go over it?"

"No."

The shortness of his answer took her by surprise. Her head snapped back to look at him, while her mouth hung aghast. His eyes seemed to have retreated into his skull, hiding their squally silver beneath heavy black shadows. His smile disappeared into a narrow, disapproving slash, and the icy lines of stress returned to sculpt his face.

What on earth had happened to cause the change? Happy children playing on the ice? It didn't make sense.

He stared at the bridge for a long moment, his jaw tensing until she thought it would break, as if he desperately tried to control boiling anger. Suddenly, he slapped the horses' backs with the reins, and they broke into a canter, calm Cirrus neighing a protest, Nimbus bucking an objection. Cathlynn hung on to the side of the sleigh for fear of falling out. Even the sleigh bells' sound changed from cheery jingles to cautious jangles. He brought the horses to a sharp halt by the river and jumped out, handing her the reins to hold.

''Whoa,'' Cathlynn said shakily to the horses, hanging on with white-knuckled force to the thin leather straps while Nimbus pawed and nodded his head. ''Jonas!''

''Get off the ice!'' Jonas shouted to the children when he reached the bank.

The startled children stopped instantly and stared up at him.

Nimbus's head jerked up. His eyes fixed on the forest's edge and grew wide. His nostrils flared. His skin quivered.

''Whoa,'' Cathlynn encouraged again. Her heart beat faster. Her mouth grew dry. She tried to look at the spot holding the horse's interest without moving her head. *Please, please stay calm.* She pulled on the reins tighter.

Shadows fluttered menacingly at the edge of her vision, and her adrenaline-soaked brain formed them into flowing black monks' robes. She turned her head for an instant, but saw nothing, except the dark branches of evergreens swaying in the breeze.

"Whoa," Cathlynn pleaded as Nimbus's fearful glances kept searching the darkness between the trees, and his antics increased. She fervently hoped Cirrus would steady his teammate, because there was no way she could handle two tons of thundering horses.

"Get off the ice before one of you falls through and drowns," Jonas shouted.

"It's solid, see!" the oldest girl said, and knocked the back of her blade against the hard slab, throwing chunks of ice into the air to prove her point.

"Off *now* before I call your parents. It's not safe. *Go!*"

Jonas's booming voice rent the air like a whip. With a fearful whinny, Nimbus took off. Cirrus nipped him. Nimbus shook his head and dragged Cirrus with him. The force of the horses' forward jerk slammed Cathlynn back into the seat, knocking the wind out of her. Her scream stuck, silent in her throat.

"Pull the reins!" Jonas's command came to her on the wind.

Cathlynn regained her balance. She pulled on the reins, but Nimbus stuck his head straight up, loosening her hold on them.

"Help me!"

The horses gained speed. The icy wind slapped her cheeks, narrowing her vision. She had no control. Panic zigzagged through her veins.

"Jump!" Jonas ordered.

Was he crazy? At this speed, she'd break her neck!

The trees on the opposite side of the clearing neared. The horses would either plow through them before they could slow down, or swerve around them. Neither situation looked too promising for her health.

"Jump, Cathlynn!" Jonas's voice grew fainter. The pounding of hoofbeats grew louder. Leather creaked. Runners hissed. The trees came closer and closer.

She was going to die. She just knew it.

Chapter Five

Cathlynn didn't want to die.

With one hand, she grabbed at the quilt tangled over her legs. She tugged and tugged, but couldn't get it free. With a frightened whimper, she let go the useless reins and freed her legs. Drawing up her courage with a breath, she closed her eyes and pushed herself off the out-of-control sleigh.

"Umph!" She landed hard on the snow, but remembered to roll to break the fall's impact. Ending up on hands and knees, she watched the sleigh fall sideways as the horses turned sharply to avoid the trees. The crack of the splintering seat as it caught trunk after trunk before bobbing impotently behind the fleeing horses reverberated through the forest like a knell of doom.

Her gaze fixed on a piece of black leather with its white stuffing sticking out, lying on the snow. One more second and she would have still been sitting on that seat. If she hadn't jumped, she could be in the same condition.

Jonas raced up behind her. He knelt before her and took her face in his hands. She saw fear and concern in his eyes as he looked her over.

"Are you hurt?"

"Just my pride," she said, regaining her breath. And a bruise or two. "I'm fine." But her body suddenly shook violently.

He clasped her hard against him and rocked her gently. "It's all right. You're fine. Everything's fine now." As he stroked her back, his hand trembled. "It's over."

She didn't know how long they stayed there, kneeling in the cold snow. She knew only she didn't want him to let her go. If he took his arms away, she feared she would break to pieces as the sleigh's seat had.

The shivers finally died away and Jonas loosened his possessive grip.

"I lost my hat," she said, latching on to the concrete in order to avoid falling apart. She touched a strand of loose hair. "And my barrette. My brother gave it to me last Christmas. I—I'd better find it." She tamped the snow with her hands, feeling the cold crystals melt against her wrists.

Jonas grabbed her arms and pulled up. "We'll find it. I promise." He smoothed her hair from her face and looked deep into her eyes. "I have to go check on the horses. Will you be all right?"

Cathlynn nodded, unable to talk. She sat back on her heels and hugged her knees with her arms, biting her lower lip to keep herself from crying.

The horses had come full circle to their departure point near the bridge. They waited, puffing huge white clouds with every breath. "I'll be right back."

He shooed the children gawking at the scene from the bank. As they ran over the bridge to the snow-filled lane beyond it, their skates bounced on their backs. Jonas ran his hands over the beasts' legs, checked their flanks for damage, then unhitched the broken sleigh. As he led the horses toward her, Nimbus limped noticeably.

"We'll have to double on Cirrus," he said, halting a generous distance away.

"No." Cathlynn shook her head, felt the shivers return in full force and rubbed her arms for warmth. She didn't want to go anywhere near a horse for a long time. "I can't."

"You'll be fine. I'll be right behind you. Nimbus is hurt. I can't leave him behind. And I can't leave you here, you'll catch your death."

"I can't." She shook her head.

Jonas let go the reins, scooped her up unceremoniously from her crumpled spot in the snow and placed her firmly on the gelding's back.

"No!" Before she could jump back down, he vaulted behind her and held her in place between the harness and his hard body.

"We'll take it nice and easy," he cooed softly in her ear, preventing further protest.

An involuntary shiver shook her body. He drew his arm tighter around her. His thighs flexed and the horse moved forward; the other followed behind, connected by a long rein to Jonas's hand. Cathlynn grabbed a fistful of mane to hold her balance. He pressed her body against his. The slow, relaxed motion of his body with the horse's movements calmed her. She allowed her head to drop back on his chest, and found it fit perfectly beneath his chin.

Then a different kind of panic filled her heart. The rhythmic thrust of Jonas's body against hers created a longing she'd sworn she'd never give in to again. A drugging, insistent yearning she knew would only lead to pain swelled like a blister. She stiffened when she felt his answering need through her coat against her tailbone and leaned away from him, placing a breath of space between them.

"The kids were having such fun skating," Cathlynn said. A snap of anger burst inside. It flared into fury—against him for confusing her, against herself for caring. "Did you have to send them away?"

"The river is fed by a mountain stream." His voice dripped icicles. "The icing is irregular. It's never safe. They know it."

"That doesn't excuse your rudeness. What's wrong with you, anyway? You yelled at those kids as if they'd committed a major crime."

"No one should have to go through the grief of loss when it can so easily be prevented."

"As opposed to leaving a completely clueless woman handling two giant horses?"

His arms tensed around her. "I—"

"And, and..." She grasped for thoughts, barely listening to his responses. Anything to forget the wave of unwanted desire cresting through the terror of her fall, which still rippled through her. "You looked at that bridge as if the devil himself lived under it."

"Maybe he does." His chin lifted and his head turned slightly in the direction of the bridge. "We've lost six children there in the past four years."

"I'm sorry. I didn't know." A wave of cold rolled through her. The sun seemed to agree; it slipped beneath a cloud and drab snow started falling like frozen tears.

When they neared the edge of the woods, Nimbus stopped and snorted. His eyes grew wide. He crowded into Cirrus's side, shoving the older horse aside. Cathlynn stiffened at the unexpected movement. She bit her lower lip to stop herself from whimpering.

"Whoa, Nimbus. What's the matter, boy?"

Jonas turned both horses to face the unseen enemy hiding in the darkness of the woods. Cathlynn hung on to Cirrus's mane with both fists.

"What's wrong?" she asked.

"He sees something."

"That's what happened when he took off with the sleigh." Her fear showed through her shaky voice, but she didn't care. She couldn't take another runaway ride. "Please, Jonas, don't let him take off again."

"We'll take it nice and easy. We'll show him there's nothing in the shadows and he'll be fine. Won't you, boy?"

Nimbus's ear flicked from the woods to Jonas and back. Icy nuggets of snow ticked against their coats, against the trunks and branches. Wicked wind wailed across the trees, sounding like the low, eerie chant the monks had vocalized in her dream. All around them, the sighs and whispers spoke of unnamed horrors and undefinable sins. The air grew cold. Shadows shifted. Like a stealthy predator, something black and shapeless swirled closer.

Nimbus started to back.

"Whooooa..." Jonas steadied the horse with his voice. "It's all right."

The wind-driven object skipped and scurried, twisted and turned.

Nimbus snorted. Cathlynn shivered.

"It's all right," Jonas said. She wasn't sure if he was addressing the horse or her, but his soft, steady voice gave her a measure of comfort. "Everything's fine. Take a good look."

The dark specter caught on a gnarled knuckle of root. It tugged. It wrenched. Then like a flag, it unfurled and revealed itself.

The base of Cathlynn's neck prickled with sudden foreboding.

Beware.

The warning echoed eerily in her mind, scattering shivers up and down her arms.

Black against the snow sprawled the desolate shell of a monk's habit.

DANGER. It floated all around him and there was nothing Jonas could do to control it.

Where had the monk's habit come from? What was it doing in the middle of nowhere? Had the horses' mad race been deliberate, or a freak twist of fate?

Then there was Cathlynn.

Kissing her had been like tasting spring after a long, bitter winter, Jonas thought as he watched her run back to the house. Snowflakes melted in his hair and ran cold drops down his neck. He was starting to realize what a harsh winter it had been living with Alana.

Watching the sensual movements of Cathlynn's running body, his desire for her grew again. A deep, dull ache pined in his heart. He slicked away the melted snow, running like tears down his face. He wanted the winter to end.

At the sharp slam of the door, taking her from his sight, he turned away and led the horses into the barn.

Cathlynn was scared. He couldn't blame her. Better that way—for her. Distance would protect her. Better for him; he couldn't afford the distraction.

He led Cirrus to his stall and closed him in without untacking him, then turned his attention to Nimbus in the crossties. Alana and Cathlynn were alike, he reminded himself as he bent over Nimbus's leg. Alana had loved the things he could give her more than she'd loved him. Cathlynn wanted only the Aidan Heart from this deal. Hadn't he bribed her with the glass to stay?

Foolish woman.

Nimbus nuzzled his pocket for a treat. Jonas patted the Andalusian's thick neck while the horse crunched on a carrot. "She should run like the devil, Nimbus. I have a feeling we'll both lose if she stays. No piece of glass is worth that much."

But his research was, and so he wouldn't chase her away.

Jonas whipped a bandage from the tack-room shelf and proceeded to clean and wrap Nimbus's injured leg. Today he'd nearly lost Cathlynn. The savage helplessness he'd felt as he'd watched her nearly crash into the trees had brought a new definition to fear. Had he ever cared that deeply for Alana? He didn't care to explore that line of thought. Cathlynn had almost died because he'd lost his temper over that blasted bridge—a constant reminder of Alana's infidelity.

The cold tentacle of danger reached for him again, wrapping around his soul like a needful thing.

As with the last part of the formula that wouldn't fall into place, he felt he'd missed something important. Something right under his nose.

Anger, deep and primal, rumbled low inside him. He led Nimbus to his stall and closed the animal in. As the tongue fit in the groove, the half door's latch hissed.

His precious control was slipping.

THE PLOW HAD FINALLY FOUND its way to the monastery on Sunday night. Monday morning, when Cathlynn

announced her intention to go to Nashua, Jonas didn't
stop her. Though she'd spent the afternoon talking to
Gram, there had been no sign of recognition in her eyes.
The doctor had tried to reassure her by telling her the
medicines were keeping Gram groggy, but she'd had a
sinking feeling in the pit of her stomach, and prayed
all the way home Gram could hang on longer.

After Cathlynn returned to the monastery, she found
a box on her bed. She opened her suitcase first, and
sighed with relief at the sight of her own clothes. She
shrugged out of Alana's dress and slipped on a soft,
cream-colored angora sweater and a pair of black wool
pants. Valentin had provided her with a few personal
amenities, but it was nice to have her own things. She
burrowed through the contents of the suitcase, and saw
Claire had packed all of her favorite things, including
her own worn but cozy flannel bathrobe. And bless her
heart, Claire had included a large Cadbury's milk chocolate bar with hazelnuts and raisins—her favorite.

About to dig into the rich chocolate, Cathlynn put
the bar in the dresser drawer instead. She'd save it for
later.

The box that had been sitting on her bed bore a label
from an exclusive dress shop in Boston.

Curious, she opened it. In the folds of tissue, she
found a ball dress fit for a queen. Except for its too-
frilly neckline and blood-red color, the dress was ex-
quisite. Standing in front of the mirror, Cathlynn placed
the dress before her and sighed dejectedly.

"What's wrong?"

Jonas's voice startled her. With a gasp she turned to
face him. She was turning into a jumpy bundle of raw
nerves. His unexpected presence and direct gaze had

her feeling very exposed despite the barrier of wool protecting her.

"What are you doing here? I thought you were in your office."

"You don't like the dress?" he asked, ignoring her question, and leaned nonchalantly against the open bathroom door.

"The dress is perfect," Cathlynn said, throwing it on the bed with a sharp snap of her wrist. "A perfect size six." With both hands she motioned to her hips. "Which obviously, I'm not."

"David's mother is a seamstress. Take it to her and she'll alter it for you."

"You don't understand," Cathlynn scoffed. "I'm not petite like Alana. I wear a size eight, sometimes ten. No one short of a fairy godmother could fix this dress to fit me."

"Have Lorraine Forester make you another."

"I don't think this is going to work." Cathlynn sagged to the bed and buried her face in her hands. This role was too emotionally taxing, she wasn't equipped to handle this much emotion.

"David's mother is a fine seamstress."

"No, I mean your little charade." Her fingers raked through her hair. "I think Sterling is getting suspicious. He keeps asking me odd questions and looking at me strangely."

"I think you're overreacting." Shadows from the doorway played on Jonas's face, hiding his expression from her. "Sterling's eyesight isn't all that keen anymore and he's too vain to wear glasses."

Leaning her elbows on her knees and her head in her hands, she gave Jonas a sidelong look. "I think you're reading him wrong."

He crossed his arms in front of his chest. "I think you're seeing ghosts where there aren't any."

"I wouldn't be so sure. Valentin seems to think the place is crawling with ghosts. He says this house has seen more than its share of death."

The lines on his face hardened once more. "Valentin talks too much."

Cathlynn snorted. "If he talked any less, he could be mistaken for a walking skeleton."

At the risk of deepening his anger, Cathlynn knew she had to ask questions he didn't want to answer. She got up and walked to where Jonas stood. She leaned on the opposite side of the door. "Talk to me, Jonas. Make me understand the kind of person Alana is."

His eyes narrowed and darkened like rain-laden clouds. "We've been over her history already."

"No, not the dry facts, not the outside—the inside, the soul. For my own protection, I need to know."

Lightning seemed to flash in his dark eyes. "Your innocence is your protection."

"My innocence didn't protect me from nearly getting killed yesterday."

"It was an accident."

"I thought so too—until I saw the monk's habit."

He straightened sharply, came close to her, crowding her against the jamb's knifelike edge. His naked anger flashed a vivid storm in his eyes. "I need you alive."

"Do you?" She didn't know why she egged him on. But she wanted to feel safe in this house that felt more like a tomb than a home. "Do you?"

His jaw twitched. His hands clawed into her shoulder. "I need a wife. Alive and well."

The sinking feeling at the pit of her stomach nearly floored her. "Did you ever love her?"

"Once upon a time." His fingers' harsh grasp eased. "What happened?"

"People change." His hands slid back to his sides.

Cathlynn growled her frustration. "Stop your damned double talk and answer me straight."

He leaned toward her until they faced each other nose to nose. "All right. She was heartless, selfish. She didn't have a soul. If she did, it belonged to the devil."

His anger rippled through her, but she refused to back away. "Why did she leave?"

"She didn't leave. She wanted to humiliate me. She never would have left without creating a scene first. There was too much hate festering in her soul for her to do any less."

His anger-heated breath against her face, the clear and deep hurt in his eyes, caused an unexpected softening in her heart. Cathlynn swallowed hard. "Then where is she?"

"I don't know." He walked into the room and stood by the window, both hands stuck into his pants pockets.

"How convenient for you."

His gaze held her prisoner. His silence weakened her. The drips, pinging from the showerhead to the shower floor, drove her crazy.

"You really think I killed her."

Cathlynn blushed, shrugged, and turned away from his piercing gaze. Jonas grabbed her shoulders and whipped her around to face him once more. "Look at me! What motive do I have to want her dead? I needed her alive until after the ball. If I wanted to harm her, I would have waited until then."

Cathlynn shook her head and stared deep into the silver of his eyes. "But she *is* dead. I can feel it."

"Well, then, that settles it. Let's call the police and

present them with this hard evidence. Cathlynn, do you realize how crazy that sounds?''

She rolled her shoulders to free herself from his hold. ''Not any crazier than a man who doesn't know where his own wife is and hires someone to replace her just so he can inherit a trust fund.''

He raised one eyebrow, then swiped a hand through his hair. ''I suppose you're right on that point. But think about it, Cathlynn, why would I want to kill Alana?''

''I don't know. Maybe because she was planning on divorcing you. I found the divorce papers in her room.''

He tensed. ''It wouldn't have mattered. We had an agreement.''

''There are so many secrets hiding behind all those locked doors. Who knows what other motive you could have? And if you didn't kill her, then what are you doing to find out what happened to her?''

''I'm doing all I can.''

''Who else has a motive?''

''That, of course, is the million-dollar question. Her cousin Geoffrey for one. Maybe even Sterling. Then there are her 'friends.' ''

''Friends?''

''The men she used for her pleasure.'' Jonas dug his hand into his pocket and came out with a key ring. He took one odd-looking key from the ring and pressed it into her hand. ''Come then. Let's alleviate your fears, dear curious Cat. This is a master key. We'll go through every room until you're satisfied I'm not keeping my dead wife's skeleton in any closet.''

Cathlynn turned the key over in her hand, inspecting its odd shape to avoid Jonas's gaze. ''Jonas...''

With a finger, he lifted her chin. When he spoke, his

voice was strangely gentle. "Would it do any good to deny I killed her?"

"I need to hear you say you didn't." Heat and longing spread through her limbs, leaving her mouth dry and her heart beating hard.

"Can't you trust me even a little?"

The wounded look in his eyes struck a chord of guilt, then one of sadness. "I couldn't even trust my own mother."

He let her go abruptly and shook his head. "You're making your own hell, you realize that, don't you?"

THE NEXT MORNING, Cathlynn stood undecided at an intersection between two halls. She started at the sound of Sterling's voice behind her.

"Lost, my dear?"

"No, of course not." On her fourth day in the rambling house, she still managed to get lost, but Sterling couldn't know that. "I just had an idea for the ball, and I can't decide whether to take care of it now or eat breakfast first."

"The brain works better on a full stomach." He eyed her curiously. She hated the way his mustache twitched at the corners when he smiled, as if he was privileged to some inside information. Maybe he was. The thought offered her no comfort.

"Breakfast it is, then." She hoped her smile didn't look as brittle as it felt.

"Allow me." He switched his briefcase from one hand to the other, offered her his elbow and guided her to the dining room.

His arm was hard and unyielding beneath her hand. Again she wondered if he suspected her of deceit, and what actions he might take to unmask her. Did she give him too much power because of the influence of his decision over the fund's dispersal? He was the family's trusted lawyer, but did he have a motive of his own to see Alana dead? Silently she chided herself. Her close call with death had her seeing monsters around every corner.

Once in the dining room, Sterling gulped a glass of orange juice and wrapped a lightly buttered English muffin in a paper napkin.

"You're not eating?" Cathlynn asked as she poured herself a cup of coffee, emptying the carafe.

"No time." Sterling glanced at his pocket watch and frowned. "I have an appointment I can't miss."

"What kind of appointment?" Cathlynn asked the question as if the answer held no interest to her, pretending instead that choosing between eggs and oatmeal was uppermost in her mind.

"Business. I want to tie everything up in a neat little bow before I retire. I fully plan on enjoying my waning years."

"How do you feel about Jonas?" She scooped up a portion of eggs onto a plate.

Sterling paused on his way to picking up the briefcase he'd dropped at his feet. "Why do you ask, my dear?"

"There's a tension between the two of you. I wish I understood it."

"J.T. will not admit defeat even when it's plainly presented to him. All these years after his parents' deaths, he's still trying to make sense out of it. You should know. I'm sure it can't be easy living with him."

She dropped a piece of English muffin beside the small mound of scrambled eggs. "No, it's not. He

keeps his feelings so tight inside, it makes me feel...
Well, I'm sure that's not what you want to hear."

"No, do go on." He twirled one end of his mustache
pensively.

She shrugged. "Sometimes, I wish things could be
different." Which was close enough to the truth,
whether she admitted it to herself or not. But wishes
were for little girls, and she was a grown woman who
should know better.

"We all do, my dear. But the past can't be erased
and we must learn to play the cards life has dealt us."
He picked up his briefcase. "Speaking of the devil,
have you seen J.T. this morning?"

"No, he was already gone by the time I woke up.
He was in a foul mood last night." She spooned up a
measure of fruit salad and dropped it in a small bowl.
"What did you two talk about all yesterday afternoon?"

"Dry, boring legalese, I'm afraid."

"Is there a problem with the trust?" Cathlynn turned
her head to watch his reaction. One cheek twitched up
into a half smile like a jackal who'd found unattended
prey.

"Not yet," he said. His implications of duplicity
came through loudly with his direct gaze. Cathlynn
couldn't hold it steadily and concentrated instead on her
breakfast selection.

She shrugged. "Oh well, I'm sure you two will figure
everything out."

"I'm sure we shall."

Sterling turned to leave and nearly bumped straight
into Jonas. "There you are, dear boy. I'm off to see
Scott MacPhearson. I'll be back for dinner."

The charged silence grew so thick and heavy, the

scrape of Cathlynn returning the serving spoon to the bowl of fruit salad sounded like the crack of a gun. Sterling's mustache twitched. Jonas's jaw tensed. A shiver ran across her scalp and raised the hairs along her arms. Who was Scott MacPhearson, and why did Sterling seem to draw so much pleasure at teasing Jonas with the name?

"Have a pleasant day," Jonas finally managed to say through gritted teeth.

"I'm planning on it." With a soft chuckle, Sterling left.

Cathlynn slid her plate onto the table and sat down, but the food held no interest. Jonas swore at the empty coffee carafe and slammed his cup back on the sideboard.

"Sorry, I took the last cup. Who's Scott Mac-Phearson?"

"No one you'd care to meet in a dark alley. What were you and Sterling discussing before I arrived?"

"The trust fund, if you must know."

"I forbid you to discuss business of any kind with him."

"Forbid?" Cathlynn slowly brought her cup back to its saucer, unable to believe what she'd just heard. "In case you hadn't noticed, I'm not six years old. You can't forbid me anything."

Jonas leaned his fists on the table and glared across at her, his presence looming tall and menacing above her. "I can and I will. Remember, the Aidan Heart won't be yours unless I succeed."

"And the trust fund won't be yours unless I can pretend I'm Alana." She dismissed his bluster with a wave of her hand. She swallowed her own anger, realizing she was a ready recipient for his temper by virtue of her presence. He wasn't angry at her, but at his fear of losing the trust. "Anything else I should keep in mind, Your Majesty?"

He looked at her long and hard, then scraped a hand through his hair as he straightened. "I'm sorry, I didn't mean to patronize you. Alana wasn't interested in business, try not to be, either." He returned to the sideboard and poured himself a glass of juice. "What are you planning on doing with yourself today?"

"I was thinking I could get started on your glass collection's appraisal." Cathlynn twisted the plate around, but didn't touch the food.

"It will have to wait until tomorrow—"

"That's what you said yesterday."

"I've got to go out this morning, and I don't know when I'll be back."

"Something to do with Scott MacPhearson?"

Orange juice spilled over the sides of the glass as he returned it to the sideboard. "My business is none of yours."

"Oh well, pardon me for asking." She sipped her coffee. "I hate sitting around doing nothing. Is there anything I can help you with?"

"No, you've done more than enough already."

With that, he departed, and Cathlynn couldn't decide if she'd been handed a compliment or an insult.

"You're welcome," Cathlynn said to the empty room and drained her coffee cup, feeling for all the world as if she'd lost another round with typhoon Jonas.

Chapter Six

Jonas paced the library's length, feeling like the tiger caged in the paperweight on his desk—a gift from his mother, the first of his collection. Weighed down by all his mistakes, he was as impotent to free himself from his tangled web as the trapped tiger was to jump clear of the glass.

Though he had no proof one way or the other, Alana was more than likely dead. Sterling had sicced Scott MacPhearson on his tail. The trust looked farther out of reach than it ever had. Had all the lies been worth it? Or were they getting him farther away from his objective? Now he'd been forced to add another lie to the web.

Scott MacPhearson was a short, squat man, with shocking-red hair that stood straight on end. His beefy jowls and sleepy eyes gave him the air of an inoffensive bulldog. But the policeman turned private investigator was anything but harmless. He was known to latch on to things like a junkyard dog and not let go until he'd chewed the situation to bits. He'd refused to drop the case after Jonas had fired him. And he would see through this latest lie as if it were a freshly cleaned window.

Ten days left until Alana's birthday. Would it be long enough?

"Is everything all right, Jonas?"

Jonas looked up from his dark thoughts to find David standing at the door. "Yes."

David sat in the chair before Jonas's desk. "Cathlynn hasn't been found out, has she?"

"No. But there's trouble." David understood the importance of the trust to Jonas's research, understood how close they were to finding, if not a cure, then at least a way to manage the ravaging disease that had killed his father and that lay dormant, for now, in his genes. Understood and shared his passion for truth. "Does your uncle still work for Customs?"

David nodded.

"See if you can find out when Sterling entered the country. And get hold of Cameron."

Ten minutes later, David handed Jonas the phone. "Cam?"

"It's been a while, big brother. What's up?"

"I need your help."

There was silence on the other end. It had been much too long—years—since he'd talked with Cameron or his sister, Juliana. Their last meeting hadn't been pleasant. *You've taken away the last of my hope,* Juliana had said, face pale and eyes brimming with tears. Cameron had laughed, but the sound had been harsh and spiteful. *Got caught on the losing end of a con after all,* he'd said, then stalked out, not bothering to finish his drink. Perhaps Jonas shouldn't have told them of his findings, of their possible doomed futures. He couldn't blame Cameron for his reluctance to help him now.

"*You* need *my* help?" Cameron said, harsh incredulity ringing in his voice. "Since when?"

"Since I find myself in need of a con man."

A LOW GRUMBLING SOUND distracted Cathlynn from her brooding thoughts. From one of the dining-room windows, she saw a plow entering the courtyard to clear the few inches of snow that had fallen overnight. Stretching her arms above her, she worked the kinks out of her stiff shoulders. Fat, white clouds glided over the sun at regular intervals, patching the ground below in a hopscotch of light and shadows. Another day, another cold storm. She had to find something to do before she went crazy.

Seeking more coffee, Cathlynn headed for the kitchen. She found Valentin, face reddened from exertion, thin hair askew, bustling about the room like a mad bird who'd flown into the house by mistake.

"Can I help with anything?" she asked, fearing the old man would die of a heart attack before her eyes.

"Non, madame." He dropped a copper saucepan on the floor and clucked disapprovingly at the dent on the side when he picked it up.

Spotting a fresh pot of coffee in the coffeemaker on the wooden countertop, Cathlynn headed for it and filled her cup. "I was wondering, how long have you known Jonas?"

"Since he was a boy, *madame*. You could say I came with the house." He poked at the dent, trying to pop it back out.

"What do you think of him?"

"He is a fair and generous employer."

"But how do you feel about him?"

He stopped poking and looked at her as if she were as appealing as a piece of rotting fish. "I am not in the position to express an opinion, *madame*."

"Come on, Valentin. Employee to employee, how do you feel about him?"

"Curiosity, *madame,* is sometimes better left unexplored."

She should have known better than to attempt a conversation with Valentin. Her previous experience should have prepared her for his creepy turn of phrase. Maybe another tack would yield better results.

"Since you came with the house, so to speak, I was wondering, do you ever hear, um…voices coming from the walls?"

"Voices, *madame?*" He hung the pot on an overhead rack.

"Well, yes, sometimes I seem to hear something that sounds like a whisper, even if there's no one around."

He shrugged, and picked up a rag by the sink. "It is an old house. Anything is possible."

"You weren't serious about the ghosts, were you?" Her hands wrapped around the filled coffee cup, seeking its warmth.

The swipe of the rag in his hand slowed on the counter, but didn't stop. "As I said, it is an old house with a long history of death under its roof. Desperation led the monks to sacrifice, which led to legend. Anything is possible." Valentin's rag redoubled its effort. Cathlynn decided to drop that line of questioning. The last thing she needed was gory details to feed her nightmares.

"Did Alana ever help out around the house?"

"*Madame* knew her place," he said, implying Cathlynn did not. He folded the rag neatly and placed it on a holder inside the sink-cabinet door, then gave her a look of pity as if she were a lost child. "She did, however, take care of the fete preparations."

"Of course, she would."

"There are still a few things left to be done. If you like—"

"Yes, I like."

She pushed herself off the counter, relieved to have something to occupy her besides the dark twistings of her active imagination, and followed Valentin down the hall to Alana's office. After opening the locked door and snapping on the light, he gave her the key, as he had in the bedroom.

Cathlynn moved about the lamp-lit room, her feet sinking into the crimson carpet's deep plush. The elaborate gold-trimmed Louis XIV desk in the middle of the room dominated the space, and made a sharp contrast with the plain-framed distorted pieces of modern art hanging on the gold-splattered walls. On the desk stood a computer, a printer and an antique telephone. What kind of woman was Alana? How could she possibly find this garishly opulent decor beautiful?

"Why are all the doors locked?" Cathlynn asked as she fingered the brass key in her hand.

"Energy conservation, *madame*."

"Yes, of course."

"*Madame* worked at the desk."

As opposed to the floor, Cathlynn thought, smiling to herself. Valentin's opinion of her definitely wasn't very high. What had he thought of the real Alana? Judging by his comments, if he hadn't liked her, he certainly had held her in higher esteem.

Valentin snapped the frothy cream curtains open, letting in light from the window. Cathlynn sneezed at the shower of dust.

"I'm sure you will find all you need," he said.

"Thank you, Valentin."

His unmoving thin line of a mouth was not reassuring as he bowed slightly. "If you need anything, there is an intercom to the kitchen by the door." He duck-walked out, closing the door behind him.

Cathlynn sat in Alana's chair and looked at her surroundings. The walls didn't dance before her. But she felt them. Watching her. Waiting.

"For what?" she asked them, but no replied whisper came back. She wished she knew what this "expectation" she felt was all about. If she did, she could get rid of the feeling of naked vulnerability which was her constant companion in this cold house.

Her call to check on Gram before she came down this morning hadn't brought any peace of mind. Gram's immune system wasn't rallying the way it should from her last bout with the flu. Overnight, they'd had to put her on a respirator. And thinking Gram so frail and helpless frightened her. How long before she was all alone?

Cathlynn shook her head. She didn't want to think about depressing things. She looked through Alana's desk and found a to-do list with the items done crossed off. Alana's handwriting was bold and thick, like a woman who knew what she wanted and went after it. Had Jonas admired her barefaced confidence? Was that why he'd married her? What had gone wrong?

She beeped Valentin on the intercom.

"Oui, madame." His irritation at the disturbance filtered through the crackling speaker.

"Have the invitations gone out? I don't see a mention of them on Alana's list."

"Non, madame."

"Where are they?"

"Behind you in the white boxes, *madame*." Cathlynn spotted them beneath a brass-footed mahogany worktable.

"Do you have a guest list?"

"In the folder in the second drawer of the desk, *madame*. The right side."

She found the file exactly where he'd said it would be, with a neatly typed list of names and addresses inside. A smile crept over her lips. Valentin needed some loosening up, and she decided to tease him. "Can I add a few names of my own?"

Silence, long and static, followed her question. "As you wish, *madame*."

Cathlynn leaned back in Alana's ornate chair and sighed wearily. Even teasing the old butler wasn't giving her any satisfaction. The house's gloom was starting to get to her.

"CAN I HELP YOU?" The voice, smooth and amused, startled Cathlynn. With Sterling and Jonas both gone, and Valentin busy, she hadn't expected to meet anyone in the narrow bowels of the mansion's basement.

She swiveled on her heels to find a darkly handsome man filling the office door. His perfectly pressed looks and evident energy made him the ideal candidate for a yuppie poster. She recognized him as David Forester, Jonas's assistant. The man who'd outbid her for the Aidan Heart. She wanted to hate him, but realized he'd only been following his boss's orders.

"No, yes. I mean, I came down looking for stamps. There were none upstairs. I saw the light." Finding David's office empty, she'd been on the verge of snooping through the desk when the young man who appeared to be in his mid-twenties had entered. "You must be David."

David stepped inside, took her hand in his and kissed her fingertips. "At your service." His warm brown eyes twinkled with mischief. "You are as beautiful as our missing mistress."

She removed her fingers from his hand, uncomfortable with his easy intimacy, yet glad to discover someone whose facial expression didn't blend in with the grim gray wall for a change. But she wasn't ready to trust anyone, even somebody with a congenial smile and a pleasant disposition. "Stamps?"

David took the file he carried to one of the three huge file cabinets in the back of the room, then extricated a sheet of stamps from a nearby utilitarian armoire. Handing them to her, he sat on the corner of the desk.

"How are you enjoying your stay in Ste-Croix?" he asked.

"It's not where I would have picked to go on a fun vacation." Cathlynn folded the sheet of stamps in three and rolled it in her hand.

"It is a strange place." David drew out a plain chrome chair with a black vinyl cushion with his foot, inviting her to sit.

She settled herself into the chair and crossed her legs. David seemed eager to talk, and she was eager to listen. Maybe she'd learn a few of the monastery's secrets. "Valentin says it's haunted by dead monks."

"The monastery lends itself so well to the battle of good and evil favored by simple village people. Long winter nights are perfect for ghost stories, no? Every little village has its own legend. Ste-Croix is no exception."

She thought she sensed anger behind his words, but perhaps she was wrong. He stretched his legs out and crossed them at the ankles, giving her a contradictory picture of ease. "I suppose. You don't seem to care for Ste-Croix too much."

"Oh, I do. I was born here. My family lives here. If it weren't for Jonas, I'd have to seek my fortune elsewhere."

"What do you do?"

David smiled brightly. "My official title is research assistant. In reality, I'm a jack-of-all-trades."

"What's he like to work for?" Unconsciously, Cathlynn leaned slightly forward.

"Depends on his mood." David waved his hands neutrally. "He can be an ogre sometimes, but I've learned a lot from him. I owe him this chance." A smile that could mean so much, or nothing at all, twisted his lips. He leaned toward her. "Some see him as a god, others as the devil himself, depending on which side of the curse you stand."

"The curse?" Was he, too, trying to scare her?

"The monk's curse."

"I don't understand."

"Haven't you noticed?" he said in a careful whisper. "There are no old men in Ste-Croix."

She and Jonas had only skirted the village during their sleigh ride, and she'd had no opportunity to visit since she'd arrived. "What about Valentin?"

"He's an exception."

"So?"

"There's a genetic weakness that kills them in their prime."

"Is that what Jonas is working on?"

David nodded. "But can a curse ever be reversed?"

The glue behind the stamps in her hand mixed with the growing dampness in her palm and stuck to her skin. The walls started their eerie pulsing. *Beware.*

Cathlynn decided to change the subject before her skin started to crawl, too. "Did you know Alana well?"

"Ah, Alana." Admiration glowed in David's eager face. "She was—"

"Was?"

"Is…quite a woman. Beautiful, witty, incorrigible. Maybe the only person Jonas can't control." He laughed heartily, as if reliving pleasant memories.

David's smile widened, showing off big, slightly gapped front teeth. "If Jonas hadn't told me about you, I might have mistaken you for her myself." His admiring gaze lingered on her breasts. She crossed her arms and leaned back in her chair. "But why would you want to take her place?"

"It's a long story." Cathlynn sighed. "I'm beginning to think I made a terrible mistake."

"It'll be over soon enough. The fete is almost here."

"Why did she leave?"

He shrugged. "Jonas isn't an easy man to live with. She needed attention. He wasn't always available." Distractedly, he picked up the daggerlike letter opener on the green blotter and slid his fingers up and down the dull blade. "There was an argument. No one is sure about what. She left slamming the door behind her, and never came back."

"Do you think she ever will?"

He eyed her curiously. "After staying here a few nights, would you?"

"I don't know." Her gaze drifted to the bare, gray stone office walls. Cold and impersonal, like the rest of the house. But her feelings for the grim house would have nothing to do with her decision to stay or come back. "I'm not married to Jonas. I don't know him very well. If I'd made a commitment to him, then I suppose once I'd cooled down, I'd come back.''

''Even if you were in the right?'' His gaze narrowed as he studied her.

''Marriage isn't something you walk away from because of one argument.''

The distant ring of a telephone lamented eerily through the basement's crisscrossing corridors.

''One of many, I'm afraid. Alana has a...fiery temper.''

Cathlynn leaned forward again, bringing her head closer to David. ''Do you think she's still alive?'' she whispered, not knowing why she did.

Suddenly, David straightened, dropped the letter opener onto the blotter and picked up a file.

''David, there's a call for you in the lab.''

Swallowing her gasp of surprise at the sound of Jonas's icy voice, Cathlynn straightened in her chair and looked at him. His eyes glowered coldly at her. What had she done wrong this time?

''Thank you, Jonas.'' David winked encouragement at her and hurried out of the office.

Cathlynn rose to leave. Jonas crossed the room to the desk. He picked up several file folders and examined their contents.

''I found your barrette,'' he said without looking up. ''Valentin took it to your room.''

''Thank you.'' She stopped at the door. Hand on the jamb, she hesitated, then turned around. ''Is something wrong?''

Slowly he looked up. The contents of one of the files floated to the desk in a disjointed cascade. ''Everything.''

JONAS'S SADNESS still echoed in her mind as Cathlynn made her way back to Alana's office later that afternoon, making her feel helpless. She'd tried to question him. She'd tried to get past the hard mask he wore, but he wouldn't respond, and in the end had ordered her away.

He'd told her just last night she was making her own hell. He was right about that. She'd have been better off sticking with her dreams of finding the Aidan Heart than dealing with the nightmare she'd mired herself in when she'd found it. Giving Jonas softness and sadness wasn't going to do her cause any good. Getting emotionally tangled with his problems would only see her hurt. To him she was a means to an end. Nothing more.

The office door stood half-open and, from within, Cathlynn heard footsteps. She opened the door farther and saw David searching through the desk.

"Are you looking for something specific?"

"Ah, Cathlynn." His smile beamed at her. "Yes, I was looking for the invitations. I thought I'd mail them for you on my way home."

"Thanks, but I haven't finished addressing the envelopes. Calligraphy isn't my forte. It's very nice of you to offer to mail them for me."

"It's nothing. I would do no less for the real mistress."

"Yes, of course. I'll get them to you tomorrow."

"Whenever you're ready."

With a friendly smile, David left. She hoped the lateness of the invitations' mailing wouldn't prevent a good turnout.

Cathlynn sat at the desk and picked up Alana's to-do list. Everything for the fete was in order. The caterers, the band, the flowers, even the decorator had been booked for months, ready to magically transform the monastery into a castle fit for a medieval fantasy. All she had to do was give them a quick call to confirm the date. Cathlynn closed the file and sighed. She was back to having nothing to do, except let her imagination go wild. Hell, indeed.

She slid the file into the hanging basket and found it caught and wouldn't go down all the way. She reached inside the jacket and her hand touched something hard.

She pulled up the slim object and discovered a computer disk. The label, in Alana's bold handwriting, read Agenda.

Fingering the hard plastic edges of the disk, she wondered if she should read it. They probably held the woman's private appointments—personal and confidential things meant for her eyes only. Yet, in a sense, she was that woman. She'd been asked to take her place, lend her skin, her spirit to a woman who'd disappeared. She had every right to read the file and feel no guilt for it. And if it yielded proof of guilt for someone else, then it would be unethical not to read it.

Before she could talk herself out of it, Cathlynn turned on the computer and fed the disk into the drive.

The blinking cursor asked for her password. Cathlynn tried the obvious—Alana, Jonas, Ste-Croix, monastery, monk. She tried a dozen more, including the names of designers she'd found on Alana's clothes, before she drew a complete blank.

Think. Put yourself in Alana's skin. What did she want more than anything else?

Money, escape, freedom. None of those words worked. What did the woman feel? Trapped. No go. Jonas had said she didn't like it much here. He'd told her she was making her own hell. She typed in the word *hell.* The computer blinked and showed her the menu. It contained three files: journal, planner, will.

Cathlynn opened the journal file. The first words she read were, "That husband of mine is going to be the death of me."

"DID MACPHEARSON BITE?" Jonas asked his brother later that afternoon.

"Like a hound on a skunk's trail. But if you ask me, what you're doing stinks just as much."

"That from a con man?" Cameron had sought to ease the pain of their parents' death by getting back at the slick swindler who'd cheated their father out of his savings in search of a miracle cure. Now he did the same for the underdog. Too bad it couldn't be on the right side of the law.

As usual, the comment slicked off Cameron's duck-smooth back. "You should have done it my way. He's not stupid, you know. He'll see through your trick."

"I know."

"What about the woman?"

Jonas's grip tightened on the receiver. His back teeth slid noisily against each other. "What about her?"

"Shouldn't she know you're rewriting her life?"

"I'll take care of her."

"She'll need to stop taking trips to the hospital in Nashua."

He took a deep breath. Cathlynn would balk at that. Her grandmother seemed to mean the world to her. "I'll take care of her. Just set the trail, and hope Mac-Phearson stays on the scent. If you do your part properly, it'll buy me enough time."

There was silence on the other end, and Jonas could have sworn his brother was smiling.

"You've fallen for her!"

"It's not like that."

"If you say so." Cam chuckled. "But if you want my advice—"

"Not on this subject." He swiped a hand through his hair. "Thank you, Cameron, for your help."

"No problem."

As Jonas placed the receiver back on its cradle, he saw Cathlynn standing at the library door. How much of his conversation with Cam had she overheard?

"Cathlynn—just who I wanted to see."

"About what?" she asked, instant suspicion visible in the growing tension of her body.

"Your grandmother."

"Something's happened?" Panic trembled through her voice.

"No, no." He rounded the desk, rushing to relieve her fear. This wasn't going as he'd planned. "We have a problem. If you keep visiting her, it'll attract Sterling's attention and put everything in jeopardy."

She turned away from him, fidgeting with the objects on his desk. She picked up the French tiger paper-weight, caressed its curves, scrutinized its surfaces. "I hope you didn't pay too much for this. It's been re-ground."

"I know, but I have a sentimental attachment to it."

She carefully placed the half globe on his desk and speared him pointedly with her gaze. "I have to go see her, Jonas. You promised—"

"Your brother—"

"Isn't dependable—"

"Cat…"

Before he had a chance to explain, Sterling's footsteps clipped loudly up the corridor.

"The traffic in the city was just beastly," Sterling said as he pushed his way into the library. He headed for the silent butler and poured himself a drink.

Jonas slipped an arm around Cathlynn's waist and led her to the sitting area. He felt her shudder beneath his fingers, along with the unnerving zing of contact between them. But whatever attraction might exist was soiled by suspicion. Her spine was rigid against his bicep, her shoulders scrunched enough to leave a stiff space between them. As soon as she could, she sat in the chair next to Sterling's and broke their contact.

Jonas stood behind her and massaged the resistant muscles of her shoulders.

"How was your day, darling?" he asked her, putting reassurance in his hands and in his voice.

"Very revealing," she answered and looked up at him. Her smile carried with it a veiled threat. Good God, not her, too. It was bad enough Sterling's visit with McPhearson had probably yielded him a sleeveful of juicy tidbits with which to trip Cathlynn.

"Really," said Sterling, "how so?" He leaned back in his seat and took a long sip from his drink. His mustache twitched. His eyes narrowed as he focused on her face.

"I realized I'd forgotten to mail the invitations to the fete. I can't imagine why I forgot. I'm usually such an organized person when it comes to things like that."

"It happens to the best of us," Sterling said. "You've been so busy lately. How did you like that new composer, Serge Montreuil? I heard you went to his premiere last month."

Cathlynn waved a hand as grandly as Alana had ever done. "His scores were ambitious and could stand some polishing, but he does have some potential in the future.''

Jonas's fingers tightened unconsciously on Cathlynn's shoulder. How had she known? Those were Alana's exact words to him the day after the premiere.

''How much money did you raise with your celebrity gala for the children's hospital last Labor Day?'' Sterling asked.

''Unfortunately, not as much as expected.'' She placed a hand on one of Jonas's and looked up at him. ''Would you get me a drink, darling. I'll skip the gin and just have the tonic.'' She smiled at Sterling. ''I've been trying to cut down. Maybe it'll help with the weight a bit.''

Jonas forced his hands to release their hold on Cathlynn's shoulder. Too spooky. It was as if Alana herself sat in that chair. Those thoughts were hers, too, not Cathlynn's. He headed for the silent butler and splashed tonic water into a glass.

''I was quite disappointed at the turnout for the gala,'' Cathlynn continued. ''But then the mayor had his golf tournament the same weekend. I guess doctors prefer golfing to dancing!''

Jonas handed her the glass. He didn't like the gleam in her eyes. Too bright, too sharp, and sliced by anger.

''I trust the spill at the gala didn't cause a permanent scar,'' Sterling said, glancing toward Jonas. Jonas wanted to loosen his tie. It felt like a noose around his neck. He headed to the bar to serve himself a drink instead, and regretted his decision when the liquor burned his throat and scorched his stomach.

''I think the dress bore the biggest brunt of the fall,'' Cathlynn said. ''It's ruined, but my knee feels much better.'' She lifted her right leg and moved the knee joint back and forth to prove her point. She'd chosen the correct one. How had she known? "It won't affect my enjoying the skiing season one bit, according to the doctors."

Watching her handle every one of Sterling's curveballs with ease was like watching Alana in action. Was he viewing a hallucination? Was Alana sitting before him, or Cathlynn? He rubbed a fist over his eyes. Had he created a monster with his ambition?

He could almost hear Alana laughing at him from her grave.

Revenge, she'd sworn she'd have it.

She'd hated this place as much as he loved it. She'd hated his decision to closet himself with his research as much as he reveled in the focus it afforded him. She'd hated his vision as much as it fired him.

Everything—his duty, his vision, his future—hung on the thin threads of fragile lies, and the complicated web he'd woven was falling around him, the strands ripping apart, the knots trapping him beneath.

Even dead, Alana would make sure she won.

Even dead, she would find a way to cut him to pieces.

Chapter Seven

Cathlynn tossed and turned all night. Even with the curtains opened and the moon's light spilling brightly through them, she'd dreamed of monks with knives and dead wives, making her feel caught somewhere between mystery and madness. The dreams always ended the same way, with a knife's silver blade searching to slit her throat, and a monk fading through her bedroom wall when she opened her eyes.

Sometime before dawn, she gave up on sleep and sat curled beneath the sheets, with the lights blazing, listening to the walls moan and weep, to the halls whisper and creak, to the pipes sigh and groan.

She reread the hard copy she'd made of Alana's disk. Her first reading of the journal file had prepared her for Sterling's grilling yesterday. Not being certain whose side Sterling was on, she'd decided to keep up Jonas's charade for the time being. This time, she read the pages to prove herself wrong.

Alana wrote of Jonas's temper, of her attempts to assuage his unpredictable storms of anger, of her fear of him. She painted Jonas as a hard, unyielding man with vengeful tendencies. Reading Alana's descriptions had filled Cathlynn with a sadness she couldn't explain, except that deep down she'd hoped Jonas would turn out to be the soft, smiling man she'd seen on that magical sleigh ride.

Once more her heart had proven her wrong. Her silent tears joined the cacophony of noisy night spirits haunting the mansion.

She picked up the last entry and reread Alana's final thoughts.

He did not take the news of our impending divorce well. He raved like a maniac about responsibility, selfishness and duty. He swore he would see me dead before he granted me the divorce. And I believe him. He was mad enough to kill. But I'll show him. I won't let him win.

I've prepared a letter with a statement which I'll have B.T. mail in the morning. Just in case. If anything should happen to me, my cousin Geoffrey will investigate the matter. If not for me, then for the inheritance. Money has that effect. And I'll still have the last word.

In the meantime, I have a date with a most interesting…friend. I may have found someone whose deep passion matches mine—at last!

Cathlynn could almost hear Alana laugh with anticipation at the prospect for bettering Jonas, at her pleasure in betraying her husband. She shivered at the viciousness of the impression. Alana and Jonas's relationship appeared to be an emotionally complex one where the wounds ran deep on both sides. It suddenly occurred to her that Alana's journal gave *one* perception of the situation, and perception was not necessarily truth. Her mother had taught her that.

She picked up the pages again. Who was B.T.? In the planner file on the disk, she'd seen several references to nighttime meetings with this person. A friend? Someone Alana trusted? She'd look for an address book and see if she could locate this mysterious B.T. Who was this mysterious date? she asked herself again. Was he the one who had silenced Alana?

Cathlynn fingered the sheets of white paper on the emerald coverlet. In the hands of the police, would this transcript be enough to get Jonas arrested, or at least get an investigation started? So why couldn't she bring herself to alert the authorities? Gathering the journal pages, she tried to convince herself she needed more evidence before she persecuted someone. Stuffing Alana's accusations deep into a drawer filled with silken underwear, she resolved to get irrefutable proof of guilt before she showed anyone these pages. The Jonas described here simply didn't match the man she was slowly starting to know.

A cold shower enlivened Cathlynn's sleep-deprived brain, but couldn't erase the dark smudges beneath her eyes. She hid them beneath the mask of makeup, and showed up to breakfast bright and shining, as a loving, rested wife should.

She had to keep up the charade, pretend everything was all right, for a bit longer. Even the cinnamon roll's sweetness couldn't hide the distaste the thought left behind, and she pushed the pastry away.

"How did you know?" Jonas asked casually.

She didn't pretend to misunderstand his question. "I found her journal."

Folding his morning paper neatly on the corner of the table he looked up. "Are you ready?"

"For what?" Cathlynn closed her eyes and inhaled the steam of the fragrant coffee in her cup.

"Your visit to the dressmaker."

She'd completely forgotten about that. "Sure." If anything, it would get her out of the thick atmosphere in these gray walls—and pretending everything was normal was, after all, part of the game.

ALL THE DUCKS were neatly in a row. *Pow. Pow. Pow.* Alana. Jonas. Ste-Croix. As for this Cathlynn, she was getting to be too big of a distraction. Jonas hadn't gone back to his work in the lab, and there was a piece still missing from the formula. His contact was on his back, and there were so few days before the house of cards started to crumble. It was imperative Jonas get back to work.

"So what do you do with excess?" he asked his reflection in the glass.

He smiled broadly. "Why, you cut it, of course!"

THEY DROVE to Ste-Croix in the gloomy silence Cathlynn had come to think of as the usual state of affairs. Valentin had taken Jonas's Jeep to run errands, so they were in her Volvo. The interior was starting to show its age, but with the heater on high, it felt warm and comfortable. It smelled old like the antique finds she often transported, but even through the mustiness, she could detect the clean woodsy scent of Jonas's aftershave.

Balancing the box of invitations on her knees, Cathlynn studied Jonas as he drove. He handled the car efficiently and with ease. With the monastery behind them, his face lost its harshness, and when he spoke of the village, a soft smile appeared on his lips. Her traitorous heart gave a leap of joy at the sight.

"The Planning Committee has worked hard to improve the quality of life here. In the summer we have a farmer's market and flea market every Saturday in the church parking lot. Fourth of July weekend, we have a craft fair that draws artists and tourists from the whole region. Labor Day we usually have a fall festival to raise funds for the school. We've got plans to restore the sugar maple industry, the tannery, and to attract several more opportunities for employment for our young people."

"This place seems to mean so much to you. Why?"

He stared blankly ahead. "The monastery's been in my family for many generations. My great-grandfather bought it when the last of the monks died. I was born here. I grew up here. When my father died, we lost it, I swore I'd get it back."

"And you did."

"I did."

"How?"

"I invested what was left of my father's estate and built it back up."

"Do you always get what you want?"

Jonas looked at her. The contact of his stormy eyes seemed to reach a tender, aching spot on her soul. "No."

When he turned his attention back to the road, Cathlynn shivered, feeling cold and more alone than she'd ever felt before.

The village of Ste-Croix had a simple layout: one main artery, four connecting veins, with the white-spindled church as its heart on top of a steep hill. Shops lined the main street, and simple square-framed houses peopled the adjoining roads. A Mobil station's single pump welcomed visitors to the village. Next to it stood a hotel sporting a vacancy sign and an invitation to try Chef Chuck's cuisine. Across the street, a hand-painted sign announced an artisan's workshop. The combination general store/post office's picture window displayed a brass bed, flannel shirts and an array of tools. The grocery store seemed to be doing a brisk business for a Wednesday morning. On the doctor's office hung a crooked sign reading For Rent or Sale. The last building before the church was a small dress shop with two aging mannequins displaying Sunday-best dresses.

"If Lorraine Forester is such a good seamstress, why didn't Alana use her?"

The lines on his face hardened at the mention of Alana's name, and Cathlynn wished she'd never brought her up.

"Too provincial in her opinion." Jonas sneered. "No designer label. She never came to the village."

Jonas did a sharp U-turn in the church's parking lot and parked in front of the dress shop.

"Here we are."

The snow along the walkway had the consistency of mashed potato and Cathlynn was glad to reach the shop's door. When the overhead jangle of bell announced their arrival, an elderly woman looked up from her sewing, squinted, then smiled broadly. She dropped the sewing on the counter and struggled to get up with the aid of a cane. Cathlynn recognized her as Bertha, the gossip from the auction. Would Bertha recognize her, or was her vision too myopic?

"Dr. Jonas! How nice to see you again!" She hobbled around the counter and squeezed Jonas with a bear hug.

"How are you doing, Bertha?"

"Oh, wonderful! With the fete coming up, Lorraine

and I hardly have a moment to breathe. We can never thank you enough for all you've done.''

"It was the least I could do after your son-in-law's death."

She released Jonas and took notice of Cathlynn. Squinting hard, she looked her over. Her genial grin faded. "You're back, I see. You don't deserve a good man like him."

"Bertha—" Jonas started.

Bertha turned toward Jonas, digging a gnarled finger into his chest. "No, no. She doesn't, and that's a fact. I don't know why you've stayed married to the likes of *her* for so long."

"Is your daughter here this morning?" Jonas asked, averting Bertha's invasion into his private life. "Alana needs a dress for the fete."

"What's the matter? Were all the shops in New York closed?" Sarcasm oozed, thick and viscous, in Bertha's voice.

"The dress I ordered arrived in the wrong size," Cathlynn said, smiling as graciously as she could while her stomach tied itself into knots. Not everyone, it seemed, held the mistress of the monastery in high esteem. "There's no time to get another."

"We don't need your business." Bertha turned her back and headed back behind the counter.

"As a favor to me, Bertha." Jonas charmed her with a dimpled smile and a tilt of his handsome head.

She hesitated. "All right, for you." Her wrinkled chin pointed at Cathlynn. "But not for her."

Bertha hobbled to a door at the back of the small shop. "Lorraine! Lorraine! A client for you."

Lorraine hurried through the door. When she saw who her client was, her eyes grew wide and her mouth formed an O. The surprise soon faded back to a blank expression. "How can I help you?"

"Alana needs a dress for the fete. Do you think you'll have enough time to make her one?"

"Surely. Come on back." The small woman wore her black hair tied back and rolled into a bun. Her chest sported an array of pins stuck in at all angles, and a measuring tape dangled from the neck of her simple black dress. Cathlynn recognized David's elegant dark looks, but he had probably inherited his spicy charm from his grandmother.

Bertha turned the Open sign to read Closed, and drew the shade over the door. "Have a cup of coffee while you wait," she said, taking Jonas's arm. "What surprise have you prepared for us this year?"

"We'll have to do with simple good food and good music this year," Jonas said.

Bertha threw Cathlynn a sharp glare. "Yes, with all your worries, simply having the ball will be a treat."

Lorraine led Cathlynn to a living room converted into a studio. The far end was filled with bolts of fabric, a cutting table and a sewing table. The other end had a round table and a set of chairs set up cozily before a fireplace. On the table lay open several fashion magazines and an album of Lorraine's designs. She invited Cathlynn to sit. Bertha bustled Jonas into a chair and left to get the promised coffee.

"What did you have in mind?" Lorraine asked Cathlynn.

"Something simple yet elegant."

After some discussion, they agreed on a design. Bertha returned with a tray of coffee things.

"Let's get some measurements, then," Lorraine said. She handed her mother a pad and pencil and removed her measuring tape from around her neck. "You'll need to take your sweater and pants off."

"I'll, uh, go wait out front," Jonas said.

"What's the matter, boy? Haven't you seen your wife without clothes on before?" Bertha harrumphed her opinion. "No, you'll stay. I want to talk to you about my David."

Jonas shifted uncomfortably in his chair. The heat of a blush burned Cathlynn's cheeks. She turned her back to Jonas and proceeded to take off her sweater. Even though she wore a camisole, even though she'd worn skimpier bathing suits on the beach, she felt utterly naked. Her fingers fumbled with the zipper of her pants. As she drew them down her legs, she felt her knees shake. When Lorraine started calling out numbers, she was mortified. Now Jonas would know just how far removed she was from the picture-perfect Alana. She couldn't remember a more embarrassing moment in her life, and wanted the floor to open and swallow her up.

Distractedly, Bertha jotted down the measurements Lorraine called out. "David's been working late for nearly a week. I take it the auction was good then?"

"Hmm," Jonas answered, his voice sounding warm, deep and distant.

"My David says that the Ryder fellow is there to cause trouble. Is that true?"

"Hmm." She felt Jonas's gaze caress her curves. Those ten extra pounds seemed to swell and magnify. It took all the strength she had to keep her arms out straight and not clamp them on a patch or two of excess hip or waist. She itched to get her clothes back on. Silently, she urged Lorraine to hurry up and end this torture.

"My David says we should close the shop and move

into the city before you're forced to sell the monastery. Get out before it's too late, David says. Do you think we should?''

''No.''

''My David says you'll be asking for blood samples again.''

''Soon.''

''We'll be standing in line to help you. Just say the word.''

''Hmm.''

''Turn, please,'' Lorraine said.

Cathlynn did as she was bid. She tried to keep her gaze averted from Jonas, but it was like the tide trying to fight the moon's pull—impossible. He was scrunched in his chair, chin in hand, face impassive, eyes stormy and dark. Her skin grew uncomfortably warm under his riveted gaze.

''My David says you're really close this time.''

''Hmm.''

She'd expected disapproval, disappointment at all her glaring imperfections. Instead it was hunger, raw and potent, she saw gleam in his eyes. The force of it nearly took her breath away. The intensity of it swirled through her with hurricane strength, eroding what little composure she might have left. Her knees wobbled. Her mouth felt dry. And a strange sensation rippled through her, hot and cold. Maybe she was coming down with the flu.

''Then we wouldn't need the yearly sacrifice,'' Bertha said.

''What?'' His forehead compressed with confusion, breaking the spell. He glanced at Bertha.

The old lady smiled. ''I wasn't sure I had your full

attention. Are you going to dress as Aurelius the Just again this year?''

He relaxed, returned his gaze to her body. ''Hmm, yes, Aurelius the Just. It's tradition.''

''He was the last abbot before the order mysteriously disappeared. I wonder what really happened to the monks. Why would they leave so much behind?''

''Circumstances.''

''The sacrifices, don't you think they really happened?''

''No.''

''That's all I need for now,'' Lorraine said, wrapping her measuring tape around her neck once more.

The torture was finally over. Cathlynn quickly donned the protective layers of her clothes.

When Jonas rose to leave, Bertha placed a hand on his forearm. ''Does she make you happy? Does she *really* make you happy?''

He didn't answer, but looked straight at her over Bertha's shoulder. The gray of his eyes was a turbulent sea that mirrored the unstable emotions still surging in chaotic breakers through her body. And as the planes of his face hardened once more, she knew with certainty it had been a long time since Jonas Shades had been happy. The thought waffled a weighty sadness through her, leaving behind an unexplainable soreness on her heart. *I'm not Alana,* she wanted to tell him. She looked away unable to bear the silence any longer. *I don't owe him anything.* But the thought was no comfort, and the strange ache to hold and heal didn't disappear.

''I'll call you when I'm ready for your first fitting,'' Lorraine said.

''That'll be fine,'' Cathlynn answered distractedly, reaching for her coat.

As they all moved to the front room, Bertha held Cathlynn back. Her fingers dug like talons into Cathlynn's arm, and her glare was as sharp as any eagle's zeroing in on an unprotected mouse. "I don't know where you've been or what you've done. But you gave Jonas quite a scare. And if you ever hurt him again, I swear I'll make sure you won't get another chance. Do you understand me?"

"Perfectly."

"We need him, but we sure don't need the likes of you."

A shiver rattled through her. Cathlynn buttoned her coat and hurried after Jonas. There was definitely no love lost between Bertha and Alana.

When they reached the car, Cathlynn spotted the invitations. Needing some breathing space and time to recover her composure before she got in close quarters with Jonas, she grasped the box. "I'll go mail these. I'll be back in a minute."

Before Jonas could answer, she trotted across the street and down the sidewalk to the post office.

HALF A DOZEN PEOPLE lingered in the aisles of general merchandise. Cathlynn spotted the post office sign at the back of the store and headed toward it. As she did, David's observation came back to her. *Haven't you noticed? There are no old men in Ste-Croix.*

A mother with two toddlers at her side stuffed disposable diapers in a cart. A middle-aged woman weighed nails into a scale. An old lady compared the virtues of Spic and Span and Mr. Clean. A young man hauled gallons of paint onto the counter serviced by a young lady preening for his attention.

She heard bits and snatches of whispered conversation, heard the resentment, the hatred.

"Is that her?"

"I heard she was back. I wonder where she went?"

"Somewhere where there's plenty of men," the young man sniggered.

"What's *she* doing here? Doesn't she usually order her boy toy to do such menial tasks?"

"Miss Fashion Plate's sure put on the pounds!"

"Who do you think will be her next conquest?"

"She should've stayed lost!"

A dozen pairs of eyes quickly pretended they hadn't been watching her cross the store. A few glanced outside at Jonas now parked before the store. Cathlynn could see their compassion for her betrayed husband, could guess their thoughts. No wonder Bertha had seemed so judgmental. I'm not Alana, she wanted to yell, but of course, she couldn't. They would never believe her, never believe the lie she lived was for Jonas, for them, not just for herself.

Cathlynn forced herself to continue to the post office window. She pushed the box of stamped envelopes across the counter and quickly made her way back outside.

No wonder Jonas was so angry. His wife had cheated on him and the village knew it. Had the good citizens of Ste-Croix made sure he was informed of her trespasses, or had they tried to protect their benefactor from the knowledge?

Any way she looked at it, it was becoming clear she was playing the role of the villain in more ways than one.

JONAS STEWED at the wheel of Cathlynn's car.

This had been a mistake. A big mistake. He should

never have asked her to play Alana. He should never have asked her to stay. The more he saw of her, the stronger his need for her grew. And he hated himself for his weakness, for wanting her arms around him, her mouth against his, her body tangled with his, for wanting the golden fire in her eyes, her hair, her skin to melt the ice on his dead soul. He didn't want to give in to temptation, and if he had any sense left at all, he'd send her away. Now—before it was too late.

But he wouldn't. There was too much at stake.

Seven more days. He could hang on for that long. Then he'd get access to the trust fund, and she'd be on her way.

So why did the prospect of her departure suddenly seem so gloomy?

The passenger door creaked open and Cathlynn sat beside him without a glance. Her purse landed with a thump on the floor. Her seat belt notched into place with a click.

He switched on the ignition. The engine raced, then purred. He steered onto the street. As if by mutual agreement, they did not speak.

The fact should have made him calmer, but it didn't. He found himself growing tenser by the minute. Black and frenzied like a starved panther, his fury stalked its cage. The low prowl of anger deep inside him metastasized like a cancer. His grip tightened. His control shook. Once on the village's outskirts, he tromped on the accelerator.

The Volvo gave a forward jerk. The speedometer's needle jogged up. Thirty-five. Forty. Forty-five. Much too fast for this twisty country road.

"Jonas?" Cathlynn shot him a worried glance.

Its effect was like a bucket of cold water. Sanity prevailed. He relaxed his grip. Fifty. Ping. He eased his foot off the accelerator.

The pedal didn't follow his foot's upward course.

Fifty-three. Fifty-five.

"Jonas?"

The speedometer's needle trembled farther up. Sixty. Sixty-five.

Adrenaline shot through him.

Don't panic. Think.

He pressed the brakes, felt the friction as they caught and dragged, smelled them burn. Still the needle quivered upward. Sixty-six. Sixty-seven. Adding the hand brake only made things worse.

"Slow down, Jonas!"

He pressed harder on the brakes. They ground their protest. The engine whined. The car shook, fought him. Sixty-five. Sixty-four.

"What are you doing?" Cathlynn asked in a high, panicked voice, grasping the sides of her seat like a lifeline.

"The accelerator's stuck."

"Jonas?"

"We'll be all right," he said with a reassurance he didn't feel. "Just hang on tight."

As the car fought him, he gripped the wheel tighter. *Downshift.*

Foot still hard on the brake, he let go the wheel with one hand. The car wobbled sideways. Cathlynn cried out. He regained control. Keeping his attention on the road, he felt for the shifter.

Jammed.

He swore.

"Cathlynn," he said calmly as he maneuvered the

car into a curve. "I want you to put your face between your knees and protect your head with your arms. Can you do that?"

"What are you going to do?"

He tried to make light of the dire situation. "I'm going to stop this aircraft, but the landing might be rough."

"All right." As she got into position, her coat rustled.

"Jonas?"

"Hmm."

"I trust you."

Those simple words frightened him more than the runaway car doing its best to slam them into the trees lining the narrow road.

"I didn't kill Alana."

"I know."

Her belief in him was like a blessing. An absolute calm came over him. Once more he freed one hand from the steering wheel. He was prepared for the wobble and kept the car in control. Hand on the shifter, he pressed hard.

No movement.

He shoved. It gave, then took. It was like arm wrestling with a rabid wolverine.

He risked a sidelong glance. "Cat, I'm going to need your help."

"What do you want me to do?"

"Put all your weight on the shifter and shove it into Park."

She uncoiled from her safe position, slipped her right arm from the shoulder restraint. Jonas's stomach clenched. She would be vulnerable. He hadn't killed Alana, but he might very well be responsible for Cathlynn's death. Curling both her hands around the lever, she glanced at him.

"On the count of three," he said. "One. Two. Three."

Cathlynn groaned with her effort. He braced himself for the sudden halt. It didn't come.

"It won't budge," she said. "What now?"

He swallowed hard. "Put your hands on the wheel."

"What?"

"Do it."

She obeyed.

"Feel the drag?" he asked.

"Yes."

"Think you can hold it?"

"I'll try."

He lessened his hold on the wheel. It bolted right, then left in her hands. She muffled a gasp. He tightened his grip again and recaptured control.

"Are you all right?" he asked after a moment.

"I'm fine. Let's try again."

He uncurled his fingers, let them hover for an instant while the car twitched once. Cathlynn held on and steered.

"I've got it," she said, attention glued to the road.

"When I say 'now,' I want you to let go the wheel and protect yourself—"

"No, I—"

"Just do it, Cat."

"All right."

As quickly as he dared, Jonas grasped the shifter. Keeping his attention on the twisting asphalt, he watched for a straight stretch. Around the next curve, it came into view. He rammed the stick forward.

"Now!"

The wound was lethal. The engine shrieked. The tires squealed. The car jerked to a grinding halt, slamming them forward, then back. Then the car spun out of control, spewing shredded and severed parts like an eviscerated dragon.

Everything was a blur. The bumper caught a snowbank. The sudden stop threw them both sideways. His shoulder thwacked into the door. Pain splintered through his arm, his chest, stealing his breath. Cathlynn's upper body landed against him. He freed his right arm and held on to her tight.

The car heaved its last rattle, leaving only the ticking of overheated metal cooling to fill the eerie silence.

"Cat?"

"I'm fine. You?"

"Yes. We need to get out."

She nodded against his chest.

"Can you open your door? Mine's jammed against the snowbank."

Though he hated to, Jonas let her go as she straightened away from him. She pushed the door open, then started to get out. She was yanked back in by the part of her seat belt still tied around her waist. Once out, she reached in to help him.

Arm in arm, they stumbled to safety.

As he held Cathlynn's shivering body, everything around him took on a hyper clarity. Cathlynn's red wool coat rough under his finger. From the cut on his lip, his blood, metallic and tangy, with each of his swallows. Snow, bright against the midday sun. Shadows crisp, falling from the trees. The pings and pangs of defeat from the car. Even through the acrid smoke of rubber, oil and heated metal, the citrus scent of Cathlynn's shampoo.

And as he surveyed the mangled remains of the Volvo, a knowing, sharp and deep, quaked through him and turned suspicion into utter certainty.

Alana was dead.

She'd been murdered.

He tightened his hold on Cathlynn. The pain knifing through his shoulder was nothing compared to the sick feeling mauling his heart.

Because of him, Cathlynn could be next.

Chapter Eight

When Cathlynn came out of the shower, Jonas was waiting for her in her room. He leaned against the window's dark stone ledge. The light of dusk, weak and gray, lengthened the shadows on his face, making him appear drawn and tired. The purpling bruises along his cheek and jaw added to the beaten appearance.

"I want you to pack your bags," he announced. "I'll drive you home tonight."

She hid her surprise, checked to see if the material of her flannel bathrobe covered the necessary parts, if the sash was tied securely, then she headed for the vanity. Even a solid half-hour under a hot shower hadn't washed away the soreness from her muscles. "I think I've had enough of the car for one day, if you don't mind. Besides, we had an agreement."

"It didn't include a death sentence."

She sat down on the lone chair before the mirror, unwound the towel turban covering her hair, tumbling the wet mass loose over her shoulders. "It's an old car and I'm way behind on maintenance. You stepped on the accelerator too hard. It got stuck. It was an accident." It had to be. Anything else was unthinkable.

"Not according to the mechanic I had go over every inch of your car this afternoon."

The hand holding her comb stopped halfway to her head, then fell with a bump to the vanity's top. She slanted him a look through the mirror. "What do you mean?"

"The accelerator was rigged to jam when the driver hit fifty."

Her pulse whooshed past her ears. The walls around her seemed to thrum to the same burning beat. *Beware.* She shook her head. "What?"

"My guess is that you were supposed to wreck your car once you hit the highway and die."

A dozen questions sprouted and wilted in her mind, but she couldn't vocalize any of them.

"You'd planned to go see your grandmother today," he said.

"Only you knew that."

He shrugged. "And Valentin, and David."

"I thought you trusted them."

"I do."

She raced her thumb up and down the comb's teeth, creating a zigzaggy chatter matching the tumble of her thoughts. "So why would they want to harm me?"

"They don't."

"Then who else?"

Jonas stuck his hands in his pants pockets. "No one knew I'd asked you to curtail your visits. No one knew I'd be driving your car to town this morning."

"But why would someone want to hurt me at all?"

He pushed himself off the wall and paced. "When Alana disappeared without a fuss, I was worried. I had a private investigator try to track her down. He found nothing. Not her. Not her car. Not a single use of her credit card. I had him keep looking, keep digging, thinking something was bound to show up.''

"Nothing did.''

He shook his head. "Nothing. Then I got angry because I thought she'd gotten herself killed by one of her 'friends.'''

"Having sex is a long way from committing murder.''

"They're not that far apart. Both are impulses. Both are strong urges. And one can easily lead to the other.''

"But if she was murdered by one of her 'friends,' why would that place me in danger?''

"Because I'm starting to think impulse wasn't the reason she disappeared.'' He paused, staring frankly at her in the mirror. "If I'd known, Cathlynn, if I'd thought there would be any danger to you, I'd never have asked you to play Alana.''

"I know.'' Unwilling to meet his fiery gaze any longer, she ran the comb through her wet hair and concentrated on untangling the knots in each strand. "Her inheritance. Other than you, who benefits?''

Jonas resumed his pacing. "If she dies before she assumes control of the fund, her cousin, Geoffrey Chandler, does.''

"Isn't he in England?''

"Which doesn't necessarily mean anything, but I'd like to know the answer to that question myself.'' He headed for the door. It creaked on its hinges. "Get dressed.''

Comb still in hand, she spun in the chair to face him. "I'm not leaving, Jonas. I can't. Not without the Aidan Heart.''

"It's yours,'' he said, glancing at her over his shoulder.

Anticipation sped her heart, making it beat a strange counterpoint to the chaotic jumble in her mind. "Are you sure?"

"Yes. I'll meet you in the library."

CATHLYNN HURRIEDLY DRESSED in jeans and a soft sweater. When she got to the library, Jonas was frowning and listening intently to someone at the other end of the phone.

"Thanks, Geoffrey. Sorry to ring you at such a late hour." He paused. "Yes, I will."

He took a key from his desk, grasped her hand and led her through darkened halls, down cold stairways, into shadowed passages to the room next to David's office.

As Jonas unlocked the door, he frowned, pausing to finger gray scratches on the black metal. He pushed the door open, flipped on a light and gestured her in.

The room held a wall of black file cabinets, two huge metal safes and several glass-fronted floor-to-ceiling collector's cabinets. Though the harsh fluorescent light didn't show them to their best advantage, through the glass she saw a magnificent collection of paperweights.

She couldn't suppress the wide smile or the laughter bubbling from her.

"What's the matter?" Jonas asked.

"Nothing. Absolutely nothing." She turned to him and gave him an impulsive kiss on the cheek, then quickly turned back to the collection.

"Paperweights!" She lifted the closest cabinet's door and reached for one of the glass globes. "Of course. What else? A man like you wouldn't collect anything with delicate stems or fancy latticework. I don't know what I'd expected. No, paperweights are perfect." They were power and grace and vulnerability all in one. Just like him. Did he realize how much of himself he'd revealed? "You thought the Aidan Heart was a paperweight, didn't you?"

"I found the original in England. I thought it was a pylon-style paperweight and looked for the matching pair for years."

"Not as long as I've looked for the original." She replaced the paperweight on its obsidian pedestal and perused the rest of the shelf. "My great-great-grandfather, Aidan O'Connell, was a glassmaker. He made the Heart as a wedding gift for his bride, Deirdre. It was a symbol of his love for her." The feelings of childhood came back in a muted ache. She tamped them down. "When they emigrated to the United States, it got lost somehow…"

"And now you've found it."

She looked up at him, and in his gaze found a reflection, an understanding of her desire. "Yes."

Jonas turned from her and crouched in front of one of the metal safes. He reached for the combination dial. It fell onto the floor, bouncing twice before it landed on its flat side. She gasped. He cranked the handle. It slipped from its cowl on the door into his hand. She crushed a fist against her heart. He thumped his fist against the door and it opened. Inside was a wooden box with a velvet lining. The drapes and folds curved and dipped into a familiar outline.

"The Aidan Heart?" Cathlynn's voice shook. Her fingertips scrunched the wool of her sweater.

"Yes."

"Where is it?" She wrapped her arms around her middle, trying to keep the chill shuddering through her from unbalancing her.

"Gone."

"Noooo," she whispered harshly, unbelievingly. Nausea billowed. *Don't panic. There's got to be a logical answer.* "Could you have stored it elsewhere?"

"No."

She hadn't come all this way, she hadn't almost died today for nothing. "Who has a key to the safe?"

"It was forced open. So was the door." His voice was clipped, distracted as he examined the broken pieces of the safe.

"Who has access to this room?"

"You, me, Valentin, Sterling, David…just about anybody who has a mind to. Valentin has a habit of leaving the kitchen door unlocked."

Gram, oh, Gram, I'm sorry. I'm so sorry. "When did you last see it?"

"Saturday."

The day of the auction. The day her life had changed forever.

"Who would do this?" On purpose? It was too cruel.

His gaze met hers, straight and true, driving home his point. "Someone who knows how much the Aidan Heart means to you."

"No one does, Jonas. No one but you."

"I keep my promises." His gaze narrowed fiercely, making her stumble back. "I have no idea who we're dealing with, but one thing is sure. If you stay here, Cat, you're placing yourself in danger."

Her emotions had been buffeted like luffing sails since she'd arrived. She was confused. She was angry. And yes, even scared. But she was also aware of time running out for Gram, and she couldn't give up.

"I can't go." Her chin rose defiantly. "Not without the Aidan Heart."

"One dead wife is enough."

"Believe me, I agree completely." Then it occurred to her through the maze of disappointment and regret that the loss of the Aidan Heart was as great for Jonas as it was for her. Without it, he couldn't assure her cooperation. Without her, he'd lose the trust fund. "I think you've got the motive wrong."

"It seems fairly obvious to me."

She shook her head. "Don't you see? It's not the inheritance that's at stake. It's not me, not Alana, someone wants to stop. It's you."

"YOU'RE WRONG," Jonas said, struggling to keep his anger in control, from lashing out at Cathlynn just because she was there. "What is there to gain?"

"How close are you to finding an answer to your research question?"

"Close, but not that close. I'm still years away from confirming something certain. Then there's the whole process of FDA approval—"

"But when you do find a cure, there'll be a lot of money to be made. And last year, you made yourself an enemy. All that research Chandler Pharmaceuticals paid for and you shoved back in their face. When you quit, you took your knowledge with you. And what did they have? Bits and pieces of what you left behind. Not enough to pay them back for what they lost."

She was right, of course. And by killing Alana, they'd insured no more Chandler money would go into funding a project for which they would see no financial benefit. Which made it more imperative than ever that Cathlynn should leave.

"I can see those wheels turning, Jonas. I'm not leaving. That would play right into someone's hand. No, what we need to do is pretend nothing's wrong. I'll keep playing the mistress of the monastery. You need to go back to your research." The gold in her eyes swirled with zeal and energy, holding his gaze prisoner. "And you need to pretend you've found the answer. Make a show of working, then just before the fete, make a big announcement that you've found the key."

As much as he'd been ready to use her to gain access to Alana's trust fund, he wasn't ready to offer her up as a sacrifice. His mission was to save lives, not endanger them. "By doing that I'd put you in more danger."

"By doing that you'd flush out Alana's killer and I'd get back the Aidan Heart."

A chance to regain control. Did she know what she was offering him? "Why are you willing to get caught in the crossfires?"

"Because I just hate it when the bad guy wins." Hands on hips she lanced him with a look of exasperation. "Look, do you want all your good work to be flushed down the toilet, or do you want a chance to find an answer?"

He ground his teeth. "I want an answer."

"IT DOESN'T LOOK like I expected," Cathlynn said as she studied Jonas's lab.

He tried to see the room through her eyes. Gleaming cabinets and drawers. Bright light from overhead banks reflecting off the stainless-steel counters. Blood-collecting equipment, neat and orderly, in racks and bins. The red biohazard can. The ugly block of refrigerator. Two computer terminals and their printers stood back to back on the work island in the middle of the

room. The lab smelled cool and remote with an under-
tone of Pine Sol.

Cold. Functional. Those would be her conclusions.

It had never seemed clinical to him until today. He'd
always thought of it as efficient, and as hope-full. This
was the only place he'd been assured of order. It had
once been an oasis of calm in the chaos of his life. Now,
because of Alana, it, too, had become touched by the
dark specter of upheaval her disappearance had caused.
How long had it been since he'd worked?

"What did you expect?" he teased. "Something out
of a Frankenstein movie?"

She shrugged and smiled softly. The gold in her hair
gleamed in the light. He wanted to touch it. The need
itched in his fingers, so he sat in the swivel chair in
front of his computer and curled his hands around the
ends of the chair's arms.

"Tell me about your work," she said, scrutinizing
the titles of the medical tomes lined up on one corner
of the island. "This disease you're researching, what is
it?"

That topic of conversation, at least, was safe ground.
Still, he couldn't stop looking at her, trying to figure
her out. She was soft like a cat, determined like a ti-
gress, and the contrast intrigued him. "It's called
Cross's Disease because it originated in the cloistered
order of the Monks of the Holy Cross. They lived in a
remote village in the mountains of northern France. One
would think that monks who'd taken a vow of chastity
wouldn't proliferate the genetic weakness, but they
did."

He smiled sardonically. "Something happened, and
in the late 1700s they were driven out of France. Marius
the Elder brought a band of brothers to the New World

and restarted the order. That's why the village here still has the French spelling of Ste-Croix.''

"What exactly does the disease do?'' She perched herself on a stainless-steel stool, leaning elbows on knees.

"It causes a hyperstormic atrophy of the cells in the body.''

"In plain English, please.''

"It causes a sudden abnormal destruction of the cells in the body. Like a chain reaction. One day the patient is normal. Two months later, he's dead—if he's lucky—disintegrated from the inside out.''

As she imagined the extent of the destruction, her eyes widened. "Wow!'' Her eyebrows scrunched. "He?''

"It's passed on the X chromosome. Females are carriers, but can't manifest the disease.''

"So if the mother is a carrier, the sons will have the disease.''

"Half of them,'' he agreed.

"There are no old men in Ste-Croix.'' Something seemed to click in her mind and she straightened her stance. "David said that to me. That's why you're doing your research here? Because there's a cluster of cases in Ste-Croix?''

He nodded, amazed she could understand this fact so easily when Alana hadn't been able to in thirteen years. "The reason the disease is so successful is that it seems to carry some sort of timer. A man has enough time to start a family before the bomb detonates, so he passes on his mutant gene before he even knows he has it.''

A cloud darkened the vitality of her face as the fact of his father's early death from a degenerative disease clicked into place. "Your father had it.''

He stared at her, tightening his grip on the chair's arms. "And my mother was a carrier."

"Oh, Jonas, no."

He turned away from her sympathy, and faced the black computer screen. Turmoil churned in him. He'd accepted his fate a long time ago, but suddenly it seemed intolerable. He flicked a switch and the computer whirred to life. "What I'm trying to do is find the bomb's trigger. Find a way to defuse it, or barring that, some way of tricking it into believing the time isn't right yet."

"And you're close?"

There was hope in her voice. He hated to shatter it.

"I thought I had the answer last year, but the computer simulation showed a fatal error. Chandler Pharmaceuticals wanted me to tamper with my findings."

"You refused. Now you're on your own." The soft footsteps of her sneakers squeaked on the hard floor. She wrapped her arms around his shoulders and hugged him. He stiffened against her compassion, against the warmth enfolding him like a quilt. "What a burden you've had to carry."

Trying to break her hold, he swiveled his chair around. When his knees hit her legs, she tumbled into his lap. He grasped her hips, intending to push her off. Instead, he held her in place. One side of her body was pressed against his, curving, female. Her hands rested softly on his shoulders, warm, tender. And her eyes, they sparkled with life, honest and true.

"Don't," he said.

"Don't what?" Her golden-brown gaze met his head-on and refused to be diverted. Alana had never looked at him that way. Not even in the bloom of fresh love.

"Don't look at me like that."

"Why not?" She touched his cheek, whispered her fingertips along the bone. He closed his eyes against the sensations storming through him. Warm. Pleasant. Soft, so soft.

"Because I have nothing to give."

"Then it's time you received."

Before he could react, she put her mouth over his, swallowed the frustrated rumble of his groan. He should push her away. He shouldn't kiss her. He should stop her. But he didn't. He drew her closer, inhaling her scent, tasting her tongue, absorbing her warmth. He touched her, the palm of his hands hard against her arms, over her shoulders, until his fingers could bury themselves in her glorious mane of hair. And when she softened against him, when her hands cradled his nape with need and tenderness, when the soft sound low in her throat asked for more, he sighed his pleasure and gave in to temptation.

He knew he shouldn't, but he wanted her, wanted to taste all of her, wanted to touch every part of her—wanted to make love to her fully, completely, until the eternal coldness resting on his soul thawed. And he never wanted to let her go.

"Monsieur?"

Valentin's voice startled him back to reality. Jonas freed his mouth from Cathlynn's, but still held on to her, felt her shaking against him. "What is it, Valentin?"

"Your guests have arrived." Valentin's mouth quirked in an amused grin.

Breath heavy and hard, Jonas struggled for control. "Thank you, Valentin. We'll be right up."

Valentin backed out, closing the door behind him.

"Guests?" Cathlynn asked, climbing awkwardly out of his lap.

The room's cool air wafted around him, dissipating Cathlynn's heat, his own momentary madness. "Uninvited."

WHEN CATHLYNN AND JONAS entered the library, three men stood by the fire. Its warm yellow light made a stark contrast with the dark clouds bruising the sky outside. It was going to snow again, Cathlynn thought.

In Jonas's absence, David was playing host. He handed Sterling a drink. Sterling's loud laughter boomed into the room at some joke they'd missed. And a redheaded man with a somber expression sipped a dark amber liquid from a glass.

"There he is," Sterling said when he noticed their entrance. "J.T., you don't mind, do you? I've invited Scott MacPhearson to dinner."

"Of course not."

But he did mind. After the day they'd shared—the mad car ride, the wild, claiming kiss, Cathlynn's senses had become highly attuned to subtle nuances that were part of Jonas. She could almost hear his muscles tightening, his mind searching for a way to cut the evening short. The lies made him uneasy.

MacPhearson appeared stiff, too, as if being here wasn't his idea. Trouble was brewing, and she had a feeling Sterling had provided the storm seed. What was he up to?

Put on your best mask, Cat. The show is about to begin. She headed for the chair closest to the fire and settled in regally as the mistress of the house. Jonas went to the silent butler and poured them both a drink. After handing her a glass of tonic, he stood behind her, one hand light on her shoulder. Like a husband would do to a loved wife. Was he playing, too, or was the role as natural for him as it had become for her?

"MacPhearson wanted to see Alana." Sterling's mustache twitched with amusement. His gaze darted a triangle between her, MacPhearson and Jonas. "It seems you played a little disappearing act, my dear. Worried your husband halfway to death."

She waved his comment away. "A misunderstanding."

"Where were you?" MacPhearson cut in. There was no polite preamble. Straight to the heart. A refreshing change, in a way.

"I hid out at a friend's." She didn't flinch. She didn't flush. When had she gotten so good at lying? She glanced at Jonas. The answer was clear. When the stakes had gotten high. She had much more to lose now than the Aidan Heart.

"Really?" MacPhearson cocked one of his big red eyebrows in disbelief. He was almost handsome in a rough sort of way. Short, but muscled, with a feral sensuality to his movements. Could he have been one of Alana's "friends"?

"New York? Boston?" he asked casually.

"California, if you must know." She smiled and hoped her expression was friendly. "We all need a little distance once in a while."

"Unless…"

"Unless?"

The fire crackled, making the flames stab sharp shadows on the walls. Wet snow slapped against the windows with the storm's first fat flakes. In Jonas's glass, ice cubes popped.

With a careless shrug, MacPhearson backed down. "Truth shines eventually."

"Yes, one would hope so," she said. "Lies tend to snag and catch. It makes for an ugly web."

MacPhearson eyed her with renewed interest. "Yes, exactly."

Sterling cleared his throat and turned to Jonas. "Where have you been, dear boy? That butler of yours has been searching for you for at least a half hour."

"I was in the cellar. It appears we've been robbed."

"A theft?" All three seemed surprised. David's mouth hung half-open. Sterling's mustache twitched. MacPhearson's eyebrows scrunched.

"Not your work?" David asked worriedly. He loosened the knot of his tie.

"No, the Aidan Heart." Jonas's fingers stroked her shoulder, sending shards of electricity shooting down her body. It was distracting. It was heaven. "Both the storage room's door and the safe were tampered with."

"That's not possible." David's arms jerked with nervous tension. "It was secure, Jonas. I swear."

"I'm not blaming you, David."

"Call the cops?" MacPhearson asked bluntly. His antagonism toward Jonas was thick enough to slice and serve for dinner.

Jonas hesitated. "Not yet."

"Going to this time?"

"Eventually."

MacPhearson gave a sneering laugh. "You're certainly having them earn their pay today."

A sudden flat *pow* from outside cut the tension in the room and doused the lights.

"Sounds like the transformer again," David said. "I'll check it out and have Valentin bring oil lamps."

"Good idea," Jonas said.

Firelight licked at their faces, exaggerating features into theater-like masks. It poked at the darkness, climbing the walls. And the tapestry above the mantel seemed to come to life. In the flickering light, knights' lances bobbed, horses' legs wavered, manes and tails fluttered. Perception changed truth.

Cathlynn decided to broach a new subject. Time to start laying down tracks for their trap. "Jonas was working today." She looked up at Jonas, entreating him with her eyes to play along. The muscle in his jaw tightened, then he gave her an almost imperceptible nod.

"He's had a mini-breakthrough," she said, studying both Sterling and MacPhearson.

Sterling stood up straighter. "Wonderful!"

"Yes," Jonas agreed. "I'll need to start my blood sample collection again to test my theory, but it does look very promising."

Twitch, twitch went Sterling's mustache. "That'll be a relief for you, won't it?"

"And many others."

"Of course, of course."

"I'll be making an announcement at the fete." Jonas looked down at her and caressed her hair lovingly with his free hand. Her heart skipped. It's an act, right? "Now Alana can spend her trust money on whatever her little heart desires." His gaze fixed Sterling. MacPhearson, she noticed, wasn't missing any of the undercurrents. "I can turn down her generous offer to fund my research."

"Yes," Sterling said uncertainly. He refilled his drink at the cart. "Speaking of the trust, how are the fete preparations coming along, Alana?"

"Very well. In a few days things will start going crazy. It'll be a madhouse until the fete is over, especially with Jonas's announcement."

Sterling took a sip from his drink. "And the height of the celebration will be the reversion of your trust."

"Complete with cake and candles and noisemakers," she agreed. "As Jonas said, the money is no longer a pressing need, but certainly a welcome addition. Now we can get some of the repairs we've put off done on the monastery."

One side of Sterling's mustache crept up into a crooked grin. "And there are many cracks yet to be filled."

A warning? No, Cathlynn concluded from the feverish burn in Sterling's pale blue eyes. Not a warning. A threat. He knew she wasn't Alana and he would expose her—at the fete, in the middle of a crowd.

Unless, of course, they exposed him first.

THE MISSING AIDAN HEART was not good. Something had gone wrong somewhere. Someone else was stirring the pot. Who? Why? It was *her* fault. Nose poking into places it shouldn't go. Dumb luck. But he had to wait just a little longer. If Jonas was on the cusp of a breakthrough, the reward would be greater, and this charade had already cost him much. She had to stay now—at least a little longer. A warning. That's what she needed. A bit of trouble to keep her busy. Easily arranged. Then, come celebration day, he would make sure she was Aurelius's next sacrifice.

Chapter Nine

The next morning, Cathlynn announced her plans to go to Nashua, and insisted Jonas drive her. They took his Jeep and shared barely half a dozen words on the long drive. Now that they stood in Meara O'Connell's hospital room with its smell of disinfectant and sickness, he cursed the impulse that had propelled curiosity into action.

Memories assaulted him, fresh like yesterday, though they were nearly twenty years old. His once-strong father, a whisper of himself, small and lost in a hospital bed. His mother at his side, crying for the future vanishing before her eyes. Himself, standing apart, impotent to change the death scenario. The day his father had died changed the direction of Jonas's life. He'd dedicated himself to study, to research, to finding a cure.

He shook his head and forced his attention back to the present.

Cathlynn reached for the old lady's hand. Meara's head with its dull white hair turned toward Cathlynn.

"Gram?"

Meara's eyes fluttered open. Her gaze remained vacant, then appeared confused. She squinted at Jonas. "Son?"

"No, it's my friend Jonas Shades, not Dad."

"Cat."

"Yes, Gram, it's Cat. How are you feeling today?"

Meara struggled as if to answer. Her mouth contorted to form words that wouldn't come. Frustration etched itself in crags on her pale, lined face.

"I'm so glad you're feeling better, Gram, breathing on your own."

As if Cathlynn spoke in a foreign tongue, Meara stared blankly.

"I found it, Gram. I found the Aidan Heart. It's as beautiful as you told me it was."

The mention of the sculpture seemed to create a hole in the fog of the woman's senility. Her eyes, so much like Cat's, twinkled, and a slack smile curved her lips. "Potato."

Her scrambled memory couldn't find the proper word, but Cathlynn understood.

"Yes, and oh, Gram, the purple heart in the center, it's simply magnificent. You can just feel the love that went into creating the piece. When I touched it, I felt it come alive against my fingers. Just like you said it would."

"See potato." Meara's sheets quivered with her excitement.

"Yes, Gram, you'll get to see the Aidan Heart, too. Soon, I promise."

Tears rolled down the old woman's sallow cheeks. Jonas couldn't bear to watch, so he turned away and left the room. Cathlynn's voice, animated and tender, trailed behind him, insinuating itself into his conscience.

He paced the hall, a rumble of frustration driving him in ever shorter passes. By coming into his life, Cathlynn had changed everything. There was no place in his life for emotions. The facts, science, would save him, save others. By feeling, he was risking everything. He shouldn't have come. Her soft voice, the life shining in her hair, and the love flowing freely from her had touched him. He stopped abruptly and shoved both his hands in his pants pockets. By coming here, he'd opened a door he'd never wanted to open again. Dreams were for fools. She had no right to tempt him into believing he could have everything.

He didn't know how long he stood there, staring at nothing, looking for loopholes and finding none. Cathlynn's hand on his shoulder made him face the inevitable.

"Are you all right?" she asked.

By tonight, she'd be out of his life. There was no other way. His work was too important. *She* was becoming too important. "I don't much care for hospitals."

She chuckled. "What a strange thing for a doctor to say!"

It was better that way. She stirred too many things into chaos. Now he could return to his research, to order. Concentrate. "Why didn't you tell me your grandmother has Alzheimer's?"

"I wanted you to see, to understand."

See what? Understand what? He led her down the hall toward the elevators.

"It's ingenious the way the disease worms itself into a life," Cathlynn said. She wound the leather strap of her purse around her fingers in a tight knot. "You don't really know what's happening. You keep making excuses. Then you can't deny there's something wrong.''

"And by that time, the disease is already established." Jonas pressed the button.

"Right. First she didn't seem as energetic as usual. Then she didn't want to leave home. She started to forget. Little things. Then she'd get frustrated because she couldn't do the things she'd always done—balance her checkbook, bake cakes and tarts, paint. I got worried because Gram was always so independent and she was turning to me more and more. It broke my heart to have to put her into a nursing home last year.''

The doors swished open. "She doesn't recognize you anymore.''

"Not really." Cathlynn shrugged. "Sometimes. Today she did. Mostly not. But I think the worst part is seeing her so depressed, so lost. It's like watching the best part of myself fade away.''

As the elevator started its descent, Jonas's stomach lurched. "I know.''

"She's been in the hospital twice with the flu since September. Her body…it's not fighting back the way it should this time. I'm scared. Not for her, really. For myself.''

She turned from him, but he saw the reflection of her tears in the polished metal of the door.

"Stay," he said. "She needs you.''

Cathlynn looked at him, face intense and determined. The hint of tears still clung to her lashes. "I can't.''

"She needs you. Stay.''

"No.''

Silence strung between them, heavy and questioning. "I promise, Cat. I'll find the Aidan Heart. She'll get to see it.'' The elevator opened onto the lobby. Jonas started toward the front doors.

''Jonas.''

He turned to face her. She stood boxed by the metallic doors. The harsh fluorescent light in the elevator's car framed her magnificent golden-brown hair in a sharp halo. ''Hmm?''

''I wanted to show you. I wanted you to understand.'' She lifted her hands in a helpless gesture, struggling, it seemed, to find the right words. But her gaze, seeking his, all warm and open, spoke volumes. ''I'm with you all the way.''

He couldn't speak through the knot lodged in his throat, so he nodded once and strode forward, wondering if the strange lightness weaving through his body was the first sign the disease that had wasted his father was now starting to consume him.

THAT EVENING, Cathlynn sat, cross-legged, on her bed, contemplating how easily she'd fallen into the habit of lying. She'd never kept anything from Claire before, but tonight when she'd called her friend and partner for her daily check-in, she'd found herself loath to worry Claire and had failed to mention the stuffed toy cat nestled between her pillows, or the fact that it had a noose wrapped with deathly intent around its neck.

She broke off another piece of her chocolate bar and popped the nugget into her mouth. She pushed the piece to the side of her mouth with her tongue and let the chocolate melt slowly. With a finger, she poked at the creature, turning it on its side. The fake orange fur was matted, threadbare in spots. Cookie goo clung to one well-worn ear, as if a child used the feline part as a pacifier. It seemed a well-loved cat and had all the branding marks of a young child on its body. In this house of adults, where could such a thing have come from?

The noose, that was the troubling part. The rope was new. And even though the cat's eyes were embroidered, the tightness of the cord gave them the appearance of bulging. The effect was brutal.

Obviously, it was meant as a warning.

From whom? It had to be someone close. Someone with access to her room. Someone no one would question should he be caught wandering the halls. Sterling?

Her flesh goosed. She crunched the nuts and raisins, concentrating on the flavors in her mouth in order to keep fear from turning into panic and eroding her determination to see this charade through.

"I find a glass of warm milk helps when I can't fall asleep." Jonas's voice came from the shadows near the bathroom door. His unexpected presence no longer startled her, as if he were a part of her now, and her unconscious was aware of his whereabouts, even if her conscious mind wasn't.

"I don't like milk."

"Won't chocolate keep you awake?"

"I'm not sure I want to sleep." She sighed wearily. "I guess we must have rattled someone yesterday." She lifted the orange creature off the green and gold coverlet. "Someone left me a present."

He came close and examined the stuffed cat. His features crisped in the soft glow of her bedside lamp. "I don't want you hurt."

"It's not exactly part of my plans either."

He plopped the cat back onto the bed. "I'd feel better if you went back home."

He tried to look commanding, to look stern and un-

bending, but Cathlynn understood him too well now to
fear the man beneath the dour look. At heart, he was
honest and good. He could glower and glare all night,
if he wanted, it wouldn't affect her. Which wasn't to
say the sheer power of his presence didn't impress her,
but the emotion he evoked from her these days was
much more dangerous than fear. It made her weak and
vulnerable and rattled her even more than the death play
evolving around them.

"If I leave, you won't lull our suspect into a false
sense of security." Silently she offered him a piece of
her chocolate. He declined. "You won't find who killed
Alana, where her body is hidden. You won't get access
to the trust fund. And I won't find the Aidan Heart."

He sat beside her on the bed, the cat and the remains
of her chocolate bar between them. "Do you really
think the Aidan Heart will make a difference?"

"Yes." She surprised herself with the strength of her
answer. "It has magic."

"Magic doesn't exist."

She leaned back against the headboard, stretching out
her legs. "Of course it does. I felt it every summer at
Gram's house. I hear it in the song of birds. I see it in
flowers in the spring. I see it in you—"

"No, don't fool yourself with—"

"In the way you give so much of yourself to others."

The twist of anguish in his eyes wobbled her heart
like a faint bruise.

"An illusion, Cat."

"Illusions are magic."

"Or lies." He leaned back, too. A foot of space separated their shoulders. "You'd make a rotten scientist."

She giggled. "Yeah, I probably would."

Silence wafted comfortably between them.

"Jonas?"

"Hmm." He sounded sleepy, and when she glanced at him, his eyes were closed. She couldn't blame him. He'd spent all afternoon and most of the evening closeted in his lab. When she'd brought him a sandwich for dinner, he'd barely glanced at her. She'd be willing to bet it was still at his desk uneaten.

"We did rattle someone yesterday," she said. "Do you think it was Sterling?"

"I find it hard to believe Sterling would get his hands dirty." He rearranged his position, stretching his legs out and crossing them at the ankles.

"He's fit for his age, strong enough to manhandle Alana."

Jonas loosened the knot of his tie. "He may be behind the plot to keep the Chandler money from me, but I don't think he killed Alana himself. According to David's uncle at Customs, Sterling wasn't here the day she disappeared."

"Which means he had help somewhere."

"More than likely."

"How well do you know Valentin and David?"

Jonas adjusted a pillow at the small of his back. "Valentin isn't merely a butler, he's as much a part of this house as the walls. He was here when my father was young. I've known him all of my life. He would never do anything to harm me or the monastery. I'd stake my life on that."

"Even if he thought it could help you?"

He shook his head. "No. Besides, he hasn't got the strength."

"I think there's more to Valentin than what he shows people." She wrapped the remaining squares of chocolate and placed the crinkled foil packet on the night table. "What about David?"

"He's been working for me for five years. I couldn't ask for a better worker. He's very bright. He's never been interested in money." Jonas yawned.

"But we're talking about a lot of money. Not just from the trust, but from whatever cure you find."

"Not everyone's motivated by money, Cat."

She pondered his comment for a minute. In David's case, that might be true enough. He was a resident of Ste-Croix. A male resident. Maybe the mutant gene was part of his DNA. A good enough reason for him to want Jonas to find a cure. "Which brings us back to Sterling."

"Hmm." Jonas's head dropped onto her shoulder.

His clean woodsy scent surrounded her, bungling her thoughts for a moment. "But something's missing."

"Hmm."

The weight of him increased against her. It was a strangely agreeable feeling. "Jonas?"

There was no answer, but the soft waft of his breath against her neck. He'd fallen asleep. They would find no answers tonight.

WHIMPERS, like the soft mewling of a cat, entered the sleepy consciousness of Jonas's mind. Disembodied images of stuffed animals hung by a rope twisted in the gray fog between sleep and dream, and for a moment, he wondered where he was.

Then he felt the unaccustomed warmth beside him and he knew. He was still in Cathlynn's room, in Cathlynn's bed. And those frightened sounds coming from Cathlynn tore at him because he knew he was to blame. He'd dragged her into this lie, and lies exacted costs.

The price for someone as good and as gentle as Cathlynn was one of terror.

He touched her shoulder tentatively, and shook it gently. "Cat, wake up, Cat. You're dreaming."

Her eyelids fluttered. Her frown deepened. Her breathing speeded up. With a twist, he stretched over her for the bedside lamp and turned it on so she wouldn't be lost in darkness when she awoke.

Then he reached for her and told himself he was a fool. Touching her was a mistake. The spring scent of her, the feel of her body soft and warm in his arms revived the need so strong inside him for this woman. But he had to do it. She was having a nightmare because she was here in his house, pretending to be his wife.

He held her lightly, stroked her hair gently in hopes he could soothe her bad dream away and ease her into deeper sleep. But the weight and the warmth of her against him created tension in his body and desire surged heavily, hungrily. He concentrated on breathing, on soothing, trying to ignore the pulse of need thundering hotly through his veins.

She seemed to calm in his embrace, then she stiffened. A strangled cry lodged in her throat. She opened her eyes wide in horror, and tried to claw away from the prison of his arms.

"It's okay, Cat." He held her tighter, kissed her temple, stroked her hair. "It's me, Jonas. You're fine. You're all right."

His voice seemed to finally reach her. She stopped fighting her nightmare ghost, blinked several times, looked at him hard in the soft lamp light, and sighed deeply. "Jonas."

"You were having a nightmare." He kept stroking

her hair, felt her shiver. She nestled her head against his shoulder as if she'd done this very thing a thousand times before. As if a match had struck, he felt himself ignite. He should leave, now, while he still could.

"Monks," she said. A snake of horror shuddered through her. "A long line of them in black robes."

He stroked her shoulder. The gown's sleeve had slipped down her arm, exposing her too soft skin. He swallowed hard, tried to concentrate on her dream. "Enough to give anyone nightmares."

"Especially when they kill every night."

She shivered again. He kissed the top of her head, tightened his arms around her, felt the sharp stab of fear rip at his gut at the thought of losing her, even if only in a dream. "Kill?"

"I guess my mind can't seem to forget all that talk of curses and virgin sacrifices."

"It's just a legend," he said, and wondered how long he could stand the torture of being so close to her without giving in to his primitive hunger. She deserved more. She deserved better.

"I know."

He tried to ease away from her. "I should go."

She clenched a handful of his shirt in her fist. "No, don't."

Looking at her, he shook his head. "Cathlynn, it's not a good idea...."

In the soft light, her eyes shone in an odd mixture of fear and want. "Stay."

"Cathlynn...."

Knowing he shouldn't, he dug his fingers into the luxurious hair at her nape. He bent his head, brushed his lips against hers. Her breath puffed hot against him, fanning the flames of his desire. He deepened the kiss, caressing her mouth, savoring her warmth, her taste, the soft and sweet texture of her. And he felt her soften beneath him, felt her heat, her rising passion feed his own.

His whole body tightened in almost painful response. He drew her closer, hip to hip, let her feel what she did to him, how much he wanted her.

Shock and pleasure and fear flickered in her eyes. "Cat?"

Her hand reached up and stroked his jaw. Shivers of pleasure raced along his skin. "I want you, Jonas."

Those soft words made desire bolt through him. He needed her the way he had never needed anyone before. He searched his mind for a way to give her a chance to say no before his control completely slipped away. "I don't want you to do something you'll regret later."

"I won't." And the truth was there, naked in the darkening of her pupils.

His thumbs stroked the delicate skin of her neck. He kissed her again—her forehead, her eyes, her cheeks. He reveled in the sweet sounds of pleasure coming from deep in her throat. He captured her mouth, felt her reach for a deeper kiss, and groaned at the swell of heat burning away his self-control.

He stripped away the soft flannel nightgown from her body. The golden fire in her eyes, her hair, her skin thawed the ice on his dead soul, heightened his hunger. His gaze never left her as he removed his own clothes then rejoined her in the sea of cream satin sheets.

He bent to kiss the hardened bud of her nipple. A shock wave of pleasure tore through him as her breath caught, her heartbeat drummed faster.

He wanted her fast and hard, wanted to sheath himself deeply into her and let the years of winter burn away. But he forced himself to slow down. He let his lips wander over her tender flesh from neck to belly. He made his fingers explore every inch of female skin. Who would have thought the slope of a back could be so sexy, that the curve of ribs could make him quiver with need, that the dip of a navel could make him lose the train of logic telling him he should leave her alone before it was too late.

He delighted in the feminine softness of her responsive sounds, in the rattling of his senses with each sweet movement of her hands along his chest.

"I want you," he said raggedly against her throat. She was spring after a long, bitter winter, and he needed her.

"Yes," she answered, eyes glittering like gold in the soft light.

His hand stroked her leg. She shifted beneath him, opening the smooth skin of her inner thigh to him. His fingers shook as they found the warm inviting moistness waiting there for him. He wanted to feel her around him, to be in her, wanted it with a fierceness that shocked him. And when she moved against him, melted against him, silently asked for a deeper caress, he groaned helplessly and removed his hand before he shattered.

He stretched himself against her, took her mouth and plundered it. Her hands moved relentlessly over him, teasing, demanding, wreaking a havoc of ravenous greed. His heart beat madly against his chest. When her hand drifted down and cupped him, he nearly lost it.

"Cathlynn!" he growled.

Eyes aglow with passion, she smiled seductively at him. "Yes, Jonas."

With a throttled groan he sheathed himself inside her,

found her hot center, and could no longer leash his wild hunger. He plunged into her again and again, heard her low moans of satisfaction with each slow, deep, delicious thrust.

Her passion-glazed eyes were fixed on him as she clung to him. He felt the building tension in her body, the gathering wave, the explosion tear through her. Her rhythmic convulsions around his rigid flesh made pleasure blast through him. Fire burned in his blood, swept over him again and again until he could feel nothing and everything and he was in mindless ecstasy.

Never before had he felt so alive, so aware of every sensation coursing through his body, so humbled. He had meant to soothe away her nightmare. Instead, it was she who had swept away the haunting loneliness of his existence.

Arms tight around him, she absorbed the shuddering aftermath of his climax. As he eased the heavy weight of his satisfied body from her smaller frame, he clasped her next to him and held her, simply held her while their pulses slowed and their hearts found their normal rhythms.

Her hair fanned like silk threads across his chest. Her heated breath wafted in small, relaxed bursts over his skin. The scent of her, spicy and alluring, spread through him, warm and wonderful. Curled against him in sleep, Cathlynn managed to make him think impossible thoughts.

Thoughts of spring. Thoughts of life. Thoughts of love.

She curved closer to him, eliciting a chain reaction of delightful memories with her sensuous movement. He reached down and spread the blanket over their sated, cooling bodies.

Then he closed his eyes against the soft lamp light playing golden life across her skin, over her hair. Placing a soft kiss against her temple, he hugged her tight.

He'd gone and done the one thing he shouldn't have. He'd fallen in love with her.

As MORNING, PINK AND GOLD, filtered through the window, Jonas woke up and left her side, taking the hanged cat with him—and his wonderful body heat. Though Cathlynn wanted to hold him back, to have him stay by her side longer, to repeat the wild and wonderful lovemaking of the night, she couldn't find the right words, so she kept silent. A few minutes later, the soft spray of water from the shower started.

She loved him, of that much she was certain. And he had to care for her to have loved her so tenderly. He'd opened to her, let her see the depth of emotions she could feel. But she'd also felt the slow, sure shuttering that had occurred as he'd woken up. He'd worried about her regrets. Was *he* having them this morning? And just as he'd retreated, Cathlynn found herself stuffing her mixed emotions into that deep, dark corner of her mind where she placed the things too painful to think about.

She shivered beneath the sheet and brought the blanket up to nose level. She shivered again. Why was it so cold?

The shower noises ended, then the ballad of Jonas's morning ritual began. She strained to hear each shuffle and sound, to recall each hard line of his body, and found herself oddly bereft at the lonesome echo of Jonas's footsteps down the corridor.

If he could pretend nothing had happened, so could she. She threw the sheets off her stiff body and stepped into the room's frigid morning air. Rubbing her arms for warmth and blowing visible puffs of breath, she hurried to the bathroom for her turn at the hot shower. She grabbed a pair of jeans, fresh underwear, her thickest socks and two layers of sweaters. It wasn't until she was drawing the second sweater over her head that she noticed the silence.

Looking around the room while braiding her hair, she spotted the source of her worry on the far wall. The radiator wasn't performing its usual dirge of creaks and groans.

She went down the stairs two by two and ran to the dining room.

"Jonas," she called as she opened the door. "Did you—"

But there was no one in the room. No food was laid out on the sideboard. No coffee steamed from the silver urn.

She pushed through to the kitchen. It, too, was silent and deserted. Same with the library, though a fire did burn in the hearth. She was tempted to stay there, warming herself, but instead kept on her quest for human life.

Following instinct more than sound, she found herself lost in the bowels of the monastery. Trailing her hand along the cold granite walls, she moved cautiously in the ill-lit passageways. As she rounded yet another corner, her fingers snagged into mortar that felt slightly damp. She stopped and examined the curiosity. The concrete was gray to match the stones, but lacked the dusty patina of age. Her gaze followed the labyrinth of the design, then she stepped back to take in its plan. At the base of the wall was a single drop of blood.

The stones outside of the arched, recently masoned maze seemed to come alive, pulsing, undulating.

"Not again," she whispered, trying to ignore the shivers skittering up and down her spine. She'd had enough fear in the past week to last her a lifetime. She wasn't going to play the victim any longer.

She confronted the pulsing wall. "What do you want from me?"

Beware. The whisper echoed eerily in her head.

Hands on hips, she defied the wavering stones squarely. "That's it. I've had enough of this. Tell me what it is you want, or leave me alone."

Beware.

"Of what?"

The monk.

"Which monk?"

Deceit.

"Care to be a little more specific?"

The walls ceased their macabre shimmering reel. Shadows retreated to their corners. The clammy feel of ectoplasm dissipated, leaving only bitter cold behind. "I guess not."

She looked around, wondering at the state of her sanity. "Talking to walls. Cat, you're losing it." She shook her head and retraced her steps down the passageway. "If you keep this up, a little white straitjacket can't be far in your future."

Still, in the back of her mind, something nagged. *What did I miss?*

A few more turns brought the sound of voices.

Jonas, David and Valentin stood in front of the black monster of a boiler, discussing their next move. Cathlynn listened for a few minutes. It became clear that heating engineers these men were not.

"Do any of you know how this thing works?" she asked.

They turned around as one.

"A kick and a rattle usually does the trick," Jonas said, massaging the back of his neck.

She chuckled. "Such a scientific technique."

He grinned. "We all have our area of expertise."

"And it seems it lies elsewhere for all of you." Time to take charge. There was too much to do before the Christmas fete to waste it on recalcitrant boilers. "Valentin, I'm dying for a cup of coffee."

"Oui, madame."

"And Jonas is going to need a hearty breakfast. He's got a busy day ahead of him."

"Oui, madame."

The butler bowed and backed out of the room. Cathlynn could have sworn there was the ragged edge of a smile on his lips.

"Jonas, I think you'd be more useful in your lab. I'll handle this crisis."

"You know about boilers?" he asked with a doubtful expression.

She gave him an enigmatic smile. "I have my ways."

"Do I want to know about this?" He frowned with exaggerated severity.

She shrugged vaguely. "Probably not." She grabbed his shirtsleeve, fought the urge to kiss him and propelled him forward. "Shoo. Off to the lab you go. I'll bring you your breakfast when it's ready."

He opened his mouth as if to argue, then shook his head. With a good-humored chortle, he left the boiler room.

"What about me?"

She looked at David. "Is there a portable phone anywhere in this place?"

"In my office."

"Lead the way. Then you can start setting up the blood sample collection Jonas needs."

He gave her an affable smile and saluted. "Yes, ma'am."

When Cathlynn turned to exit the room, she noticed drops of blood close to the wall. "What's this?"

David looked down, then at his hand, seemingly surprised to see a cut on his palm. "I guess I must have cut myself on the access panel when I tried to get the pilot light going again."

"First-aid kit?"

"There's one in my office."

They started down the hall. "David, when I was looking for Jonas, I got lost and found some fresh masonry work."

"We had some work done a couple of months ago. The west wing is closed in the winter, and Jonas didn't want the freezing-cold air from that side of the house to filter through to this one, so he had the cracks along that wall filled."

"That makes sense."

In his office, Cathlynn spotted the dusty first-aid kit on top of one of the cabinets. She motioned David to sit down, sprayed the wound in his palm with antibiotic and applied a Band-Aid. "There, that should take care of that."

David's smile brightened his boyish good looks. "It's been a while since I've had anybody take care of me."

"Jonas needs you," she said, whisking the bandage wrapper into the garbage can. The warm and inviting look in his eyes worried her. She fervently hoped he hadn't taken the small gesture of efficiency as interest.

"Of course." David handed her the portable phone. "It's good what you're doing."

She grabbed the local phone book from a pile of directories on David's desk and started to riffle through the pages. "What?"

"Getting Jonas back to work. Putting a smile on his face. Do you know how long it's been since he's done either?"

"Too long. He's got too many people depending on him, asking the impossible of him."

Gliding a finger down the yellow page, she sensed more than saw David frown. She paused her finger and looked up. He shrugged.

"Well, I for one, am glad you're here. You're very good for him." He took a binder from one of the file cabinets behind him. "I'd better get started on this. I'll be upstairs in the library if you need me."

Cathlynn called the heating company and badgered the poor receptionist until she was passed on to a supervisor, who got rid of her only when he promised he would have someone at the monastery within the hour. After making sure Jonas ate his breakfast, and installing the promised heating technician in the boiler room, she busied herself by starting her inventory of Jonas's paperweight collection. With the Aidan Heart's theft, this task could no longer be put aside.

Safely carrying the paperweights by the half dozen, cushioned by layers of thick towels in a large basket, she took them to the library where she could work by the fireside without shivering from the cold.

Between each trip up and down the icy stairways to the basement, she checked on Jonas and forced food on him at regular intervals.

She sat contentedly with the last batch of paperweights she planned on cataloguing today. After David left for the day, after Sterling and Valentin retired for the evening, she and Jonas would set out their plan of action for the next few days. Timing would be critical.

Melting snow dripped from the roof, carrying on a pleasant chatter. The sun sparkled each globe of glass, showing off its beauty. Valentin had supplied her with a pot of coffee, and the full-bodied aroma helped give the room a feeling of warmth.

Jonas had quite a range of paperweights—swirls, crowns, flat flowers, fruit, bouquets, close millefioris, sulphide portraits—representing most of the major glassmakers from Scotland to Italy. With his wide-ranging interest, it was no wonder the Aidan Heart had gotten his attention.

Who had taken it? Where had it gone? *Somewhere safe, I hope.*

The more she measured and noted and photographed, the more she understood Jonas. Just as the artists had captured a moment of pure beauty in the glass, so Jonas was trying to recapture something, too. Although they'd experienced vastly different upbringings, both their hopes for the future reflected themselves in pieces of glass. For her, Gram and the Aidan Heart were one. For him, continuing his mother's paperweight collection kept her alive.

"Where is everybody?" Sterling asked as he entered the library later that afternoon.

"Busily exploiting their individual expertise," Cathlynn answered, not quite feeling up to a battle of wits with the British solicitor.

Pouring himself a drink, Sterling shot her a quizzical glance.

"Jonas is researching. David is coordinating. Valentin is cooking. The heating technician is still trying to perform a minor miracle. And I'm cataloguing Jonas's paperweight collection.''

He sat in the chair closest to the fire and reached to the occasional table, where sheets of her work lay in a neat pile. ''I didn't know you were interested in J.T.'s glass.''

''Oh, yes. I find it fascinating.''

''Since when?'' he asked, dropping the sheets back to the table.

She lifted the eighteenth-century Venetian millefiori she held and gave her best imitation of Alana. ''Since I found out a small piece like this one is worth as much as that gold watch you're wearing.''

''Money is important?'' He stroked his mustache pensively.

''Money is security.''

His stare was long and hard. ''Of course.''

Had she been wrong? Had Alana not cared for riches as she'd assumed? Had she overacted her part?

As she turned back to her task, she couldn't quite shake the sharp stab of uneasiness piercing the space between her shoulder blades, or the smile on Sterling's face, which reminded her too much of a jackal's glee.

''Tell J.T. I won't be in for dinner tonight,'' Sterling said.

''Sure.''

His glass rattled on the table's top. As he rose, the material of his suit swished. His footsteps retreated with muffled shuffles on the carpet and determined clicks on the stone floor.

When Cathlynn reached for her coffee cup, it was gone.

Chapter Ten

After enduring an explanation from the heating technician about the boiler's age and how it wouldn't last another winter and needed to be replaced, Jonas was surprised to see the lights still on in his lab. Even more surprised to see David at work.

"I thought you'd be gone by now." Jonas sat in his swivel chair and entered his password onto the prompting computer screen.

"Just wanted to make sure everything was ready for the blood sample collection in the morning." David ejected a disk from the far computer and slipped it into his shirt pocket, then walked over to the printer to pick up a stack of papers. "I've got the release forms ready and the supplies arrived this afternoon. We're all set."

"Great. I'll see you in the morning."

"Bright and early." David gave a halfhearted salute and left.

When this was all done, he'd have to make sure David took a few days off. At his age, David deserved a social life, and working nights and weekends wasn't going to get him much of one.

Calling up a file, Jonas tried to regain the thread of his research thought, but it kept straying to the missing

Aidan Heart, the possible plot to steal his work, and inevitably, to Cathlynn and the mess he'd dragged her into. How could he keep her safe if she insisted on staying here in the thick of things?

He could understand chemical formulas, statistics, data of all sorts. He could wander through mathematical mazes and create order out of seeming chaos. But he knew his limitations. His investigative skills did not extend to murders and villains. He wished for the hundredth time since he'd fired MacPhearson he could have retained the private investigator's services. But Mac-Phearson would have asked too many questions, and Jonas had long ago figured out he was MacPhearson's prime suspect. Husbands usually were—especially estranged husbands with millions to gain. He saw no point in paying to be crucified.

"Time for a break," Cathlynn called as she entered the lab. Her presence seemed to throw a warm new brightness into the room.

She arrived with a tray laden with pizza, salad and drinks. After placing the tray on the desk, she rolled the other swivel chair around the desk to face him and coiled herself into it with her feet tucked under her. Contented like a cat, she looked, and he found he liked her there all nice and comfortable, had unconsciously looked forward to her arrival and their promised conversation.

Jonas propped his feet on the edge of the desk. He reached for a slice of pizza and took a hefty bite. When was the last time he'd eaten fast food? Or even enjoyed eating? "Valentin made this?"

"With a little coaxing." Her smile was Mona Lisa mysterious.

Jonas couldn't help his answering chuckle. He could

just imagine Valentin's disinclination at having his pre-planned menu tampered with. "I'm not sure I want to know your methods of persuasion."

"There were a few grumbles."

"I'll bet."

They ate in comfortable silence for a while. He was glad Cathlynn didn't feel she had to fill every quiet space with chatter.

After polishing off her second piece of pizza, she gave a satisfied groan, then placed her plate back on the tray. "It turned out amazingly good, considering Valentin was so reluctant to try something new."

"He actually enjoys cooking." Not that Jonas had tasted anything in a long while. It was strange to reacquaint himself with the tang of tomatoes, the crunch of fresh bread and the richness of melted cheese. "A lot more than cleaning."

"I noticed that." She sipped from her glass. Her mood shifted, signaling the end of the pleasant part of the evening. He'd hoped to extend this quiet mood longer before plunging once more into murder and mayhem. "Claire is keeping an eye on the market for the Aidan Heart. I have a feeling it's still close at hand, but if it's in the monastery, I haven't found it yet—"

"Yet?" Just the thought of her snooping through the vast emptiness of the monastery was enough to slash in half his already short life expectancy. He wished he'd never given her the master key. He'd have to get it back tonight—before she got herself into any trouble.

"I still have Sterling's room to search—"

"I don't think so."

"Don't worry, I'll be surreptitious."

"That wasn't what I was worried about. I don't like the idea of you snooping on your own. What if—"

"So join me."

Ignoring his grumble, she continued as if the original thread of conversation hadn't been lost. "But then, if Sterling is indeed the thief, he'd have been smart enough to remove the Aidan Heart to a safer place. With all his trips outside the monastery, he could have done that easily enough."

"Exactly," Jonas said with a sigh of relief. "I doubt it'll appear on the market either."

She shrugged. "Probably not, but if it does, Claire will know about it."

"We'll get it back." He wasn't sure how, but he'd find a way. He'd made her a promise and intended to keep it. *One thing at a time.* "If we find the murderer, we'll find the thief."

"Sterling borrowed my coffee cup today," she said, draining the contents of her glass.

One more spice into an already too-hot stew. "Are you sure?"

"Quite. One minute he was there. The cup was there. Then they were both gone."

The back of his neck was feeling stiff again. He kneaded the knots to no avail. "Have you ever been fingerprinted?"

"No, but Alana would have to get her resident-alien card, and our prints will definitely not match."

"She was a child when she entered the country."

"Wouldn't she still have been fingerprinted?"

"I'll take care of it."

"How?"

It was his turn to pretend mystery. "I have my ways."

She cocked her head. "Share."

How could she, with just a movement of her head, a

flow of her golden-brown hair, cause so much internal turmoil? "My brother's already helped rearrange a few things in your life."

Both her eyebrows surged up. "Such as?"

"Your car's registration, for one thing. It was put in Alana's name. Alana's driver's license—"

"Was changed to reflect the heftier body?" she asked wryly.

"To reflect the improvement. You'll notice all the cards in your wallet have been altered."

She stared at him, blinking twice. Was she thinking how easy it had been for him to get rid of her on paper? Was her open trust of a few days ago crumbling? Why couldn't he just reach out to her like he wanted and let her know the toll the lies were taking on him?

Shifting her gaze to her hands, she cleared her throat and changed the subject. "Do you know who B.T. is?"

"No, why?"

"I, uh, found mention of that person in Alana's journal."

The pain in his neck increased. A tendril of fear unfurled deep inside him. He squashed it fast. It was too soon. He still had a few years. Right? "I'll bet she didn't paint me in a pretty light."

"No, not really." She uncurled one leg and swung her foot in a restless rhythm. "I couldn't find anyone with the initials B.T. in her address book. Thought you might know."

"I didn't know any of her...special male friends by name."

"Can't say I blame you." She swept away nonexistent crumbs from her lap. "So you think this B.T. might be one of her lovers?"

He flinched. "More than likely."

"She mentioned she was going to have him mail a letter to her cousin Geoffrey."

"Yes, I thought she might have." He pushed the remnants of his food away. The cheese on the pizza was congealed and unappetizing. "I'm sure that's why Sterling arrived early and why he's been trying to snoop into your past."

She cocked her head once more, scrutinizing him with twinkling curiosity. "What exactly does your brother do that he can rearrange the evidence of my life so easily?"

"He's one of the best con men around."

The can of worms had been opened, and Cathlynn, judging from her brightening expression, was dying to delve into it. "A con man? Really? Is that why you haven't talked to him in a long time?"

"One of the reasons," he said sharply.

"You're right. Now's not the time to talk about family difficulties. We'll have plenty of time for that later. How's the research coming along?"

"It's looking good," Jonas said, relieved she wouldn't pursue Cameron's occupation, worried about the "later" part of her comment. "The blood sample results should finalize everything."

"You'll be ready to make the big announcement by Friday?"

"Yes."

This would be the biggest lie of all. The thought of it lumped the dinner in his stomach into an ironlike mass. He'd be giving false hope to many people, and that was a bitter pill to swallow. How else could he protect his work? How else could he assure safe results? He needed time to find the right answer, and right now, there was none. A lie now for the greater good later. If this plan backfired, his credibility was at risk. He would get no more chances to find the key to this disease. His whole life's work would have been for nothing.

He shook his head and started to speak.

From the hall, as if someone had bumped against the wall, came a thump and a soft scrape. Then a silence that was somehow too still. The stealthy sound repeated.

Without making a noise, Jonas stood and went to the door. As he rounded the jamb, he saw a dark figure hurrying down the hallway.

He turned to look at Cathlynn. "Stay here."

He sprinted down the corridor. Who would sneak around his house? The thief? Alana's murderer? A shadow, flat and dark, scurried against the wall and was sucked around the corner.

Jonas would not let him escape.

Discovered, the trespasser no longer seemed to care about noise. His shoes thwacked against the granite. His clothes brushed against the walls. Jonas could easily track the invader. The one thing Jonas had going for him was familiarity with the cellar's mazelike corridors.

What if Cathlynn was right? What if it was someone close to him? Valentin or David? But no, Valentin couldn't run this fast, and David had no reason to betray him. And the trespasser was heading away from any exit—straight into the wall separating the west wing from the main house. Whoever this was, wasn't familiar with the cellar.

Closer. He was getting closer. Through his own pounding heart, he could hear the intruder's labored breathing. One more corner.

Got him!

Jonas slowed, then stopped.

The figure, dressed in a black monk's habit, was trapped by a dead end. The cowled hood and the nearly nonexistent light gave the impression the man had no face. Hard breathing filled the tight space. Frantic scrabbling on the wall and frustrated growls came in bursts. A start to the left, then the right. Then the monk stilled. There was nowhere to go. His only escape route was straight ahead through Jonas.

"You might as well show yourself," Jonas said. Cautiously he approached, crowding the monk's space.

"Jonas?" Cathlynn called from down the hall.

Jonas turned his head to call back, "Stay away!"

Out of the corner of his eye, he saw the monk move his sleeves up.

Before Jonas could react, the monk lunged forward. *Whoosh.* The metal buckle of a leather belt whipped across his face and snapped hard against his temple.

Jonas felt himself falling.

Steps retreated. Others advanced. Cathlynn gasped. Something thumped.

Just as he felt the cold hard floor smack against his body, everything went black.

"JONAS!" Cathlynn cradled Jonas's head in her lap. A long red welt swelled from his temple to his chin. And he was out cold. *Please let him be all right. He has to be all right.* Feeling for a pulse, she held her breath. His carotid artery bumped beneath her finger. Her relief whooshed out of her. She wanted to run for help. But she couldn't leave him. She shook him lightly, afraid to hurt him, afraid to let him linger in unconsciousness. "Talk to me! Please, Jonas, wake up, say something."

He moaned. She stroked his hair, kissed his temple. "Are you all right? Say something, Jonas."

"I'm fine." He struggled to get up and reached a hand to the welt on his face. "I told you to stay put."

"No, don't get up yet. He knocked you out." She helped him lean against the wall. "I thought he might have a knife or a gun. And you were defenseless."

"Thanks for your vote of confidence," he said, rubbing his temples.

"Unarmed, I mean. I—I—"

"And just what were you planning to protect me with?"

Sheepishly, she showed him the dinner tray.

"How effective would that have been against a gun or a knife?"

She shrugged and fussed over him. "Not very, but I just couldn't leave you alone to face him." She waved a couple of fingers in front of his face. "How many fingers do you see?"

"Two." He brushed her hand aside and tried to get up. "Did you see who it was?"

She supported his elbow and helped him to his feet. "No, he just shoved me aside, and I was too worried about you to run after him. I thought he killed you."

"It's going to take more than that," he said lightly.

She frowned. "It's no laughing matter, Jonas."

He seemed contrite, but maybe it was pain twisting his face. She fussed at him once again. He clasped both her hands and placed them against his heart. The steady *thump thump* against her palms reassured her.

"Can you remember any details?" he asked.

"Not really. All I saw was someone wearing a black monk's habit."

"Could have been anyone." Jonas leaned against the wall. His lips curved with a mirthless smile. "Although I think we can safely discard Valentin as a suspect."

"Yes, this guy was going much faster than a penguin shuffle." Her brief smile faded. She brushed aside the lock of hair falling across the welt. "I think you should see a doctor."

"I *am* a doctor."

"So you are. I've heard they make the worst patients."

"I'm fine. Just a simple contusion."

"It's more than a bruise."

"I said, I'm fine."

"All right. Let's at least get some ice on that 'contusion' of yours."

Jonas grumbled and pushed himself off the wall.

She wrapped her arm around his waist, half expecting him to push her away. Instead, he held her close. The warmth of him, the strength of his grip calmed her further. The brief unconsciousness seemed to have no weakening effect. They started down the dark corridor.

"Do you think he heard us discuss the research?" she asked. If he had, then their careful plan to restore order could be ruined.

"We'll find out soon enough."

"What if he realizes the results are false? Do you think he'll stay hidden?"

"There's a lot at stake here. If Sterling is behind all this, it'll all come out on Saturday."

"Yes," she said. "That's what I'm afraid of."

And if the monk knew the research results weren't going to give him the promised riches, the one who would lose the most would be Jonas.

HE SLAMMED the phone back on the receiver. The bastard was here. Didn't he trust him? Hadn't he produced everything he'd promised? And more, too. Ungrateful twit. He paced in a tight circle.

The prissy idiot thinks he's better than me. Well, I've got news for him. Blue blood doesn't always equal smarts. Doesn't he realize he could blow everything by showing his face?

There was only one way to handle this.

He picked up the phone again and tendered an invitation.

As CATHLYNN WAS APPLYING a cold towel to the welt on Jonas's face, the phone beside one of the lab computers rang. He answered. It was the hospital.

"Jonas, it's started." Andy Trask was trying hard to hide his fear, but it wavered through the phone line. Andy was alone. He'd never married, had no family left, and the friends he'd had had slowly abandoned him over the years. He had no one to help him face the painful death awaiting him.

"It's all right, Andy. I'll be right over."

"What's up?" Cathlynn asked when he hung up the phone.

Jonas rested both his hands on the edge of the desk. Andy was only two years older than him. The disease was striking early. His head dropped to his chest. Was this what he had to look forward to? "A friend is dying. I've got to go to the hospital."

"Cross's Disease?"

He nodded.

"I'll go with you," she said softly.

And as she slipped her hand into his, he was shocked by the sense of relief her quiet offer flowed through him.

AT DAWN THE NEXT morning they made their way to the parking lot.

She insisted on driving. Once on the highway, Jonas

fell asleep. Lines spidered from his eyes. Color had drained from his face. His vigil with Andy had drained any reserve of energy he might have had.

As she threaded her way back to the monastery, fingers of daybreak tickled at the somber light of night. Today, they had much to do, but she'd make sure Jonas got some sleep before they tackled their plan.

Just as she passed the monastery gates, the sun broke over the ridge of woods, illuminating the courtyard with its warm golden-pink rays. The white crosses sparkled in the sudden light, flinging shadows behind them like cast cloaks.

Something moved, shifted. A long black shadow twitched out of place. Cathlynn braked the car. The heater whirred. The engine purred. She turned off the ignition with a click. Silence fell frigid and heavy. She peered through the windshield. Her heart tripped. Her hands clasped around the steering wheel. She grew cold all over.

"Jonas." She shook him awake with one hand. "Look."

Before them, a monk's habit swayed gently back and forth from the middle cross.

Jonas swore and shoved open the Jeep's door. "That's too low even for Sterling."

Cathlynn followed him. As they neared the cross it became evident the robe was filled with a body. Shivering uncontrollably, she clutched Jonas's arm. A tumbled chair lay on its side. Black dress shoes poked from beneath the robe's hem. Hands were linked together loosely by a length of rope twirled around the stiff fingers like a rosary. A dark red face, framed by thin blond hair, gaped down at them from the monk's hood.

Jonas raked a hand through his hair and swore again.

"Who is it?" she asked shakily.

"Geoffrey Chandler. Alana's cousin."

Her heart thundered at the implication. "But if he's dead, then... What's going on, Jonas?"

"I don't know."

He turned toward the monastery.

"Aren't you going to cut him down?" she asked, hurrying after him.

"There's nothing we can do for him. It's best to leave the crime scene untouched for the police."

"Right."

Bleakly, she followed him inside, into the library.

"Do you think it was suicide?" she asked, recalling the tumbled chair.

Jonas picked up the phone. "No. Geoffrey wouldn't have come all this way just to kill himself. He was far too lazy for that kind of effort. Someone flushed him out."

"And murdered him...." Her knees suddenly felt weak and she flopped into a chair. "Who gets the trust fund now?"

"Chandler Pharmaceuticals."

The company who'd lost out on Jonas's genius. Geoffrey's murder at once made too much sense and too little. The whys mushroomed fast and furious, making her dizzy.

While Jonas placed his call to the police, she huddled by the fireplace. But even the blazing flames couldn't seep any warmth into her chilled bones.

Soon the courtyard swarmed with activity. The ambulance's red and white lights swirled a macabre dance around the scene. A plainclothes detective directed the action. Flashes exploded at regular intervals. Possible evidence was bagged and tagged. As she and Jonas stood arm in arm on the edges, Sterling came out of the monastery.

"What's all the commotion about?" he asked.

Jonas turned to him. "We found a body hanging from a cross."

"A body?"

From the knot of police officers near the cross, the detective barked, "All right, you can cut him down now."

A ladder was brought. The sound of the knife sawing through the rope ratcheted on the breeze. As the body was lowered, the robe's hood fell back, exposing the monk's congested face.

"No!" Sterling howled. He raced toward the body.

Jonas tried to hold him back. "Sterling, no, stop."

Two paramedics lay the corpse on a black body bag. As one started drawing the plastic folds around the body, Sterling shoved him aside.

"Geoffrey, Geoffrey," Sterling moaned, and collapsed to the ground. Swaying back and forth, he cradled Geoffrey's grotesque head in his arms.

"Sterling," Jonas started. He extended a sympathetic hand to Sterling's shoulder.

Sterling's head snapped up. He ripped his shoulder from Jonas's hold. His murderous gaze skewered Jonas. "I'll get you for this. I'll get you both."

Chapter Eleven

Some of Jonas's work notes were found in Geoffrey's pockets, and Jonas was taken away by the police for questioning. Sterling insisted on accompanying the body to the coroner's office in Concord, and making arrangements for the corpse's return to England.

Cathlynn was left to handle the influx of volunteers who'd come to give blood samples. She thought of sending them away, but realized that without something to keep her busy, she'd go crazy with worry. Instead, they were rerouted to the kitchen entrance to avoid the crime scene. With David efficiently seeing to the sample collection, she checked off names from the master list, obtained signatures on the releases and kept the queue of people plied with hot coffee and orange juice. The one thing she refused to do was feed their curiosity and give them fuel for village gossip. Medical questions were deferred to David; weather and Christmas fete questions were answered to the best of her ability; personal and dead-body questions were glossed over with nonanswers and a polite smile.

Even the day's bright sunshine and unseasonably warm temperature couldn't lift the gray gloom encasing the monastery's walls. The day passed in a blur of activity, yet it seemed to crawl on interminably. Any minute, she expected Jonas to walk through the front door. The longer his return took, the bigger her sense of dread grew.

As David cleaned away the last of the used supplies, Cathlynn wiped an already spotless counter with vigorous circles.

"Do you think Jonas'll be back soon?" she asked David.

"I'm sure everything will be fine. It's easy enough to check that he was at the hospital all night and couldn't have killed anyone."

"Yes, one would think so." She frowned. "Why is it taking so long? How can they even think he's guilty?"

"He'll be fine. Don't worry." David punched holes in the signed release forms and filed them in a binder. "Do you need me for anything else?"

She slowed her nonproductive cleaning. "I guess not."

"Do you want me to stay?" he asked.

She didn't miss the hopeful glint in his eyes. "No, thank you, David. I'll be fine."

Locking the lab carefully behind her, she followed him upstairs. Darkness had descended in the courtyard, creating a hushed stillness that seemed both dead, yet somehow alive. When David's headlights arched away from the monastery, Cathlynn felt very much alone. With the sun gone, a chill permeated the air. She closed the heavy front doors. The low boom of the action echoed down the hall. The silence inside the house became suffocating.

Unable to stand the quiet anymore, she headed for the library and called the hospital to check on Gram.

Her condition had worsened and she'd been placed back on a respirator.

She placed a second call. The officer who answered told her absolutely nothing helpful. Growling her frustration, she slammed the receiver back on its cradle. She'd half made up her mind to take Jonas's Jeep and head to the station, when she heard the front door open. She flew down the hall. "Jonas!"

When Sterling came through the door, she skidded to a halt. "Oh, it's you."

He smiled coldly, and his gaze speared her mercilessly. "Yes, it's me. And I think it's high time you and I had a chat."

Turning away, she dismissed him. She had too much on her mind right now to deal with Sterling. "It'll have to wait till later. Jonas—"

"Will be a while longer."

Her head snapped back. Her imagination created and discarded a dozen dire scenarios. "Do you know what's happening?"

The ends of his mustache twitched with pleasure. "My dear, he's paying the piper."

"I don't understand."

He took her elbow and led her to the library. She shook him off and went to the fireplace, where she offered her cold palms to the fire's heat.

"Why did you say Jonas was paying the piper?" she asked, surprising herself with the steadiness of her voice.

Sterling clinked ice cubes in a glass and splashed whiskey on them. "Though Geoffrey's death was sloppily made to look like a suicide, the marks on his body tell another story."

"What does that have to do with Jonas?"

"Geoffrey is dead because of Jonas."

She spun around, turning her back to the fire. "Jonas couldn't have killed Geoffrey. We were at the hospital all night—"

"Nevertheless, he murdered him indirectly."

She shook her head. "But—"

"Jonas tried to perpetuate a fraud. Because Geoffrey came to investigate the situation, he was killed."

Goose bumps riddled her arms. She tried to rub the chill away, but it only became more dense. "How much did you feel obliged to tell the police?"

"Just doing my duty."

She quirked an eyebrow. "Of course, *you'd* never lie."

He smiled and raised his glass to her. She fought her urge to punch him. What was going on at the station? Why was it taking so long? Was Jonas next on the killer's list? Was she? And just what was Sterling up to? "What did you tell them?"

"Don't worry, my dear, I'm not ready to expose him quite yet. I just gave them enough innuendos to keep him in custody for a while."

She sat and crossed a leg over one knee and pretended a calmness she didn't feel. "Why?"

"Because when I've gathered all my proof, it will be all there in black and white—irrefutable. And Jonas will spend the rest of his life in jail."

"Why do you hate Jonas so much?"

"Hate?" he scoffed. "I don't hate him. I hate lies. I hate deceit. I hate murderers."

"He didn't kill anyone," Cathlynn said with certainty.

"He hasn't exactly been honest."

"Neither have you, for a man who claims to prize

honesty so highly." She leaned forward. "What's your deep dark secret, Sterling?"

"It wouldn't be a secret if I shared it, now, would it?" He leaned forward to meet her across the occasional table separating them, and whispered, "But I know yours."

"And what would that be?" she whispered back with the same mock intensity.

"You're not Alana Chandler."

"Can you prove it?"

"Soon." He took a satisfied gulp from his drink and leaned back. "So, tell me, my dear, who are you?"

As if modeling a gown, she waved her hands down her body. "Exactly what I appear to be. How about you?"

"I'm a trusted family lawyer, paid to make sure the family money is dispersed at the proper time, to the proper person."

She was heading into dangerous territory, launching accusations she couldn't back, but something was definitely wrong with Sterling's involvement. It was too personal somehow to simply be a paid executor's duty. If he could badger her, she could return the favor.

"But you don't want that person to be me, do you?" She placed a finger on her lip and gave him a contemplative look. "I wonder why. Is it because Chandler money would go to finance a project for which a competitor would eventually benefit?"

His expression iced. "How much were you paid for your part in the charade?"

"Not a penny." Which, at this point, was the truth. "How much do you have to gain by stealing Jonas's work? Is it worth more than my life? Than Geoffrey's life?"

He stared at her frostily, then smiled. "Now I know you're not Alana. She would never have fought for her husband this way."

She shrugged. "Maybe I've changed."

"Maybe I, too, am just what I appear to be." He refilled his glass.

"Then I guess we're at an impasse." She rose to leave.

"Alana."

She glanced at Sterling over her shoulder.

"Soon, the truth comes out."

"Yes, Sterling. *All* of it."

THE BASTARD had ruined everything. Why couldn't he have stayed at home, all nice and cozy? He paced hard and fast across the small room. Now he'd have to start negotiations all over again. Who to trust? Geoffrey had come to him all those months ago, offering him a better revenge than he could have engineered on his own.

He stopped and tapped a finger across his front teeth. But the prize was still good. Surely there were a dozen Geoffreys not only within Chandler Pharmaceuticals, but at other companies. With Jonas in police custody, things would start unraveling fast.

He'd have to steal and strike quickly and soon.

He went to the closet and snapped open the door. Wicked laughter echoed in the room. "Aurelius, I've got one last job for you."

IT WAS PAST MIDNIGHT, and still Jonas wasn't home. Cathlynn had gotten ready for bed, but couldn't seem to make her way beneath the sheets. Lying there un-moving, her mind would whirl with bleak possibilities. She sat before the vanity, brushing her hair, but even that movement couldn't quite stop her restlessness. What if Jonas didn't come home? Was he all right? What if…?

So lost was she in the twist of her thoughts that she didn't hear Jonas walk in. When he took the brush from her hand, she gave a cry of shock and half jumped out of the chair. Seeing Jonas's reflection in the mirror, she settled back down.

She smiled at him and didn't care that her relief showed through the breathlessness of her words. "You're here."

"Yes," he said. Gently he caressed her hair with the brush.

In the quietness of his movements, in his somber silence, she sensed he didn't want to discuss whatever had happened at the police station. Suddenly, neither did she. She wanted to whisk away the sadness from his eyes. She wanted to hold him. She wanted to love him. He placed the brush back on the vanity and headed for the bathroom door.

"Jonas?" she called anxiously, as if his departure would cut her adrift on a vast, endless sea.

"I'll be right back."

When he returned a moment later, he held a pendant in his hands. The tiger's-eye cabochon caught the light and gleamed rich topaz stripes in the stone's warm brown background. Surrounding the three-inch cab was a filigree of gold, its scrolled design gave the appearance of cat paws tenderly protecting the dancing light in the stone. Jonas held the necklace in front of her.

"Lift your hair," he said.

She did, and he clasped the chain around her neck. The mirror reflected the tiger's eye as it lay heavy on the skin of her chest exposed by the V of her burgundy flannel robe. The gold-wire design brushed the edges of both breasts. She let her hair fall back down and reached a hand to touch the pendant.

"It's beautiful."

"My mother loved to make her own jewelry. This was one of her favorites pieces."

Gaze fixed on Jonas's strangely doleful face, she wasn't sure what to say.

"The first time I saw you," he said, "I thought of this necklace." Into the mirror, he looked deep into her eyes. "You wear it well."

A storm brewed hot and violent in his intense gaze. She couldn't seem to breathe. "I—I—"

"Any man would have to be blind not to notice the fire in your hair." He buried his hands in the thick strands, showering a warm ripple down her spine.

"Or in your eyes." He kissed her temple, tripping her pulse into a tempest.

"Or on your skin." He lowered his hands to her shoulders, exposing the skin beneath her robe when his fingers cupped the roundness at the point of her shoulders. He kissed her there, too, electrifying every one of her nerve endings.

"I hate you," he said softly. The stormy desire darkening his eyes betrayed his words. "I hate what you do to me."

She twisted in her seat and looked up at him. "I know."

"I don't want you," he whispered, and reached for both her elbows, drawing her up to him. "I don't want to need you."

"I know." She twined her arms around his neck. The longing coursing through her was exciting, and frightening with its power. Yet she wanted him in a way that was all-encompassing and held no logic. Just like the last time.

He raked his fingers through her hair until they were buried at her nape. Desire washed over her, hot and strong. Closing her eyes, she sighed her pleasure.

"Don't do that," he rasped. "Tell me to go. Tell me to leave you alone."

"No, Jonas, stay."

"Cathlynn—"

She touched his lips with one finger and shook her head. "Don't talk. Not now. Later."

He opened his mouth to protest. Lifting herself on tiptoe, she leaned forward and kissed him. There was a heartbeat of hesitation, then his arms tightened around her, and he kissed her back with drenching passion. She was stunned with the wave of piercing need rolling around her, over her, through her, buffeting her senses with aching anticipation.

He guided her to the bed, tumbled them both into the satiny sea of sheets.

"Save me from this improper obsession." A haunted expression clouded his face.

She reached up and brushed his cheekbone with her fingers, felt the raspiness of his beard, the tension in the muscles. "I can't save myself."

Then she unknotted the tie holding her robe closed, and opened herself to him. "Jonas."

She loved him. Always would.

With a husky groan, he shed his clothes and accepted her invitation. With his hands, his mouth, his body, he sailed her straight into the hurricane of his need. She forgot her fear. Shock waves of pleasure tossed her. His kisses seared her skin like bolts of lightning. The taste of him, heady and hot, thundered through her. The woodsy scent of him ensnared her. His touch pitched her senses to new heights. She was reeling in a dangerous vortex, spiraling closer and closer to the center of a powerful whirlpool. Never had anyone made her feel this way.

Suddenly she cried out, afraid she would drown in the sensations he incited in her, afraid she would lose herself, find herself floundering alone. Tears brimmed her eyes as heart and head battled. *I love him. I can't help it, I love him.*

He stilled, and the stillness was worse than the storm.

"Cathlynn?" He stroked her hair, tenderly, needily.

She saw the worry in his eyes, tried to speak of the strange, wondrous things she was experiencing, but couldn't. With a finger, he gently stroked the tears away. "Cat..."

She saw the affection, clear and exposed, and understood the risk was as great for him as for her. She reached for him, soothed the worry lines crinkling his forehead with her fingertips, lost herself in the deep gray of his eyes. She unlatched the tight little box in her mind where she stuffed the feelings she feared, and exposed her vulnerability to him, her love. And she did love him, with her heart, her body, her very soul. "Love me, Jonas"

At his renewed caresses, she sighed her delight, lost herself in his touch. Then she was caught in an uncontrollable undertow, and she did drown, and drowning was wonderful, and he joined her there in the tossed seas of their climax, and the waves rolled one on top of the other, like surf on the sand, lulling them on a warm, pleasant buoy. She wanted to stay like this in his arms forever.

He relaxed against her. The haunted look was gone

from his face. His breathing slowed, became regular. The tension unwound from his muscles.

"Cat?"

"Shh. Later." She didn't want to shatter the pleasant dream just yet.

Morning would be here soon enough to talk. He needed to rest. She needed his arms around her for just a bit longer.

She snuggled close to him, head cradled against his shoulder, hand on his heart, one leg between his. His fingers caressed her hair. The lub-dub of his heart was a gentle lullaby. And his warmth wrapped her in comfort.

Safe, secure, in the harbor of his arms, she fell asleep.

ON THE MORNING of the fete, Jonas was sleeping soundly, exhausted from long hours in the lab and nights of mindless passion. Drawing the blanket snug around his shoulders, Cathlynn kissed his temple and decided to let him rest a little longer.

Though the previous few days had been unseasonably warm and had melted most of the snow away, the cold returned on Sunday. The skies were gray, threatening snow. Cathlynn hoped the leaden skies weren't a portent of things to come. Bright sunshine would have made her feel much cheerier today.

She hurried down the stairs and cornered Valentin in the kitchen. He was busy getting the breakfast platters ready. The scent of bacon and eggs and buttered toast filled the room.

"Is Harry here yet?" she asked, snatching a cup from a cupboard and filling it with coffee straight from the pot.

"He is in the stables, *madame*. Seeing to the horses."

As opposed to the goats. She smiled. Valentin really didn't have a high opinion of her intelligence. "How about David?"

"*Non, madame*. He has not arrived." Valentin transferred the platters from the counter to the rolling cart.

"I'll have to call him." She snatched a sheet of paper from the thin, long pad Valentin kept on the fridge and a pencil from the cup on the counter, and jotted down a list. Call David. Call television station. Prepare front room. "I'm trying to get an interview set up for Jonas this afternoon before the official start of the fete. He has a big announcement to make. I'll need extra coffee for the crew, and maybe muffins."

"Muffins?"

"Yeah, you know, those little individual-cake things. I'm sure you can find a recipe somewhere. A couple dozen at least."

"Very well, *madame*." He clanked glasses and plopped a pitcher of orange juice onto the cart.

"How about Christmas decorations? There must be extra decorations somewhere."

"In one of the storage rooms in the cellar, *madame*."

He raised an eyebrow in question, but Cathlynn decided to ignore him for now.

"All right, you can show me later." She hiked on her coat. "I'm going to go out to talk to Harry. I'll be back before the caterers and decorators arrive to set up for the fete."

Having assured herself Harry was up to the task of safely cutting down a Christmas tree, she returned to the house, installed herself at the library desk and phoned the research assistant. She felt bad about waking David so early, but promised him some time off in the near future. David chuckled and told her he was on his way.

The television station agreed to send a crew out at three. That left her less than six hours to turn the cold front room with the portraits of dead monks into a festive showcase. And supervise the fete set-up.

"The impossible is my specialty!"

After making sure Jonas ate breakfast, she left him alone to prepare for the interview. Briefcase in hand, Sterling had come down and left.

Harry and David dragged in a huge Christmas tree and set it up. They also cut swaths of greenery, which they helped Cathlynn install along the mantel and on top of the windows and doors. With Valentin, she unearthed boxes of decorations and filled the tree with lights and color. From the decorators, David borrowed pots of red poinsettias and white mums, which now dotted the room. Harry wasn't too keen on running the vacuum cleaner, but she promised him he could climb the ladder to set the star on top of the tree in exchange. With a good polish, the old furniture gleamed.

At two o'clock, Cathlynn looked around the front room to make sure everything was just so. It had come to life. The reds, greens and whites, the scent of pine and cinnamon created a festive atmosphere. The decorators had transformed the rest of the monastery into a festive showcase. Had the monastery looked this way when Jonas was young? Full of color and brimming with comfort? No wonder he'd fought to get it back after his father had lost it to debt.

She glanced at her watch. Just enough time for a quick shower and a change into her new dress. Putting up her aching feet would have to wait until after the fete.

As she turned to exit the room, her attention snagged on the portrait over the fireplace. In the firelight, the monk's face seemed to come to life under the shadow of his black hood. She could have sworn the thin lips curved into a mild smile. Had he just winked at her? She peered closer. No, it had to have been a trick of the light.

"You look familiar," she told the portrait. Then shook her head. "You're really losing it, Cat."

With a last look of approval, she headed upstairs to see if Jonas was ready.

THIS WAS SHEER FOLLY, Jonas thought as he frantically searched through the contents of his closet. He was crazy to think this would work. What if everything backfired? What if—

"What's all this banging around?" Cathlynn asked.

Jonas looked up. She stood arms crossed, leaning against the bathroom door. From the earful he'd received from Valentin, she'd been quite the dictator today, ordering everyone around. Funny, though, Valentin hadn't seemed to mind. If anything, there had been a certain amount of pride in his voice as he'd recited her accomplishments.

"What banging?" he asked distractedly, shutting yet another drawer.

"You're slamming drawers all over the place. Is everything all right?"

"I'm fine. I just can't seem to find a tie." As he shoved shirts aside, the hangers clattered.

"There's one around your neck."

He ripped it out of his collar and threw it onto the ground. "I don't like ties."

"Then don't wear one."

"There's a certain etiquette—"

"And we wouldn't want to break a sacred code of etiquette, now, would we?" A Cheshire cat grin lit her face.

"It's no laughing matter." He tried to sound serious, but felt his lips curve at the corners. She had that effect on him, calming and exciting all at once. "I can't afford to give a less than professional appearance."

"Then I guess that leaves out the monk's robes." She quirked a smile, then walked into the room, picked up the discarded tie and dropped it on the chair holding a week's worth of dirty clothes. "How about if I fix you up so you look acceptable, but you don't have to wear a tie?"

He grumbled, longing to reach for her, to lose himself in her and forget all about the press conference and the fete. "It won't work."

"So negative." She pushed him backward until he sat on the edge of his bed. "Sit."

She riffled through his things, plucking out a sweater here, a jacket there. He hadn't anticipated the intimacy of her invasion into his room, how right it would feel, how much he would want it. She held combinations up, added and deleted, and he found himself envious of his own clothes. With a nod, she seemed to come to a decision.

"Take off your shirt," she ordered. "Put on this sweater, then your jacket over it. *Voilà.*"

He did as she asked and had to admit the results worked. He felt comfortable, and looked professional but not stuffy.

Her irises flared with a warm flame. "Simply dashing, sir."

She hugged him from behind. He drew comfort and warmth from her embrace. "Are you ready?"

"As ready as I'll ever be." On an impulse, he turned around and pulled her close. He speared his fingers through her hair, harvesting the sheer life it exuded, and kissed her hard. He drew a long breath in, inhaling her scent, then let it out slowly. Calmness and confidence now swathed his body. "Let's go."

As THEY NEARED the front room, Harry intercepted them. Cathlynn tried to rebound him away until later, but he wouldn't be put off.

"Can I take Nimbus out for a ride?" he asked expectantly.

"No, he's still a bit sore." Harry's face melted in disappointment, but soon brightened again when Jonas continued. "Take Cirrus."

"Thanks." Harry was already running out the door.

"Don't run him too hard," Jonas called after him. "It's getting cold out there. And the fete will start right after the press conference."

"I won't," he promised, and disappeared.

Excitement crackled in the air. David was helping the television crew set up. When he saw Jonas and Cathlynn, he brought the regional anchor, Dani Sands, over to meet them. She was a small, wiry woman with short blond hair and a fresh, freckled face that spoke of a love of the outdoors. Her manner was easygoing, and Cathlynn hoped she could put Jonas at ease.

The next half hour passed in a flurry of activity. Cathlynn stayed out of the way, but was always close by when Jonas sought her attention. With a confident smile and a touch or a word of encouragement, she tried to keep him relaxed.

It would soon be over. Then what? But she didn't want to think about possible failure. If greed was the motive, Alana's murderer would be flushed out.

Jonas and Dani were ushered into chairs. Microphones were clipped onto their jackets. Soon the harsh television lights were turned on. Dani introduced herself and her guest. Then the questions started.

"What exactly is Cross's Disease?" Dani asked.

Jonas, voice confident and strong, answered. Cathlynn thought she heard screams from outside. She edged her way around the room.

"How long have you been working on finding a cure?"

A car's engine droned in the courtyard.

"For over twelve years," Jonas said, and gave more details.

A car door slammed shut.

"Weren't you associated with Chandler Pharmaceuticals?" Dani asked.

The sound of galloping hooves came closer and closer.

"Until last year, yes," Jonas answered.

She slipped into the hall.

"What happened?" Dani asked.

"We didn't agree on ethics," Jonas said. "But this week, I made a great discovery."

The hoofbeats jagged in tempo to ragged shouting.

Sterling entered, grinning jackal happy. "I'm not too late for the show, I hope."

Cathlynn blocked his path. "I won't let you interfere."

"I'm afraid you can't protect him any longer, my dear. I've got an announcement of my own."

The horse clattered to a halt on the courtyard's cobblestones.

"What did you find?" Dani asked.

Through the open door, Cathlynn saw Harry vault off Cirrus's back.

Jonas said, "I discovered the key that locks the mutant gene and tricks it into believing it's too early to manifest."

He had barely finished making his announcement when a breathless Harry burst through the door.

"Jonas! Jonas! Come quick. Some kids have fallen through the ice on the river."

Chapter Twelve

Shouting orders, Jonas raced out the door, vaulted onto Cirrus's back and galloped to the rescue.

At Harry's announcement, the cameraman had disengaged the camera from its tripod. Now he was heading toward the river with the rest of the crew.

Cathlynn ran to the phone and called for help. She glanced out the window. Winter solstice—the year's shortest day—and here at the foot of the mountains, night was arriving especially early, as were the guests for the fete. In the growing twilight, the scene reminded her starkly of her nightmares.

The rising full moon cut the three crosses in the courtyard with scattered shreds of light. As they made their way onto the snow trail left by Cirrus, the news crew and the guests wearing winter coats, not robed monks, snaked a chaotic queue around the fluttering crime-scene tape surrounding the crosses. Shouting replaced chanting. Fog swirled around the forest's edge, giving the courtyard a surreal quality. A thick, heavy gloom and a sinking sensation of doom wrapped around her like a lead shawl. Once again, the river would bring sorrow to the village.

Grabbing her coat, Cathlynn rushed to join the fray.

David was running back toward the monastery and stopped her.

"Get some blankets for the kid in case it takes the rescue squad a while to get here."

"Good idea. He'll be soaked and freezing. He'll need something to keep them warm. See if you can get Valentin to put something hot in a thermos."

"I'll be right back."

Quickly she raced upstairs, snapping lights on as she went. From the linen room, she gathered as many blankets as her arms could hold. Struggling backward out of the closet, she dropped half her load. As she bent down to pick up the fallen blankets, she heard the creak of a door opening and closing.

"David, I'm glad you came up. I'm going to need help with this."

She staggered up and turned to share her load. Not David. Someone else. From the doorway, a black-robed monk stepped forward. His hands were buried in opposite sleeves. His hood was pulled forward, creating a dark shadow across his face.

"Who are you?" she asked.

He took a slow step forward, then another, like a ghostly monk on the way to vespers.

The gray granite stones of the walls seemed to come alive. They pulsed and shimmered in a feverish dance. *Beware. Beware. Beware.*

Her skin crawled from the sudden chill permeating the room. She hadn't needed the wall's warning to know this monk's intentions weren't pious.

"Who are you?" she repeated, backing away.

No answer.

The monk took another step forward. His sleeves

slowly separated. With a snap, a rope jerked between his black-gloved hands.

Claire was right, she thought. All those self-defense classes are going to pay off. Rule number one. Stay calm. Rule number two. Take the aggressor by surprise.

Cathlynn threw her load toward the monk, pitched herself against him, bowling him off balance, and rushed to the door. She grabbed the iron handle, pulled, and smacked into the door when it didn't budge. Frantically, she jiggled the knob. It was locked.

When she turned around to face the monk and give him another dose or two of defensive moves, he hit her square against the side of the head with the thick rope.

She fell into his waiting arms.

JONAS SKIDDED Cirrus to a halt by the river's edge. Two children huddled and cried by the bank, looking forlornly at a jagged hole in the ice where a girl was desperately trying to hold a little boy afloat. Dark water churned below. The kids by the bank looked up at the noise and ran toward him, both talking and gesturing at once.

"William," a boy of about nine said, sniffing. "He fell in, and Ashley, she went after him. We were skating. And William just fell in. Then Ashley, Ashley... He's in the water. And...and..."

The other child started wailing.

"It's going to be all right," Jonas said. "Here." He handed the boy Cirrus's reins. "You hold Cirrus and take good care of him. I'll go help your friends."

"Hang on," he shouted to the girl on the ice. He stripped out of his jacket and sweater, shucked his shoes and headed toward the water.

As he stepped onto the ice, Ashley shifted her weight

to look at him. The ice beneath her cracked and gave way, plunging her into the water. The current below swallowed her shriek and dragged both children into its icy flow.

Jonas dived after them.

The water was a frigid insult. It needled his skin, stole his breath, wracked his body with snaking chills. He was stinging hot, numbing cold. Blackness surrounded him. He bobbed to the surface and took another long breath. Getting his bearings, he dived beneath the surface again. The current carried him forward. This wasn't good. At this rate the children could already be too far downriver to help. Their only hope was to hang on to something along the course— a root, a boulder, a pylon from the bridge. Jonas fought the current, tried to stay in control of his path. In the ink-black water, he could barely see his own hand in front of him.

Then something fluttered ahead of him. Something white. He swam harder. The white blob took on the shape of a snowsuited girl. She held on to the smaller boy. Both were stopped by an object at a right angle to the current. A car. In the murky water, the red was dull, but the feminine curves of the sports car left no doubt.

It was Alana's car.

He hadn't reported Alana's disappearance to the police. There had been no search for clues other than his and MacPhearson's. Neither of them had thought to look in the river.

Someone tapped him on the shoulder. Jonas swiveled to see another man. He grabbed both kids, handed one to his helper and fought his way back to the hole with the other.

His lungs burned. His muscles cramped. Though

small, the child was a dead weight. Straight ahead light flashed. With a last burst of effort, he surfaced.

He gasped for breath. For a moment, he couldn't see anything in the powerful beams of the rescue lights pointed at him. Clapping and shouts of joy exploded around him. Two paramedics reached for the kids and whisked them away from their rescuers for first aid. Someone hauled him and his helper out of the water. Someone else handed them dry coats, boots and blankets. Sirens blaring, the ambulance carrying the children left.

Uniformed police officers entered the fray of agitated guests. Then the questions started flying. The camera rolled on. Between wildly chattering teeth, the other man talked. The car was mentioned.

A paramedic interrupted, insisting the man needed care before hypothermia set in.

"Car. What car?" a policeman insisted.

"A red Miata," the man said.

"Alana's car!" Sterling barked. He spun toward Jonas and grabbed the blanket Jonas was holding tightly around him. "Where is she? What have you done with the real Alana Chandler?"

Thick clouds spirited the moon's remaining light. The cold stuttering through his body had nothing to do with the icy water or the wintry night's air, and everything to do with loss.

Sterling tightened his hold on Jonas's blanket. "I want an answer, Shades. I want it now!"

"I don't know."

A tall policeman with a no-nonsense face approached them. "What's going on here?"

"What do you mean, you don't know?" Sterling asked, ignoring the officer. His face was mottled red with rage. "That's her car down there and you put it there."

Stiffly Jonas jerked away Sterling's hold. "Alana left six weeks ago and didn't return. I had no idea where her car was. I have no idea where she is."

"I don't believe you."

"Believe what you want," Jonas shot back. With warmth returning to his body, his reddened skin hurt, his head ached, and he didn't have the will or inclination to contain the fury churning through him. "You don't care about Alana. You don't want her to get the trust. You'd do anything to see Geoffrey got it."

"Geoffrey's dead." Sterling's face puckered with hatred. "You killed him, too. For greed—"

"You did it to get a bigger share—"

"Don't be an ass!" Sterling roared. "I'm paid to do a duty and I take that duty seriously."

"Especially if you can make it benefit your son."

Sterling looked stunned. "You don't know what you're talking about."

"No lawyer I know has established himself so well into a family as you did with Geoffrey's."

"What has a good relationship got to do with you murdering Alana and Geoffrey?"

Shivering, he ignored Sterling's comment. "I always wondered why. I asked Cameron to check into it. And sure enough, he charmed Geoffrey's mother into telling him all about her little indiscretion twenty-nine years ago."

As if someone had punched him in the stomach, Sterling took a step backward.

Jonas drove in another nail. "Barret Chandler was sterile."

The officer cleared his throat. "Now about the car—"

"He needs to get into dry clothes," a paramedic interrupted.

"The car in the water belongs to this man's wife," Sterling said venomously, pointing at Jonas. "He killed her in order to inherit her trust fund."

Jonas crammed Sterling's space. "Think about it, Sterling. If I'd wanted to kill her, wouldn't I have waited until after the trust fund reverted?"

"She'd already filed for a divorce." He tapped his briefcase. "I have the letter to prove it."

"We'd already settled."

"You wanted more."

Jonas pressed closer. "You had her killed so you could make sure no Chandler money paid for any more of my research. You had her killed so Geoffrey could inherit, and you could spend your retirement in ease."

"That's simply not true."

"Stealing my work, that was an added bonus. More money in the Chandler coffer, more money for you."

"All right," the officer interrupted in a stern, commanding voice. "That's enough out of both of you. We'll straighten this out at the station. You, take those clothes and change in the back of the squad car."

Disgusted, Jonas started turning away. "Later."

"Now," the policeman insisted. "We don't take murder lightly around here. And we like to keep our suspects healthy."

"Yes," Sterling agreed. "Let's get this settled once and for all." He dusted his coat. "A murderer belongs in jail."

"Then be prepared for a long stay, Sterling, courtesy

of the state of New Hampshire. You won't see England for a good long while.''

As Jonas was being led to the waiting police car, it occurred to him he hadn't seen Cathlynn. Night had fallen, cloaking the landscape in darkness, making it hard to see. Flashlights beamed an eerie, strobing dance in which he caught flickers of activity. Harry was fussing over Cirrus. The news crew was shooting eyewitness accounts. Valentin poured coffee. David circled the edges of the crowd. No Cathlynn.

He tried to turn back. The policeman wouldn't loosen his hold. Jonas spotted David.

"Have you seen Cat?" he shouted.

"I thought she was out here somewhere, handing out blankets."

A long line of dread shuddered through him. Something was wrong. Cathlynn wouldn't have stayed away if she could help. If she wasn't here... She was all right. She had to be. "Go find her, David. Make sure she's all right."

"I'm sure she's around. Don't worry."

But as the first blast of heat from the police cruiser gusted onto him, the feeling of failure renewed the intensity of his shivers. If he could just see her, talk to her, know she was all right, he could endure the hard questions and answers waiting for him at the police station. *Cathlynn, where are you?*

"How long is this going to take?" he asked the officer.

"As long as it takes."

He hadn't felt this helpless in nearly twenty years.

HEAD POUNDING, body feeling cramped and stiff, Cathlynn awoke. What time was it? How long had she been unconscious? Her eyes fluttered open, focused on something blue at her side. A hand. *Cold. So cold. Must be really cold if my hand is blue.* She tried to shake it to revive the circulation, felt her arm pinned against her back. The red fingernails drew her attention. *When did I paint my nails?* She shifted and moaned at the hammer of pain pounding in her head. Two fists dug into the small of her back. She froze.

Slowly, she fixed her gaze on the elegantly curved hand with the bluish skin and blood-red nails, followed the stiff wrist up the naked forearm to the bare shoulder, saw the long matted brown hair, took in the slashed neck, and screamed. Her cries echoed and reechoed against the stark walls, adding torture to her already aching head.

"Go ahead. Yell all you want," a voice said.

Alana. She'd found Alana. She couldn't stop screaming.

"No one's here to hear you," the voice continued.

Where was she? What had happened? Then she remembered the blankets and the monk, remembered trying to run away and falling.

Her throat was dry. Her scream no longer had voice. Through the frantic tripping of her pulse something registered. The voice. It was familiar. She'd heard it before. *Calm down. Calm down.* Turning her head from the corpse at her side, Cathlynn forced her ragged breath into a semiregular pattern, her tumbling thoughts into a semblance of order.

"That's better," the voice said.

Staring ahead, she took in the lone bulb hanging from a wire in the ceiling. Its light was dimmed by dust and cast long shadows on the gray granite walls. The room was small, dark and freezing cold. A figure moved slowly, rhythmically before her. A soft scraping sound came from that direction, but she couldn't see the cause.

"Who are you? What do you want with me?" she asked.

"All in good time."

Her hands were tightly bound, but her legs were free. If she could distract him from the noise, she could stand up and run. Where was the door? "What are you doing?"

He chuckled. "A little interior redecorating."

Recognition slapped her. "David, is that you?"

"Oops, caught in the act. Not that it matters."

Pressing her hands onto the frozen floor, she pushed herself up in a straighter position against the wall. "You killed Alana."

"An unfortunate necessity." Slop, crunch, scrape.

Slowly, carefully, she bent her legs. "Why?"

"One good turn deserves another." Slop, crunch, scrape.

Tentatively, she rocked forward. "I don't understand."

"You don't need to." Slop, crunch, scrape.

One. Two. Three. Feet under her, she launched herself up to her knees, tried to carry the momentum farther up, but fell back down.

"Now, now, Cat. There's no need to struggle. I promise it won't hurt. I'm not as cruel as some people around here. Relax. It'll be over soon."

From her new crumpled position, she could see past the dusty beam of light to the yawning hole in the wall. David, dressed in a monk's habit, his face still hidden by the cowl, was slopping mortar onto squared stones and lapping away the excess like an expert. Soon, there would be just enough room in the wall to admit one person, if he stepped high and hunched over.

He was going to kill her. Just like he'd killed Alana. He was going to strangle her and leave her here, entombed in this small chamber with Alana's dead body for eternal company. She had to buy time. *Talk. Get him talking.*

"Where are we?" she asked.

"The infamous west wing with all its hidden chambers." David's words steamed in the cold air.

A phone shrieked. David extracted the portable phone she'd used in the boiler room from the pocket of his monk's habit. "I expect that's Jonas checking up on you. I'm surprised it took so long. Good thing you're awake to reassure him."

Pulling his hood back, he pressed the On button. "Jonas, yes, she's here. Busy keeping everyone warm and happy. Sure. Hang on a second."

David placed his hand across the speaker. "I'm going to put the phone next to your ear. I want you to talk to him in a normal voice and make him think you're all right. No tricks. Got it."

She nodded. David should have known by now that falling meekly into place wasn't her style.

"CATHLYNN, you're there." Relief flowed through Jonas. She was at the monastery safe and sound. And he was wasting the precious five minutes the police had allowed him on stupid observations.

"Yes, of course. Where else would I be? Are the kids okay?"

The relief didn't last. Something wasn't right. He heard it in the edgy tone of her voice. "They're scared, but they'll be fine. They both swallowed water and suffered hypothermia, but they're warm now and resting. They're going to stay at the hospital overnight for observation. Are you all right?''

There was a second of hesitation. "As well as Gram.''

His heart started hammering. Gram had been put on a respirator. Gram was not doing well. David had answered the phone. David had assured him everything was running smoothly. "Oh my God, David.''

David had her. His grip on the phone, on the counter's edge, tightened. David was going to hurt her.

"Yes. How much longer will you be?'' Her voice was overly bright.

"I'm on my way.''

"As long as that? Won't they let you go sooner?''

She was trying to give David a false sense of security. Smart girl. His throat constricted. "Hang on, Cat. I'll be right there.''

He slammed the phone down and raced down the station hall.

"Hey, you can't leave yet.'' An officer rounded the counter and rushed after him.

He grabbed Sterling, who was coming out of the men's room, by the collar and shoved him against the wall. "Give me your car keys. *Now!*''

Stunned, Sterling obeyed.

Sprinting out the front door, he shouted back. "David. He's the one who killed Alana. Cathlynn's in danger.''

Chapter Thirteen

While David continued masoning her tomb, Cathlynn searched furiously for a way out. Dying in a freezing monastery basement wasn't part of her long-range plans. The fingers of her tied hands palpated the walls until they found the edge of a stone jutting out slightly. Fanning her hands as far apart as the rope would let her, she started sawing at the taut cord. She would not show him the sheer terror zigzagging through her. To hide her activity, she started talking.

"The horses?" Cathlynn asked, surprised at the calmness of her voice. "Were you the one to scare them?"

"An accident." David shifted from the outside of the wall to the inside and continued his work. "I was getting the monk's habit from the cottage. Not that there's a lack of them around, but..." He shrugged. "Then those damned horses saw me and panicked and the wind got hold of the robe. I couldn't just run after it. Not with you there to see me. So I had to let it go."

"The car? That was you, too."

He gave a pleased grunt. "I have a cousin in Manchester who's a mechanic. He was willing enough to trade what-ifs for a few beers."

"The cat on my bed?"

"Ingenious, eh?" He paused and grinned sheepishly. "A client's daughter left the thing at my mother's."

"Why did you steal the Aidan Heart?"

"I didn't." He heaved a sigh of regret. "But whoever did, saved your life. For a little while anyway."

His answer halted her surreptitious sawing. If David hadn't taken the Aidan Heart, then who had and where was it? And how had its disappearance given her a temporary reprieve from death? She found the sharp edge of stone and resumed her sawing. *Keep him talking.*

"You were the intruder in the basement a couple of nights ago?"

He lifted a square stone and placed it on the ledge he was building. "No, that was good old Geoffrey. Son of a bitch nearly ruined everything."

"So you killed him."

"The greedy little bastard left me no choice." He shoved the trowel into the bucket of mortar. "And Jonas will rot in jail for the crime. What lovely irony!"

"What if he's not convicted?"

He shrugged. "Well, he'll still die, won't he? A painful, horrible death."

"Why are you doing all this?" The skin of her wrists burned, but she didn't dare stop sawing.

"He killed my father."

"What?" She missed the stone with the rope and scraped a palm.

David banged the trowel's handle on the stone to set it firmly. "My father crawled to him, begged for help while he was bleeding to death from a gunshot wound. What did Jonas do? He killed him. Let him bleed. Let him die in cruel agony like an animal."

"That doesn't sound like Jonas," she said softly, trying to calm the mounting madness in David's voice.

"Well, it is." He gave a bitter laugh. "You know what he did?"

"I can't imagine."

"He gave my mother money to open a dress shop." David sneered. "As if a dress shop could replace a father!"

"What was wrong with your father? Did he have Cross's Disease?"

His face suffused with fury. "My father wasn't one of *them*. He wasn't from around here. He wasn't going to croak at forty."

She played on a hunch, hoping against hope she could make him see reason. "But your mother is from the village. Her father died from the disease. Aren't you afraid you'll die from it, too?" she pointed out desperately.

David patted his pocket, partially extracted a computer disk for her to see, then let if fall back into its hiding spot. "I've got the cure. What does it matter if Chandler Pharmaceuticals or some other company manufactures it?"

"It won't solve your problems." The skin of her wrist was raw, broken. Still she continued.

"He owes me. With his work I can buy myself peace."

"Do you really think so?"

"Of course! I've got two buyers interested already. I've wasted five years trying to find the best way to make him pay. Now the time is right."

"Why kill Alana?" Another of the rope's cords snapped. *Just a little longer.* "What did she have to do with this?"

"I couldn't let Jonas get the trust fund money. I wanted him to get close to finding the cure, but not too close." He paused his ghoulish work. As his gaze pierced hers, his eyes burned with malevolence. "Don't you see? He has to die. He has to die slowly, painfully. Just like my father."

"But why kill her, why do so much damage to her body?"

"Because of the monk's legend." He bent back to his enterprise. "The monks weren't stupid. It didn't take them long to figure out only men got this curse. They figured if they sacrificed a young woman and drank her blood it would cleanse theirs."

"So you slit her throat to make it appear like a monk's sacrifice."

"And the river cleansed me of my sins."

"So why did you hide her body?"

"Because I wanted to wait for the Christmas fete. I wanted to have my revenge in public. I wanted Jonas to be humiliated. I was going to make sure the highlight of this year's festivities was the police finding Alana's abused body. He managed to ruin that, too."

"Why kill me?" Another string pinged dully against her hand as it broke. "Jonas won't get the trust fund now. What have you got to gain?"

He laughed. "That's the beauty of this, Cat. He can watch you die—just like I had to watch my father die."

"I don't understand."

"You will."

"What are you going to do?" She quivered with renewed fear.

He lopped off the excess mortar and lobbed it into the bucket, then smiled at her. "Why, I'll have Aurelius perform one last sacrifice—and leave enough evidence for the police to blame Jonas.''

She wanted to argue. She wanted to plead. But she could only stare while her words stuck in her throat.

In David's cold, dark eyes, she saw the certainty of her own death.

JONAS DROVE as fast as he dared on the twisty country roads. Wrapped around a tree, he wouldn't do Cathlynn any good. Questions stormed inside his mind. Why was David holding Cathlynn? What had he to gain? When had David turned on him? How could he have entrusted Cathlynn to the care of a murderer? Why? Why? *Why?*

Please, Cathlynn, be all right.

The research, which had seemed to mean the world to him only hours ago, now appeared insignificant. All the secrets. All the lies. And he was no further ahead.

He'd failed again.

And because of him, Alana was murdered. Because of him, Geoffrey was hanged. Because of him, Cathlynn might die.

So much for saving lives!

The work, it would always be there. Somehow, he'd keep his research afloat. But if Cathlynn died, he could never forgive himself. She hadn't asked for this. All she'd wanted was that damned Aidan Heart. A piece of glass to see her grandmother smile again.

And he'd trapped her into living a lie. Then he'd lost the sculpture. What had she gained for all her trouble? She was scared for her life and alone with a murderer.

He growled his frustration. "He won't get away with this, Cathlynn! I promise you."

The monastery gates loomed before him. He braked

and darted out of the car without bothering to turn off the ignition.

As he shot through the door, the first thing he noticed was the quiet. No guests laughed and drank in the decorated house. The caterers were gone but had left behind heaping platters of food. His first instinct was to call out loud, but he didn't want to warn David of his presence and force the bastard to act too quickly.

Following the bright trail of festive lights, he raced upstairs. Room by room, he searched for evidence of Cathlynn. He found nothing but a discarded pile of blankets in the linen room and a spot of blood on the floor.

Cathlynn!

He bolted down the stairs.

Library, kitchen, office.

Empty. Empty. Empty!

Where the hell was Valentin?

He paused in the front hallway, uncertain where to go. Had David had time to take her elsewhere since he'd called? *Cathlynn, where are you?*

A surge of terror propelled him forward. With hurried stealth, he headed down the stone stairs to the cellar. With each step he took he grew more terrified. He'd been powerless to save his father, his mother, even Alana.

Cathlynn!

Images raced through his mind, each more dire than the previous one. And with them the cold dread that he'd be too late for Cathlynn, too.

Lab. Empty. David's office. Empty.

Where could she be?

"Cathlynn," he whispered harshly. "Where are you?"

She hadn't asked for this. He *had* to find her. He *had* to save her.

I'd trade my life for hers. He wasn't sure if he was making a bargain with the devil, or asking God for grace.

Then he heard something coming from the dark. A soft scraping sound. Through the hammering of his heart, the ripping of his breath, he tuned in to the noise and followed where it led.

AS THE LAST OF THE ROPE gave, Cathlynn's hands thudded against the granite wall.

"There. That should do for now." David plunked the trowel into the bucket and wiped his hands on his habit. "I've got a few things to set up before Jonas comes back. I really don't want him to miss out on the show."

He extracted a length of rope from his pocket. "I'd like to trust you to stay put, but I've learned not to trust anyone. So, I'll give you a conscience." He chuckled. "Alana is in dire need of a friend. Wherever you go, you'll have to take her with you."

"No!" He was sick. The man had to be absolutely unbalanced to want to shackle her to a corpse.

David started in her direction. The tip of his shoulder caught the lightbulb and set it swinging. Shadows spun like dervish ghosts on the walls.

Her heart thundered. Her throat went dry. She wanted to charge and run free, but she had to bide her time. She would get only one chance.

All's fair when your life is in jeopardy, the self-defense instructor had said. *You're not a martial artist. It doesn't have to be pretty. Strike and run.*

She watched him, concentrating.

Closer. Come closer. She coiled energy in her legs

by stiffening them. *One more step*. She shifted her balance. *Just one more step*.

David advanced.

She kicked her legs straight out, smashing her heels against David's forward kneecap. He howled. She scrambled up, stumbled over the raised edge of the partially masoned wall, knocking bricks aside in her rush, and ran for her life.

Bellowing his anger, David raced after her.

The hall was dark. She couldn't see far ahead of her. A corner came up too fast. She bounced against the wall, pushed herself off, rebounded too hard. Her upper arm caught the opposite wall's sharp corner. She had no idea where she was, where she was going, but she ran.

Footsteps jackhammered behind her. *Keep going*. Her lungs burned. *Faster*. Her legs hurt. *Keep going*.

David caught her arm and jerked her back. She fell, slamming down hard on her hip. Swiveling on her rear, she aimed her feet at his shins. He jumped back.

"Oh no you don't."

He kicked savagely at her legs, unbalancing her and swinging her feet away from him. Then he reached down and hauled her up by the scruff of her sweater.

"Let me go!"

"I can't."

Before she could regain her balance, David wrapped the rope around her neck and held her tight against his heaving chest.

"Let her go, David." Jonas's voice was low, gruff, commanding. She had never been so glad to see anyone in her life. "She doesn't have anything to do with this."

The rope tightened around her neck. She yelped.

"She has everything to do with this."

Jonas, Jonas, look at me, she silently begged. But he was intent on David, watching his every move like a predator stalking a kill. She prayed he understood the distraction she'd try to give him.

She made horrible, gurgling, gasping sounds. Jonas's gaze didn't shift from David, but his pulse jumped at his throat. She blasted David's shins with kick after kick of her heels. She raked his hands mercilessly with her nails, drawing blood.

Then, with a final rattle, she went limp.

"TOO LATE, Jonas!" There was cold glee in David's voice. Jonas fought his urge to lunge at the man he'd once thought of as a friend.

"What does it feel like to have the person you love the most killed before your eyes?" David cackled, loosened his hold of the rope around Cathlynn's neck. On her white skin was a rude red mark. Jonas swallowed hard. "Now you understand. Now you understand!"

David dropped the body. Cathlynn fell in a heap at his feet. Jonas's heart skipped a beat. He wanted to wail his despair. He forced himself to focus on David.

David came toward him. Cathlynn hooked her feet around his ankle. He fell into Jonas's arms. With all his strength, Jonas shoved David against the wall. Bones cracked. David's head lolled sideways. He slumped and sank to the floor.

Jonas ran to Cathlynn, gathered her in his arms, hugged her, held her. "Are you all right?"

"I'm fine, I think." Her voice was hoarse, but when she smiled up at him, all he could see was that golden life in her eyes, and a long shudder of relief rolled through him. "What took you so long?"

He kissed her, then rested his forehead against hers. "Oh, Cat, I thought, I thought—"

A swishing sound interrupted him.

They both looked up.

David stood over them, blood dripping from one side of his face. In his hands was a knife.

"You shouldn't have done that," David said, lips curled in a vicious sneer. "You really shouldn't have done that."

Jonas swiveled, placing his body protectively before Cathlynn's. "It's too late, David. The police know where I am. They know you killed Alana. They're on their way now."

"You're lying! Like you've lied to me for years."

"I've never lied to you. Valentin—"

"Is tied up in the pantry. Don't count on him. Don't count on anyone."

In the dim light, the knife's sharp blade gleamed.

"David," Jonas started.

"You said you couldn't help him. You said it was too late. He was in pain and you did nothing."

"What are you talking about?"

"His father," Cathlynn whispered.

Armand Forester? He'd died seven years ago, shot accidentally by his own hunting partner—David, who was then only fifteen. "He was shot in the chest, David. There was nothing anyone could have done."

"You're a doctor. If you'd tried to stitch him up." The echo of David's pain was like a wounded animal's cry.

"It was an accident, David. It wasn't your fault."

"Of course it wasn't. If you'd tried—"

"There was too much damage."

David's grip tightened around the knife. Tears

streamed down his face, mixed with the blood. "He begged you for his life. *Begged* you."

"And I did my best to ease his pain. You can't bring your father back by killing us."

"They'll never find Alana's body and Cathlynn's body, and you'll be blamed." His voice was hard, cruel. In his eyes, a renewed determination flared. He strode forward. "You'll pay for what you did to me. They'll curse your name. But they'll never find your body. They'll assume you ran like the coward you are."

Just as Jonas steeled himself to lunge at David, a deep, melodious chant floated down the corridor. *"Adhesit in terra venter noster."*

A black-robed monk glided into view.

David whirled in surprise.

When he did, the monk's fist met with David's face. *"Adhesit in terra venter noster."* The sound of David's falling body strangely imitated the melody the monk chanted. Before David could get up again, the monk sat on him. Jonas took the rope the monk handed him and tied David's hands back.

"You must always remember to incapacitate the villain before you rescue the damsel, *monsieur*."

As the monk lifted his head, his face came into view. Cathlynn gasped. He looked just like the monk over the fireplace. *Valentin is more than a butler, he's as much part of this house as the walls.*

"Valentin!" Cathlynn said hoarsely, massaging her neck.

"Oui, madame." He smiled.

"Valentin, just how long have you been a member of this household?"

His answer was the same mysterious soft smile she'd hallucinated on the monk's portrait this afternoon. Was the impossible thought prickling her mind a result of her choking experience? It couldn't be. Was Valentin some sort of supernatural being? She shook her head. No. He was too real, too dense to be the ghost of her shimmering walls. Or was he? No, impossible. Then what? It simply didn't make sense.

"Valentin?" she pursued. "What's your first name?"

"Aurelius, *madame.*"

"As in Aurelius the Just?"

"*Oui, madame.* My ancestor. *Protecteur du secte loyaliste de la Sainte Croix.* Protector of the loyal order of the Holy Cross. And all who enter its gates with a pure heart."

Chapter Fourteen

Once in police custody and faced with the evidence of his crimes, David confessed to Alana's and Geoffrey's murders and his plan for revenge against Jonas, but rationalized his actions. He couldn't take responsibility for shooting his father seven years ago, or for the recent killings he'd committed. It was plain to everyone who heard David's confession that he felt no remorse for the lives he'd taken, the ones he'd nearly destroyed.

By the time they had given their statements to the police, tended, per Jonas's insistence, to the bruises around Cathlynn's neck and the rope burns around her wrists, it was morning. They said little on the ride back to the monastery. In the library, Jonas took Cathlynn's coat and sat her by the fire. He wanted to take her upstairs, fill the tub with bubbles and hot water, take care of her, love her. Instead, he asked Valentin to bring her a pot of tea.

"What happens now?" she asked in a croak that tore at his conscience. "Who'll get the trust fund?"

Her gaze darted at him warily, uncertain. She looked pale and tired. Who could blame her after what she'd gone through last night? At her neck, the purpling ligature mark blazed his failure at him. She could have died. And it would have been his fault.

"It's going to take the courts a long while to unravel the mess," Jonas said. He'd convinced the police that Cathlynn had been blackmailed into cooperating. Now his lawyer was doing his best to keep Jonas out of jail, too. "I don't expect I'll see any of the money."

"I suppose you're right." She sighed wearily. "What about Sterling?"

Jonas sat on the opposite side of the fire. It was best to maintain distance. "Since he wasn't part of the plot, just an innocent bystander caught in the mess, like you were, he's free to leave and return to England."

"How are you going to continue your research?"

He stared into the gyrating flames. "I'll find a way. The television coverage should bring some interest to the cause."

Valentin, dressed as a butler once again, squeaked his cart into the library.

"Madame." He handed Cathlynn a cup of hot tea.

Jonas bounded up and poured himself a drink. He needed something stiffer than tea. The whiskey burned and tasted bitter. This was going to be harder than he thought.

"Thank you, Valentin." She wrapped her hands around the cup, inhaled the fragrant aroma and took a long, satisfied taste. "What's under the dome?"

Jonas blasted himself. He should have thought she'd be hungry. All she'd had to eat since breakfast yesterday was a soda at the police station. Good thing Valentin wasn't as dense as his employer.

Smiling, Valentin uncovered the platter. On the silver tray lay a wooden box. Jonas's glass stopped halfway to his lips. Where had Valentin found it? At least he could stop feeling guilty on one point. Cathlynn would have her prize, after all.

Cathlynn gasped and put her cup down on the occasional table with a clatter. "Valentin?"

"*Oui, madame.*" His grin was wide and pleased. The old guy certainly had taken a shine to her.

Valentin lifted the cover, and inside the box, amid the layers of protective foam and silk, lay the Aidan Heart.

"You took it?" she asked. Her hair tumbled forward as she bent to examine every facet of the sculpture. Jonas stared at the life weaving in the golden-brown mane, memorizing, savoring the image, the sensation.

"I had to, *madame*. I knew you would not leave the monastery without it, and you had to stay. Jonas needed you. And Ste-Croix needs Jonas."

Without further explanation, Valentin squeaked his cart out of the library.

"You're free to leave," Jonas said. It sounded stupid and arrogant, but he didn't know how else to broach the subject. He was setting her free, and it was breaking his heart. He braced himself with another stiff gulp from his glass. "Take the Aidan Heart and go back to your grandmother. I hope one day you can forgive me for what I put you through."

"Jonas—"

"No, don't. I had no right to place your life in danger. It was selfish."

She was silent for a moment, then she rose from her chair. "I've never done anything I didn't want to do."

In the golden light of her eyes, he saw a reflection of his own confusion, longing and regret. Unable to stand the resonance, he turned to the window. The skies were heavy with gray clouds. It would probably snow today.

"Take Sterling's rental car," he said. The words scratched at his throat. "It'll take me a day or so to replace yours."

"You want me to leave? After everything, you want me to leave?"

He closed his eyes to gather his strength, then he looked at her straight and true. "Yes."

She swallowed hard, and the pain in her eyes nearly crumbled his determination. He tightened his grip around his glass, but said nothing.

Without another word, she shrugged on her coat. Cradling the boxed Aidan Heart in her arms, she left.

It took everything he had, but he didn't stop her.

His father hadn't been much older than he was now when the disease made its presence known. He couldn't bear the thought of Cathlynn watching him die the way his mother had watched his father die. He loved her too much for that.

He'd once believed in happily ever after. Thought he'd found it with Alana. But his parents' very real, very tragic deaths by disease and by grief, and Alana's infidelities had woken him from the haze of dreams, shaken him into accepting reality for what it was—harsh and irrefutable.

Now everything needed facts, needed proof. And when he looked at the cold facts, the proof in black and white, he couldn't deny the absolute evidence. For him, there was no future.

It was better she leave.

The front door's boom echoed unchallenged in the hall. He emptied his drink. Never had his home felt so icy, so lifeless.

CATHLYNN DIDN'T KNOW how she made it all the way
to Nashua in one piece. The car's windshield wipers
had worked furiously all the way, but they were helpless to keep up with the blur of her tears. Her mind
refused to think. Even with the heater on high, she
couldn't thaw the ice that seemed to clog her veins. She
was hurt, numb. The last thing she wanted was to be
alone. Neither did she want company. Claire would ask
too many questions Cathlynn wasn't ready to answer.
So she drove straight to the hospital, to Gram.

A nurse was monitoring all the machines connected
to Gram, and the action was yet another bruise to Cathlynn's already battered emotions. Gram had always
been the strong one. Gram had carried her through her
chaotic childhood with her love and her care and her
stories. Gram had given her hope when she could find
it nowhere else. To see Gram so helpless tore at what
little resilience she had left.

Tears choked her once again. Would they ever end?
Angrily, she brushed away the falling drops. They were
selfish tears. She was crying for her breaking heart. She
was crying for the loneliness that would fill her life
without Gram—without Jonas. Enough was enough.
There were plenty of people with worse problems than
hers. She'd get over this. She always did.

Adjusting the cowl neck of her sweater to cover her
bruises and the cuffs to cover her burns, she pasted a
smile on her lips and entered the room.

For a moment Gram's eyes flashed with recognition.
She struggled to say something, but nothing came out.

The nurse turned to Cathlynn. "Good morning, Miss
O'Connell. Nice to see you. Your grandmother is doing
much better today. We took her off the respirator again

this morning.'' She adjusted Gram's blanket. ''For good this time, right, Meara?''

''That's great to hear,'' Cathlynn said, glad she would have Gram around for a while longer.

The nurse made an entry on the chart, then left.

Cathlynn dragged the visitor's chair next to Gram's bed and sat down. ''I brought you something.''

She opened the box and lifted out the glass sculpture. ''Look, Gram.''

''Potato!'' Gram rasped.

''Yes, Gram, it's the Aidan Heart. Isn't it beautiful?''

She didn't have the heart to tell Gram the magic wasn't there after all. After years of searching, she finally had her treasure, but the glass felt cold and hard in her hands.

Gram looked from Cathlynn to the sculpture and back, then became agitated. ''No potato, no potato, no potato.'' She spat and struggled for the right words, and finally grasped Cathlynn's hand and squeezed hard.

In Gram's eyes, Cathlynn saw the bright, warm light of love. Something stirred in her. She was once again in that circle of pine in Gram's backyard, the picnic table laden with scones, and tarts, and cakes. Gram's storyteller's voice echoed on the breeze of her memory. Aidan and Deirdre's story. Their love. Their loss.

But they always had their love, Cathlynn. And that's what's most important.

The look lingered. The memories flooded. Then Cathlynn understood.

With tears of joy in her eyes, she kissed her grandmother.

Gram had given her the Aidan Heart's real magic after all.

AIDAN HEART IN HAND, Cathlynn stormed into the monastery. No one was in sight. She stomped her way to the library. Empty. In the kitchen, she startled Valentin.

"Where is he?" she asked without preamble. She'd apologize later. This was too important to wait, and she didn't want to lose her nerve.

Valentin smiled. "I would try the laboratory, *madame*."

"Thank you, Valentin."

The lab door was open. Through it, she saw Jonas sitting at his desk, before the computer, scrolling line after line of data. His back was rounded. His shoulders were slumped.

"Back at work already," she said.

He snapped his head to look at her. "Yes." He turned back to his work. She walked over to his desk and plunked the Aidan Heart in front of him. "I want you to have this."

Sculpture in hand, he spun in his chair. "It's yours. You've earned it."

She shook her head. "I want you to sell it and use the proceeds toward your research. It's not much, but it's a start."

Without a word, he touched the glass. He fingered the purple heart in the center of all those translucent layers of glass. Then he handed the Aidan Heart back to her. "I can't accept your gift."

Turning back to face his computer, Jonas dismissed her. The back of his chair caught the fingers of one of her hands. Before she could stop the tragedy, the sculpture slid from her hands. It exploded on the gray granite floor. Shards scattered all around her feet.

"Oh, God. Oh, Cathlynn." Jonas stared in numb disbelief at the shattered glass strewn about the granite floor.

"Cathlynn..." He looked up at her and in his stormy gray eyes, she saw his despair.

"I used to think there was magic in the glass," she said. She ran her fingers along his jaw, shaking her head slowly. "But you were right, Jonas. It was just an illusion. The magic of Gram's stories wasn't in the folds of the glass, but in Aidan and in Deirdre, people who dared to share their love against all odds."

She scattered the shards of glass with the toe of her shoe, kneeled before him and took his hands in hers. "I love you, Jonas. I know you care for me, too. You and me together. That's the real magic. How can you throw something so wonderful away?"

"You're already suffering watching your grandmother wither away. Do you really want to go through that ordeal again with me?"

Squeezing his hands tighter, she looked hard into his eyes, willing him to see the depth of her feelings. "My grandmother is a very special woman. I wouldn't trade any of my summers with her even if I had to live ten more years watching her die. Taking care of her is not a burden. Don't you see? I'm with you all the way."

"All I can offer you is an uncertain future."

"But Jonas, the future is uncertain for all of us." Her eyes burned with unshed tears. "Have you ever thought that *I* might be the one to get sick? That you'll be the one watching me become a shadow of myself? My grandmother has Alzheimer's. That's genetic. I could very well suffer from that, too."

She pulled at his hands until they both stood and circled her arms around his waist. "We can't control what our mutant genes might or might not do. But we can control our actions. I love you, Jonas. I want to spend whatever days we might have left together. I would rather have a few tomorrows filled with joy than a lifetime of being alone.''

Cathlynn had infiltrated his life in little ways, injecting warmth and love into his dead soul. For the first time, as Jonas stared into the whirling gold in her soft brown eyes, he understood the bond that had tied his parents so tightly and provided the glue for their family. Given the chance to live their lives over again, his parents would have chosen love in the present over the certainty of a distant future.

Cathlynn was offering him what he'd searched for with his dedication to research—a chance at life. It was time to follow the truth of his heart.

''I accept your proposal.'' His breath caught in his chest. His heart swelled, crowding his rib cage. His fingers trembled at his sides, but he made no gesture toward her.

She cocked her head and gave him a quizzical look.

''You asked me to marry you, didn't you?'' He couldn't stand the separation any longer. He crowded her, plunged his hands in the golden life of her hair, smiled into the topaz of her eyes. ''I'm saying yes. I'm choosing happiness with you.''

''Oh, Jonas.'' She flung her arms around his waist and held him so tight he could hardly breathe. A burden seemed to lift. He felt light, giddy. He laughed and drew her closer. Then he kissed her slowly, thoroughly, as if they had a lifetime to savor the sensation.

Epilogue

A year later. Christmas Day.

Morning had dawned with a fresh fall of snow on the ground and sunshine turning each flake into a shining jewel. Soon the house would be a bustle of activity as Jonas's brother and sister and their families joined them for dinner, but for now, Cathlynn had her husband to herself.

A fire glowed in the hearth. The Christmas tree twinkled with bright lights and colorful ornaments. A bayberry scent wafted from the candles on the mantel. Their opened presents lay at the base of the tree, the ripped paper in a pile beside the boxes. But none of the purchased gifts could please her more than having the grand jury dismiss the charges of fraud against Jonas. It was a heavy burden lifted from both their shoulders, and now Jonas could devote his full attention to his research.

Cathlynn sipped her coffee, content in the warmth of Jonas's arms.

As Jonas reached forward, she made a small noise of protest.

"There's one more present," he said and plucked it from the branches of the spruce.

"For me?"

He smiled, and Cathlynn's heart hitched with joy. She would never get tired of Jonas's smile.

"Go on. Open it."

She placed her cup on the small table beside the love seat and ripped at the silver bow and blue foil paper, exposing a fancy jeweler's box. Inside the box was an ornate, old-fashioned-looking key made of gold.

"The key to your heart?" she teased. Over the past year, he'd surprised her time and again with his sentimentality.

A serious expression crossed his face. "No, the key to the future."

She gasped, bringing a hand to her mouth. "You found it! You found the key to Cross's Disease!"

He nodded. "There's still years of FDA red tape to go through, but I found the key."

"Oh, Jonas!" She threw herself at him and kissed him long and hard.

He rested his forehead against hers, wrapped his arms around her waist, bringing her hips close enough to feel his desire for her, and rocked her gently from side to side. The gray of his eyes darkened, softened, stormed with emotion. "Want to go make a baby?"

Pressing her hands against his nape to bring his mouth closer to hers, she smiled. "I can't think of anything I want more."

Shh!

HARLEQUIN®

I N T R I G U E®

has a secret...

It's *confidential!*

September 2000

You loved Gayle Wilson's original
MEN OF MYSTERY *series so*
much that we've brought it back!

HARLEQUIN®

I N T R I G U E®

presents

Coming in August 2000

#578 RENEGADE HEART

Another exciting new story by
Gayle Wilson!

Former CIA operative Drew Evans is a man on the
run. His only chance at life is Maggie Cannon, a
beautiful but vulnerable widow with a young
daughter to raise. But is she willing to help a
mysterious stranger...?

HARLEQUIN®
Makes any time special ™

Visit us at www.eHarlequin.com   HIMMM1

What can be stolen, forgotten, hidden, replaced, imitated—but never lost?

HARLEQUIN®

I N T R I G U E®

brings you the strong, sexy men
and passionate women who are
about to uncover...

SECRET IDENTITY

LITTLE BOY LOST
by Adrianne Lee
August 2000

SAFE BY HIS SIDE
by Debra Webb
September 2000

HER MYSTERIOUS STRANGER
by Debbi Rawlins
October 2000

ALIAS MOMMY
by Linda O. Johnston
November 2000

Available at your favorite retail outlet.

HARLEQUIN®

Makes any time special™

Daddy's little girl... **THAT'S MY BABY!** by

Vicki Lewis Thompson

Nat Grady is finally home—older and wiser. When the woman he'd loved had hinted at commitment, Nat had run far and fast. But now he knows he can't live without her. But Jessica's nowhere to be found.

Jessica Franklin is living a nightmare. She'd thought things were rough when the man she loved ran out on her, leaving her to give birth to their child alone. But when she realizes she has a stalker on her trail, she has to run—and the only man who can help her is Nat Grady.

THAT'S MY BABY!
On sale September 2000 at your favorite retail outlet.

HARLEQUIN®
Makes any time special ™

Some secrets are better left buried...

Yesterday's Scandal by Gina WILKINS

A mysterious stranger has come to town...

Former cop Mac Cordero was going undercover one last time to find and exact revenge on the man who fathered, then abandoned him. All he knew was that the man's name was McBride—a name, that is synonymous with scandal.

...and he wants her!

Responsible, reliable Sharon Henderson was drawn to the sexy-as-sin stranger. She couldn't help falling for him hard and fast. Then she discovered that their love was based on a lie....

YOU WON'T WANT TO MISS IT!

On sale September 2000 at your favorite retail outlet.

HARLEQUIN®
Makes any time special ™

COMING NEXT MONTH

#577 A MOTHER'S SECRETS by Joanna Wayne
Randolph Family Ties

Kathi Sable was in danger. The threat of harm to loved ones had caused her to flee...not realizing she carried Ryder Randolph's child. Now, almost two years later, the forces that sent her on the run drew Kathi back to Ryder's side. Determined to reveal the truth, she needed Ryder's help to end the threat—and make their family reunion last a lifetime.

#578 RENEGADE HEART by Gayle Wilson
More Men of Mystery

Ex-government agent Drew Evans was being hunted for a crime he hadn't committed. The man who could clear Drew's name was dead, leaving his wife and daughter to take up Drew's cause. Though Drew didn't want to involve Maggie Cannon or her daughter, his life depended on questions only she could answer. But once involved, would Drew be able to let Maggie walk away? And would she want to?

#579 INADMISSABLE PASSION by Ann Voss Peterson

Five years ago, secrets shattered Brittany Gerritsen's engagement to Jackson Alcott. Now, opposing attorneys on a high-profile murder case, their exchanges heated up the courtroom—and ultimately blazed in the bedroom. Though a murderer threatened their lives, this time love just might be enough to keep them together.

#580 LITTLE BOY LOST by Adrianne Lee
Secret Identity

When someone stole her identity and her son, Carleen Ellison immediately turned to Kane Kincaid. Though she'd never told him, the child they were searching for was his and the love they'd once shared still burned in her soul. To save his boy and reclaim Carleen's love, Kane would do anything...even if it meant risking his life.

Visit us at www.eHarlequin.com

CNM0700